MW01134639

The Fall Back Plan

MELANIE JACOBSON

Copyright © 2023 by Melanie Jacobson

All rights reserved.

No portion of this book may be reproduced in any form without written permission from the publisher or author, except as permitted by U.S. copyright law.

To the Sweater Weather girls,
thank you for letting me
be part of the fun

Chapter One

LUCAS

Sometimes, a sign from heaven falls and hits you right on the head. Other times, a sign falls off the roof of the new bar on Maple and almost hits *me* right on the head, except my finely honed instincts from coaching my niece's softball team kick in, and I jump out of the way just in time.

I stare at the sign on the sidewalk in front of me, then up at the two workmen who are supposed to be installing it, both gaping at me with wide eyes. "Whoa, sorry, man!" one of them calls.

The crash brings the owner of the bookstore next door running out, and she looks from it to me, then up at the workmen.

"You good, Sheriff?" she asks.

"I'm good," I tell her.

She narrows her eyes at the workmen. "That's what happens when you don't hire local."

This bar—specifically its renovation—has been a bone of contention for the Chamber of Commerce for five months. The businesses here pride themselves on hiring locally and contributing to the economy that way. Whoever bought Sullivan's—the bar I'm standing in front of—is changing the name to "Tequila Mockingbird."

Enough people are annoyed about that. Sullivan's had been open longer than I've been alive, and I'm thirty-one.

The new owner is also definitely not planning on keeping the scruffy ambiance acquired from decades of dusty blue-collar workers sitting on its worn barstools. We've watched for two weeks as boxes and furniture got unloaded from trucks and carted inside, and no one has been invited to come and check out the progress. It's not the kind of furniture a blue-collar guy wants to sit on while killing some time before he heads home.

Best I can tell, it's the kind of furniture ladies who drink fancy wines will like sitting on.

But most people's hides are more chapped over the buyer's contracting choices.

Wayne Oakley, current Chamber president, researched the name on the notice of intent to sell liquor posted in the window. It lists a "Karma LLC" as the business owner, and whoever is running Karma has failed to use a single local business or worker in the renovation. It would have made a nice profit for some of our local contractors and interior designers and furniture makers and gallery owners.

"Sorry again about that, officer," one of the workers calls down.

I shrug. "I'm not hurt, but y'all best be careful when you try again. Barricade the sidewalk first, keep people out of this space."

"Good idea, sir."

They're my age or older, but I get "sir" a lot when I'm in uniform. Or maybe it's my sidearm that keeps them minding their manners.

The bookstore owner goes back inside, but Ruth Wilson emerges from the gift boutique across the street and crosses over. "How are you doing, Lucas?" Using my first name is old-person privilege. No one who's known me since I was in diapers ever calls me sheriff, even though I've had the job two years.

"I'm good, Miss Ruth. How's the store?"

"Fine, fine. Busy getting all the shelves filled for the Harvest Festival."

Harvest Hollow's big fall festival is still a month off, but the average attendance over that weekend will swell the city's population by more than fifteen thousand, all visitors ready to eat good food and buy harvest-themed tourist crap.

Er—merchandise.

Don't know why someone needs an apple-shaped toothpick holder, but Miss Ruth sells out of them every year.

The whole city is getting ready for it. Ribbons the color of fall leaves have been up on the Maple Street lamp posts for a couple of weeks and we're barely into September.

Miss Ruth nods at the sign, which one of the workers has moved out of the center of the sidewalk. "Did you see the ad today in the *Harvest Times?*"

"What ad?" I skim the newspaper sometimes in the morning, but generally I already know about anything related to city news before it goes to press.

"Half-page ad announcing an opening date for this place next week," Miss Ruth says.

This seems to remind the worker of something because he suddenly straightens and disappears into the bar.

"Better have Rolly stick around here that night," she adds.

"You think it'll be busy enough to warrant an extra patrol?" I'm only asking to be polite, but of course I'll send a deputy that night. Public safety calculations change when liquor enters the equation. No one had dared cross Janice Sullivan, not even after Tom died, and if ever an out-of-towner got too uppity, the locals schooled them right quick. Without knowing what kind of security or policies this new owner has, the smart play is to have a deputy in the area until we get a feel for what kind of trouble will find the Tequila Mockingbird and how the bar will handle it.

Miss Ruth shrugs at my question. "Don't know what kind of crowd it'll get. But you'll wish you'd had someone here if it's big, and that's worse than sending a deputy you don't end up needing."

"You're right." I nod like I'm grateful for this wisdom.

The worker reappears with a poster, which he unfurls and sprays with adhesive before sticking it to the window. A large serif font announces that Tequila Mockingbird will be opening in a week.

So far, I'm taking the sign that nearly hit me in the head as a figurative one as well: Karma LLC does not have all its crap together, but it's my literal job to make sure that doesn't cause problems for Harvest Hollow.

Chapter Two

JOLIE

We're open.

After all the negotiations, ordering, renovating, staffing, and training, it's here.

I sit at the table in the farthest back, nearest the hall leading to the restrooms and my office, a shadowy corner that couples will no doubt claim in the future for whispered conversations and kisses.

Sullivan's was built in the old shotgun bar style, and we had to stay with that floor plan, but everything else is different, the interior stripped and remodeled from the ceiling down. If I had to describe the previous aesthetic, it would be "Have you ever seen a 1970s movie scene shot inside a bar?"

Now it's boho contemporary with light woods and natural textures wherever we can use them. Wicker shades in modern funnel shapes on black iron pendant lights, stone and jute covering the walls, lush plants in harmonious places. In a nod to the town's full embrace of fall, some of the tables have small pumpkins filled with succulents.

Ads have run in the *Times* and all over social media for a week now announcing our opening night. It's 5 PM on a Monday, typically the slowest night of the week in the restaurant and bar industry, but that's intentional. It gives my staff a chance to get some experience and work out kinks before the weekend rolls around and we become part of the modest Maple Street pub crawl.

We have a full month to get our act together before the Harvest Festival, when the crowds descend and our taps—and their cash—will flow freely.

Harvest Hollow is a "just big enough" town. Big enough for two high schools. Not big enough to expect a long wait at your favorite restaurant most nights.

Still, I don't expect an empty bar fifteen minutes after our official opening time. I exchange nervous glances with my cousin Ry in his spot behind the bar when no one has come in. Our servers, Tina and Precious, shift from foot to foot. They're both experienced waitresses, single moms who need the tips that pay them better than any salary job will get them.

My security, Mary Louise, stands by the door wearing an inscrutable expression. She looks as if she's always thinking hard, but you can't ever tell if it's good or bad. It's how she looked on the court as Valley League All-Star basketball forward for three years straight in high school.

After another five minutes, even Mary Louise fidgets, her fingers drumming against her thigh the only giveaway that she's got some reservations about how this opening will play out.

Ry shoots me another look. "Rethinking not sending those invitations?"

I shake my head. Not even a little. He'd been on my case for the last month to invite the Harvest Hollow VIPs for complimentary drinks on opening night to help get the word out.

"The mayor? The Chamber of Commerce? They love photo ops showing them caring about local businesses. They'll post it all over their social media. Free advertising for you while they tell everyone what good citizens they are." He'd made several versions of this argument, and I shot each one down with a look. He'd drop it for a day or two. Then he'd start up again, even though he knew exactly why I didn't want an Oakley or his spawn in here.

It had been plenty satisfying to know they were probably popping blood pressure meds every time an outside vendor or delivery truck pulled up to Tequila Mockingbird. It would drive them crazy knowing I hadn't spent any of my renovation funds in town.

I am in my petty era. The kind of petty that has a long memory, and now has the money to act on it. But I learned from the best. Namely the biggest snobs in this town.

Finally, nearly a half hour after we unlocked the front entrance, the door swings open to let in the waning daylight and two women in their late twenties who I don't know. It isn't surprising. Harvest Hollow is the kind of place where you always see a few people you know at Walmart but even more who you don't. I'd probably graduated two or three years ahead of these two, but if they'd gone to Stony Peak and not Harvest High, there wasn't much chance our paths had crossed.

One was in a black pencil skirt and light blue blouse, the other in a navy pantsuit. Bankers, I decided. The account rep level. They'd probably started as tellers and graduated to desk jobs that allowed them to wear heels that no teller would put on for a full shift on her feet. I had a whole closetful of designer versions of both their outfits.

Tina goes to greet them, her dark box braids swaying softly from her high ponytail as she leads them to the center table.

Precious sweeps in next, bearing two flutes of champagne, her halo of blonde curls catching the soft bar light. "Welcome to Tequila Mockingbird, ladies. You're our very first patrons, and we want to celebrate with this complimentary champagne."

They happily accept and admire the decor as they drink. Within minutes, Pantsuit has her phone out, telling Tina she's putting out the word to her friends to come in and check us out.

By seven, Pantsuit and Pencil Skirt are leaving, but our tables are half-full, and more than half the barstools are occupied as well. I stay in my corner to watch it all, periodically slipping into my office to pull up the sales report and see how we're doing.

We'd given the first twenty customers free champagne, but even still the sales are adding up. Tina especially is doing a good job of pushing our signature cocktail while Precious keeps our house ale selling. I'll have them compare notes to see what they can learn from each other.

Mostly, though, I watch. I recognize some of the faces that come in, even though it's been several years since I've seen anyone but Ry and a handful of cousins in person. I don't worry that any of them will recognize me, but I hang back anyway. If anyone realizes that Jolie McGraw bought Sullivan's, I'll have to field more questions than a deck of Trivial Pursuit cards.

Around 8:00, the office crowd thins, and a different type of customer starts drifting in. Jeans instead of slacks. More flannels than Oxfords. Unshaven versus groomed scruff.

Loafers give way to boots with heavy, worn treads, and this later crowd heads straight to the bar rather than claiming tables. They nurse beers or sometimes whiskey and don't talk as much. Not sure how many of them will come again. This was my dad's crowd, and he would have hated this place.

Which is why I bought it. I'd been called to fetch him far too many times from Sullivan's. If Janice had known I was behind the purchase of the property, she would have declined, probably thinking I'd only buy it to burn it down. It wouldn't have been a terrible guess.

A disturbance at the entrance around 9:00 draws my attention, but Mary Louise is already on it, moving toward a group of men coming through the door who have clearly already been drinking. I recognize the look in their eyes, the way the liquor makes them small and mean.

Mary Louise moves in front of them, speaking too low for me to hear. Her body is relaxed, but no one paying attention would be fooled. At least, no one who knows a thing about Mary Louise. If she doesn't want to let them in, they haven't got a shot of getting through her.

"—want a drink is all. Wanna try the house ale," one of them says loudly enough for the entire bar to know their intentions.

Mary Louise glances over her shoulder to Ry, who nods. She moves out of the men's way and welcomes them in with a polite wave of her arm.

They head to the bar and claim stools, making it nearly full. Only about four of the tables are occupied, and at one table, two middle-aged women exchange looks with each other. They appear to have reservations about these latest patrons. I wonder if it's because these guys would look more at home in a honky-tonk or sports bar, or if they know something more.

It doesn't matter. Mary Louise and I will watch them closely either way.

The one who spoke to Mary Louise wears a gray hat with the local hockey team logo. It's a minor league team. The Appies, short for Appalachian. It's clever, but I always read "apple" instead of "appie" at first glance.

Apple Hat's voice has an arguing-with-the-ref tone and volume as he declares, "They wussified Sullivan's."

This gets grunts and mutters of approval from his friends. No, his *cronies*. One of the middle-aged women glances over again and takes out her phone to send a text. They signal Precious to come over and she nods and returns a minute later with their check.

It's what Apple Hat wants. I know this belligerence. They're trying to start something. I catch Ry's eye again and he gives me a tiny head shake to tell me he's still got it handled.

It's more satisfying to me to overcharge them for their drinks and stick it to them that way. Ry will make sure they pay what we call the "jerk tax."

The tax climbs when they start griping about the ale, which is a craft beer from a microbrewery in Asheville I partnered with. "PBR is better than this," one of the other guys says, using an impolite word to describe the beer.

Ah, yes. This carefully curated microbrew is definitely not as good as the cut-rate sour beer of high school keg parties. I allow myself an eyeroll in my private corner, then watch the rest of this drama play out. I don't know these dudes, but I've known these kinds of dudes my whole life. They can be trouble, but so long as you pay attention, you can usually head it off before it bubbles over. Mary Louise knows this even better than I do, so I'm not worried.

"Y'all come in here with fancy lights and do some dusting and think that'll keep us from noticing that you're serving the cheap stuff?" Apple Hat demands. One of his sidekicks scoffs.

I notice the table closest to them gesture for their check too.

Another one of Apple Hat's wingmen, maybe because of the liquid courage he's drained from his whiskey glass, straightens and turns to run his eyes around the bar, sliding right over me like I don't register on his radar. "Dang shame when Asheville hipsters come infesting the Hollow like stiltgrass. Good thing y'all do poorly at our altitude. Won't last."

"Gentrification," Apple Hat spits. "Janice Sullivan is a good woman, and it's going to break her heart when she sees this place. Old Tom is rolling in his grave."

I rise and cross half the floor before I speak. "That's enough."

I must look like I materialized from the low lighting like a ninja in my black sleeveless shirt and black Calvin Klein wide-leg trousers, my dark hair pulled into a low bun at my nape. I'm average height but wearing three-inch heels, and I stare them down with the cool "do not mess with me" expression I used for eight years in the storied boardrooms of Blue Slate Investment Management. These men are right to see me as a silent assassin.

"Who're you?" Apple Hat demands.

"I'm the owner, and the woman who paid Janice Sullivan a generous price for this bar." I stop in front of him, out of arm's reach, and give him a slow scan from head to toe, letting him know I'm not impressed. "Generous enough to guess she doesn't miss it. And she definitely doesn't miss the likes of you."

He straightens, his jaw jutting forward in a way that's supposed to signal aggression. All he's doing is offering Mary Louise an easy target if he doesn't back down.

"You can't talk to a customer like that," he says.

"Of course I can." I offer him a slight smile. "What's more, the longer you talk, the higher your tab climbs, so I'd shut up and pay up if I were you."

"You can't do that," one of his wingnuts—wing*men*—says.

I nod at the sign posted directly behind Ry, a chalked slate that states *Prices vary depending on your attitude. Behave or leave.* "What do you think, Ry? Are they following the rules?"

He shakes his head. "They are not, Jo."

A new person walks in, but I don't pay them any mind. I've got Mary Louise to keep an eye out.

"You heard my bartender," I tell the Bad Apples. "You're not man enough for my wussified establishment. Get out." I don't raise my voice. The remaining patrons can definitely hear Apple Hat but not me. Not unless Precious or Tina drops the volume on the alt-country music playing loudly enough to give the bar atmosphere without drowning out conversation.

The servers won't, of course. Like total pros, they're offering more complimentary champagne to the tables who haven't asked for their checks yet. We probably ought to be giving them popcorn for the show too.

Apple Hat hears and understands me just fine. He glances at his friends, and when a couple of them don't meet his eyes, he puffs his chest out and zeroes in on me again. "Who's going to make me?"

I barely repress another eyeroll. I like a good action flick as much as the next person, but the greatest disservice those films have done our culture is giving the bad guys weak dialogue for unimaginative Apple Hats to parrot.

"I am," a deep male voice answers before I can.

The whole group turns like their heads are mounted on the same swivel, and my gaze slides past them to realize why Mary Louise didn't react to the new arrival.

I take in the tall, powerfully built man in a sheriff's uniform, the firm jaw beneath the short-cropped beard on his startlingly handsome face, and meet the flinty eyes of Harvest High's legendary holy terror, Lucas Cole, above the badge.

I never asked when I moved back who the current sheriff is. I really should have.

Chapter Three

JOLIE

There is no recognition when Lucas Cole's eyes meet mine before settling on the Bad Apples.

"What's the problem, Hardin?" Lucas asks.

Here's what it means if the sheriff of a town the size of Harvest Hollow knows your name on sight: this isn't the first time you've raised hell. Sounds like the Bad Apples turn up like bad pennies.

I can't see Apple Hat's face now, but the sneer is clear in his voice when he answers. "I'd like to report vandalism at Sullivan's. Paint all over the place. Interior defaced."

"I've got this," I inform Lucas.

He quirks an eyebrow, a subtle sign of disbelief.

"Mary Louise?" I turn my head when I say her name. She pushes away from the wall she's been leaning against and straightens to her full six-foot-two height. There's a reason she was the most feared forward in the Valley basketball league. She's got two inches on Lucas, and he's taller than any of the Bad Apples.

Mary Louise walks over to stand beside me, her arms folded across her chest. She looks at Apple Hat for two full seconds before she says, "Pay up and go, Shane."

She knows him, then. I suspect lots of people know Apple Hat now for the same reasons that everyone knew Lucas Cole in high school, none of them good.

Apple Hat, aka Shane Hardin, clearly knows what Mary Louise can do. He looks at his wingnuts and says, "My allergy to hipsters is acting up." They all produce cash and toss it on the bar, following after Apple Hat as he brushes past the sheriff on his way out.

I turn to address the remaining customers, all seven of them. "Thanks for your patience as we took out the trash, folks. Please enjoy a Cherry Bounce or a pint of our house ale on us."

This is greeted with low-key applause, and the last of the tension leaves the room. Good. Tension is the last thing you want customers feeling in a bar.

Lucas extends his hand for a shake. "I'm Sheriff Cole. I'll step out to make sure Hardin and his crew aren't sticking around, but I wanted to say congratulations on your grand opening."

"I know who you are, Lucas." I slide my hands into my pockets, ignoring his outstretched one.

Confusion crosses his face as he studies mine. He's got a beard now, close cropped and the same warm brown as his hair, no early grays. I see the second recognition strikes when his jaw goes slack, but he catches himself before it drops open.

"Gappy." His tone is both surprised and certain as he uses my hated high school nickname.

"The one and only," I agree. I'd knocked out my right incisor when I was ten on a particularly bad night after retrieving Dad from Sullivan's. His drunken staggering on the icy sidewalk had pitched us both against a garbage can, the kind maintained by the city in a concrete holder. I'd gotten a black eye from that too. But we had no insurance, so after my dad sobbed his apologies and passed out, I googled first aid for black eyes and how to stop your mouth from bleeding. The eye got better. The permanent tooth stayed permanently gone.

On the advice of the woman who'd recruited me to work at the hedge fund, I'd gotten a dental implant with my signing bonus for joining their firm. Got expensive skin care and Invisalign too. Now I looked like I'd come from a wealthy family—the kind who got their kids braces and skin care that didn't smell like the Irish Spring bar soap shoplifted from the dollar store.

"Call me Jolie," I correct Lucas.

"Jolie McGraw," he says. "It's been a minute."

"Twelve years, actually." That was the last time I'd tutored him in the high school library. The last time he'd tortured me with his scorn while I did a job I couldn't afford not to take.

"So you're Karma LLC?"

"I am."

"Didn't know you were back. Congrats on the opening."

Why *would* Lucas Cole know I was back? We'd never been friends. I hadn't bothered to keep up with Lucas once he graduated—or possibly even dropped out of—Harvest High. I hadn't kept up with anyone from high school. It's not like I could forget it, but I could—and definitely did—leave it behind.

"Thank you. Can I help you with anything?" It's a clear invitation to leave.

His forehead furrows. "That's my line. Let me know if Shane Hardin or any of his thug buddies turns up. We'll handle them."

It's rich to hear him call anyone else a thug. I glance at his badge before meeting his eyes again. "You must have better things to do than handling customers that no one asked for your help with, Sheriff. Mary Louise can show you out. She'll do any handling around here."

Ry's eyebrows shoot up, but he knows how much I hated working with Lucas Cole in high school, and he says nothing.

Lucas freezes for a second, like he's not sure how he's supposed to respond to his dismissal. Then he gives me a nod and touches the brim of his hat. "Evenin', Jolie."

He gives Mary Louise knuckles on his way out of the bar. She meets my eyes and gives a small smile and a head shake before she resumes her spot.

The rest of the grand opening goes well. Only about a dozen more people wander in by the time we close at midnight, but we'll have a bigger crowd tomorrow as other locals see pictures from tonight in their feeds. By this weekend, we'll be full.

After everyone is tipped out and Ry and I wipe everything down, we stumble upstairs to the apartment over the bar. Ry is living there rent free, and I'm crashing on his couch for a few days until I close on the house I bought.

It takes a long time for me to fall asleep. Between the rowdy bar guy and the sheriff who threw him out, it's the sheriff who's got me stressed.

How in the world did Lucas Cole ever end up on the *right* side of the law?

Chapter Four

LUCAS

Harvest Hollow is the kind of place where your past is always present. You're always running into people you grew up with. Sometimes I have to arrest former classmates who probably feel like they're in the Upside Down when it's Lucas Cole, of all people, slapping cuffs on them. I run into past teachers at the grocery store and old neighbors in restaurants. They knew me when, but most of them are kind enough to forget it.

Clearly, Jolie McGraw isn't one who's forgotten, and I don't blame her. I've thought of her over the years, because if ever there was someone who hadn't deserved my teenage contempt, it was Jolie. I've owed her an apology for a long time, but whatever I thought might have happened to the mousy sophomore who'd tried to haul my butt through geometry as a senior, she is the *last* person I would have expected to see in Harvest Hollow looking flat-out beautiful.

She'd put on badly needed weight, fleshing out her scrawny frame with curves a man couldn't help noticing, her dark hair much longer than the short cut she'd kept it in during high school. Her makeup wasn't heavy, but she'd applied it well, drawing attention to the long lashes around her dark eyes and to her full mouth.

Good for her. Everyone should get a chance to redefine themselves. A chance as often as they needed one, in fact. I wouldn't be sheriff if people hadn't made space for me to grow up and change. Not that *everyone* did, I think as a group spills out into the street from the restaurant ahead. I recognize the mayor's voice because no one loves to hear himself talk more, so he always does it loudly to make sure everyone else can hear him too.

He's talking about the high school football season. "Of course, as mayor, I'm impartial and only want to see these young athletes give it their best, but go, Bobcats!" This is met with laughs from the suck-ups he's with. I recognize a local real estate agent and the restaurant owner in his entourage.

"Evenin', George," I say, knowing it will bother him that I don't use his title. I stop, not because I want to talk but because the mayor will expect me to.

"Good to see you, Sheriff," Mayor Hinder says. This is where he'll try to look important by bringing up some point of city business to remind our audience that he has a Very Important Job that means he gets the sheriff's ear. "On patrol? Thought you got yourself elected out of that grind."

"Checking on the new bar," I say. "Some of the old Sullivan's crowd were trying to start something tonight, but it's settled."

"Did you find out who owns it?"

I'd heard through the grapevine that the mayor had been right peeved when he couldn't find the name of the true owner of Karma LLC.

"Jolie McGraw," I tell him. He frowns like he's trying to place the name. "She was a couple of years behind me in high school. Probably Hailey and Holden's class." Those were his twins, both of them grown, married, and living elsewhere.

He frowns. "McGraw. Was her dad the one who crashed into the Harvest Festival?"

"Yeah." I'd had to bring him in a few times for public intoxication when I first got on patrol, and by then he was notorious. No doubt I'd have dealt with him even more, but he died several years back.

"Does she seem like the type who might have some of her father's same . . . tendencies?" the mayor asks.

The question bothers me. It's bad enough to have your own past held against you, much less someone else's, like your father's. "She does not. She was the valedictorian of her class and went to Duke on a full scholarship. I knew her back then. She seems even more pulled together now."

"Perhaps we ought to stop in and say hello," the mayor says, glancing around at his group. "I'd have done it before opening if she'd been forthcoming about how to get in touch with her as the new owner."

"It's a nice place," I tell him. "Y'all have a good evening." I move on with the murmurs of their polite "You too"s following me.

I'd only come out tonight because Jennifer Lee had texted me on my personal number to let me know there was trouble brewing at Sullivan's. Make that Tequila Mockingbird. I'd radioed Rolly to let him know I'd handle it.

This sort of thing happens a lot—friends and acquaintances bypassing the dispatcher to reach me directly. Usually it's when they want something handled off the books, like a difficult relative they want managed without pressing charges. Or like tonight, when something has the potential to go bad but the presence of law enforcement could tip it the right way.

Once, about a year after I'd joined the department, I'd been standing in line to order at Cataloochee—they had the best coffee on Maple—and a young mom had told her little girl to thank me.

"For what?" the kid had asked.

"Do you know what a police officer does?" the mom had asked.

"Takes people to jail." The little girl had given me a nervous look even though I'd made it a point to smile at her.

"No, honey. Police officers are here to keep people safe."

The girl had come over then with a shy smile to say thank you.

That interaction stuck with me because most people don't make that distinction. A peace officer's primary responsibility is to de-escalate any situation. That's the main way we keep people safe. Detainment and arrest are always a possibility if a suspect doesn't comply with our directions, but in general, we're always trying to keep a situation from boiling over.

Heaven knows I didn't learn that particular skill in my own home.

But I'd trained under good officers, and we still lead with that philosophy now. All good police do. In high school, I'd been collared by enough good cops and a couple of bad cops to recognize the difference immediately, and it was the good cops—who were by far the majority—who'd ultimately helped me turn my life around.

I glance down at the shiny star on my chest and snort. There are days where I still can't believe I'm the law-and-order guy in this town. Not after being a literal juvenile delinquent with a record of petty crimes from shoplifting to vandalism. But dang, I love this job.

Still, it's been a long day. I try to get home by supper most nights to eat with Brooklyn and Pops, but at least once a week something will come up that keeps me away. Even before the problem at the new bar tonight, I'd been running behind. I'd gotten caught by an old woman named Beryl Griggs coming in right before the end of official lobby hours at 6:00, telling me some wild tale about a psychopath on the loose and china dolls. It was about the fourth wild conspiracy she'd brought to me since I'd been elected. Nice lady, but she watches too much BritBox. She comes in and lays out her whole theory of the case like she's writing an episode of *Midsomer Murders*. It never amounts to anything, but I hear her out anyway. I think she's mostly just lonely.

Police work. So glamorous.

Chapter Five

JOLIE

I stumble out of the Mockingbird Thursday night—Friday morning?—exhausted but pleased. The week has unfolded exactly like I thought it would, and why wouldn't it? Business analysis is my whole thing. I hadn't gotten into the bar business lightly. We're at about sixty percent of our capacity each night, and that's right on pace. Within a couple of months, we should be nearly full most nights.

Tonight, instead of slogging upstairs to sleep on the sofa at Ry's place, I get to go to my own house. The title cleared right before 5:00 yesterday, and I had my new key in hand before lunch. I'd had furniture delivery already scheduled for weeks.

I climb into my truck and pull out. It's past midnight, and the bar will still be open until 1:00, but technically it's staffed so that I don't need to be there at all. Tonight, I'm letting myself leave early as the only official celebration I'll have of getting my house. It's not my first; I own two rental properties in Chicago, including the townhome I moved out of when the rest of my life fell apart.

This newest house is outside of Harvest Hollow proper, in an older area that never became an official neighborhood. City lights and sidewalks disappear, and I'm driving along roads bordered by drainage ditches that front large pieces of property and houses built to suit the owners' tastes without an HOA to tell you how big or what color anything can be.

It's an interesting mix of custom homes in everything from Georgian style to modern farmhouse and a fair sprinkling of double- and triple-wide mobile homes with vinyl roofs in bright colors mixed in.

I'd been stubborn about what I wanted; as a kid, I'd longed for even a modest rambler, built in the sixties, beige brick, small windows, most of them showing outdated mini-blinds. And I'd have killed for an invitation into one of the bigger houses, like the Georgian ones with two stories and long windows looking out on groomed yards. But Jolie McGraw hadn't been the type of person that kids who lived in those houses invited over to play. My life could have been scripted by a television writer who never had the imagination to rise above movie-of-the-week dramas.

The streets are empty this late at night, and I pick up some speed as I get closer to my property, a "nouveau Craftsman revival," according to my realtor. All I know is that even though it's way bigger than what I need at three thousand square feet, it still looks cozy. Cottagey, maybe? Like a place to burrow as the weather cools, for sure.

The roads here are narrow and dark, but not busy, and the curves are gentle enough not to risk any loss of control. I watch the speedometer climb to five over the speed limit and smile at the feel of my Ford F-150's engine handling it like a boss. It's so overpowered for what I need, but if you're going to be a stereotype, might as well go all in. I'd even had it lifted and fitted with mudflaps.

I'm only a mile from my place when red and blue lights flash behind me. I shoot a glance in the rearview mirror and curse. That is, in fact, a police car, and it is, in fact, pulling me over. For going five over the speed limit? What a joke.

I signal and pull to the narrow shoulder, reaching for my license and temporary registration. The permanent one hasn't come in from the state, and I've still got an Illinois ID.

When I catch sight of the officer in my sideview mirror, I groan before schooling my face into bored indifference. Of course it's Lucas Cole. Why wouldn't it be?

I enjoy the height my lift kit gives me when he reaches my door and has to look up, shining his flashlight inside before he steps back in surprise.

I roll down my window. "Sheriff Cole," I drawl. I'd worked hard to smooth out my Appalachian accent in college and got it pretty close to neutral by the time I started at Blue Slate, but I could summon it at will. "Surely you have people you can send out for country road patrol. Or do you do *everything* in your department?" It comes out with dropped *g*'s, long *e* sounds rolled more into long *a*'s, and a "surely" that sounds like "shorely."

"Jolie," he says, nodding. "Got called out and happened to be returning when I saw you driving."

"Honestly, Sheriff, you're about the last person I'd expect to stop someone going five over."

"Guess you think you know why I stopped you. License and registration, please."

I blink at him. "Are you joking?"

"No. License and registration, please."

I hand them over, my face telling him exactly how stupid I think this is.

"Illinois?" he says, his eyebrows going up.

"I have thirty days to get a North Carolina license."

He looks up at me, and I wonder if that's part of the problem; he's used to towering over people, and it ticks him off to look up to me, of all people. "How long you been back?"

I give him a cool smile. "Not thirty days."

He nods and walks back to his cruiser, settling into the driver's seat and doing who knows what. Does he have a computer in there? Does he have to call dispatch to run my license?

I settle into my seat and wait, my hands curled around the steering wheel.

When he returns, he hands back my registration but not my license, even though I know for a fact my record is clean.

"Can you step down from the vehicle?" he asks. But it's not really asking. He says it in a calm voice, but he's used to being obeyed. I can tell. Maybe it's in the way he says it with total certainty that I'll comply.

But why should I? "No thanks. Write me the ticket so I can get home."

"That wasn't the option I offered you." His voice is the same level of calm.

I lean out to meet his eyes and give him a hard stare. "You think I'm drunk? I'm not. You'd smell it on me. I don't even drink."

He furrows his forehead. "A bar owner who doesn't drink?"

I lift my chin slightly. I don't have to explain myself to him any further.

"Are you driving home from the bar?"

"My *business*? Yes, I am."

"So you're returning from a bar at 1:00 in the morning in a vehicle with registration tags that aren't easy to see." He steps back to make room. "As I was saying, please step out of the truck."

The one thing Lucas Cole did for me in high school was burn up every last bit of patience I may have ever had for fools and people who waste my time. He's both, and he knows it. I cut the engine and swing my door wide so fast that he has to hop backward to avoid getting hit.

I just look at him, giving him the same "go to hell" stare he'd give me when I tried to help him with geometry proofs. I will be making no apologies.

I climb down from the cab and land on my feet, light and easy, even in my heels on the dirt road, steady as can be. I cross my arms and wait for whatever foolishness he comes up with next.

"You ran a stop sign about a quarter mile back," he says.

"What stop sign?" There's no stop sign back there.

"I will never understand why people who run signs and signals think admitting they didn't see it is some kind of defense."

I turn and stare back down the road, visualizing that stretch in my head. Did I really run a stop sign? "I've only driven this stretch twice before. It's possible I missed it. These roads aren't exactly well lit."

"Even better reason not to cruise over the speed limit on the way home from a bar. I'm going to perform a field sobriety test on you, Jolie. Please stand on one leg and count to ten using Carolinas."

"Are you freaking kidding me, Lucas? Is this because I didn't ask you to turn around so I could kiss your butt when you interfered, uninvited, on Monday night?"

He sighs. "I explained why I'm doing this already. Are you refusing?"

I glare at him again. "I'll even keep my heels on for this." I lift a foot behind me and stay rock solid on the one still planted. "One Carolina, two Carolina, three . . ." I keep going until he stops me at five.

"That's enough," he says. "One more quick check. Walk a straight line, heel-to-toe, ten steps ahead, then the same thing backward."

"Legally, I don't have to do that."

He dips his chin in acknowledgment. "You do not."

I would like to punch that chin. Hard. Just knock the smug off his face. But I'm not a violent woman, and I don't actually know how to throw a punch. "I'm glad you realize that, because I'm not going to do it. Here's what I *am* going to do for you: recite every theorem you couldn't understand when I tried to tutor you through geometry until you get bored and leave me alone. Reflexive property: a quantity is congruent to itself." I use the hand motions I'd once tried to come up with to help Lucas remember them, making them as precise and energetic as a Bobcat Kitten's cheer routine.

Yes, our cheerleaders are called the Kittens. I hate it, but I wasn't one, so it's none of my business. "Substitution postulate"—hand motion—"if equal quantities are—"

He holds up his palm. "All right, Jolie. You can stop."

"I'm not under the influence. Give me back my license and go catch some real bad guys."

"Not under the influence of alcohol," he concedes. "But we don't write DUIs here anyway. We write DWIs, and while you're in the clear on that too, you probably need a DWA."

A what? "Driving while . . ."

"Angry," he says. "Not good for you either."

You know who the last person I want lecturing me about anger management is? Lucas Cole. This is definitely a pot and kettle situation.

"Lucky I wasn't driving angry until you pulled me over, *Sheriff*," and I curl the title in my mouth in a way that makes it nearly a profanity. "Now give me my license, and I'll drive exactly forty-five all the way to my house."

If it surprises him to hear I've got a house out this way instead of living in town, he doesn't show it. Instead, he nods and hands back my license. "You're clearly not drunk. And if ever someone deserved a break on running a stop sign, it's you. I owe you after what I put you through in high school. Just watch for it in the daylight tomorrow so you don't make that mistake in the future."

He nods and heads for his cruiser, and I stare after him until he's climbing into his seat, and then I snap into action.

"Lucas, wait!" I call.

He pauses. "You need something?"

I walk toward him, stopping a few feet from his open door so I don't have to shout. "I'm sorry for the attitude. I know you were doing your job. It's what I'd want you to do for anyone you thought was driving drunk."

It's too dark to make out his expression, but after a couple of seconds, he nods. "Appreciate that. Night, Jolie."

He shuts his door but doesn't pull out until I'm safely back in my truck. Then he gets on the road headed in the direction I'm going, and I watch his taillights until they disappear, my own engine idling.

I've seen Lucas Cole twice now, and he hasn't sneered either time. If Lucas Cole doesn't sneer, is it even really Lucas Cole?

Because the Lucas Cole who showed up at my bar to calmly deal with the bad apples last night and the Lucas Cole who courteously did his job tonight even when I gave him attitude both times?

That is *not* the Lucas Cole I remember.

Chapter Six

LUCAS

When you have a ten-year-old at home, it doesn't matter that you didn't fall asleep until 3 AM; you still have to get up and take her to school.

Which I'll do, without complaint. I knew what I was signing up for when I became my niece's legal guardian. Pops and I go out of the way to give her a consistent routine, and that routine doesn't care about traffic stops I make in the middle of the night, or if they keep me up for an extra hour.

My brain still isn't done with the subject of Jolie McGraw, because she's the first thing I think of when I wake up. That woman really stood on the gravel shoulder last night in high heels and recited geometry theorems with those freaking hand motions like we were back in high school.

That is one of those days I most regret. She'd come into the library, looking determined and maybe even proud of herself as she'd shown me the gestures she'd come up with to help me remember. But I wasn't about to do them. It had made me feel like I was in kindergarten.

So instead of at least thanking her for trying, I'd acted like a bigger dirtbag than usual and told her she looked like a loser, and I would never care enough about math to do something that stupid looking. Her cheeks had scorched red as I turned to walk out of the library.

I'd been the worst.

Watching her do them last night, her face defiant, her motions sharp and almost angry, it had been hard not to smile. I'd had that coming for years.

It had also been impossible once again to ignore how well those years had treated her. She'd had her tooth fixed. In general, I like scars and marks that add character to a person's face, but that missing tooth had been about more than the look. It had advertised her poverty in a solidly middle-class town.

Stuff like missing teeth goes uncorrected when you're poor. I knew this because I'd been that poor before I'd gone to work in construction and then into law enforcement. Maybe I'd resented her back then for trying to make something of herself with her good grades, while I only came to school to escape the chaos at home.

Anyway, I'm glad Jolie fixed her teeth. I'd have done the same thing if it were me. Brooklyn would say Jolie is fancy now.

I smile again. I can say for dang sure that her shiny hair and carefully made-up face were not what I had expected to see looking down at me from that lifted good old boy truck.

It's sexy when a woman drives a truck. But when Jolie climbed out of her brand-new one looking like she'd be equally at home stepping out of a top-of-the-line Mercedes?

Whew. That had been next level. Stopped my breath for a second until I could pull myself together.

She's a contradiction, and everything about her appearance raises questions. Why is she back? Is she here to stay? Why all the secrecy around opening the bar?

Does she like a man in uniform?

I shake my head as I walk into the kitchen, the smell of strong coffee hitting me before I even reach the doorway. Brooklyn hasn't come out of her room yet, but she will soon, and the morning can truly begin.

I like my time with Brooklyn before I take her to school. It used to be that she'd chatter to me all the way there; there's less of that lately and more of morning grumpiness. But I still love the time.

In addition to the coffee, Pops has scrambled eggs and toast ready for us. Between my grandfather and me, we're getting by with raising Brooklyn since my brother went to prison. Barely.

Anyway, it's better than what my brother could do and far better than what he actually did. If Brooklyn had been mine to start with, I would never have done anything to risk losing her. But my brother had decided armed bank robbery was easier than holding down a factory job, and he'd given up the next fifteen years with her.

I accept the tumbler of black coffee Pops hands me and take a few fortifying sips before I tackle the most dangerous creature in the Smoky Mountains: a cranky tween.

Our place isn't big; it's the house Pops built for him and my grandmother who passed in an accident before I was born. He'd been left to raise two kids, my dad and my aunt, by himself. I'm certain a big reason he's helping with Brooklyn is because he feels like he did such a poor job with his own kids. Grief had made him an absent father, even when he was there. More often than not, he was off overseeing the Oakley Orchards as the farm manager for two decades before a fall from a ladder sent him into early retirement twenty years ago. The Oakleys had paid off his mortgage as part of his retirement.

I cover utilities and property taxes, and while it's a small place, it's enough for the three of us. I'm sure Brooklyn would be happier not sharing a bathroom with her uncle and great-grandfather, but she has her own room. We fit. It works.

I knock on her door at the end of the hallway. "Brooklyn? You up?" I get a grunt. I use my police training to decide that this means yes. "We leave in twenty minutes. Come on and get your breakfast so Pops doesn't worry." Another grunt. I decide to go eat and give it a few minutes to see if she emerges. It's hit-and-miss whether that will take more coaxing. I hope it's a non-coaxing day.

Pop's eyebrow goes up when I come back in. "Still sleeping?"

"I think she's up. Probably."

He nods. "What do you think is wrong with her?"

I sigh. "I don't know. Is being ten a psychological condition?"

Now he grunts.

Ten minutes later, Brooklyn materializes in the kitchen wearing a thick hoodie that's too warm for the early September forecast, pajama bottoms, and her backpack.

"I'm not hungry," she says.

Great. I've got two battles to fight right now, but I'm already learning to pick one. Pajamas or food?

"You need regular pants," I tell her, keeping my tone neutral. "Pops washed some laundry yesterday."

"Jeans in there," he says.

"Not comfortable," she mumbles.

Makes me wonder how early is too early to let her drink coffee. I should google it, because if ever someone was born for the habit, it's this kid. At least lately. But google will tell me no. Anything I ask google about raising Brooklyn basically returns a result of "it will ruin her forever." White bread. Nylon. Cartoons. Probably just breathing.

"You can't go to school in pajamas," I tell her. "You need to show up dressed ready to learn."

"I hate jeans."

This is a newer complaint. For the last week, we've gone back and forth until she changes, but she's later than usual this morning. That means Uncle Boss has to come out, and he's my least favorite version of myself.

"No pajamas to school. Go change."

"I just won't go to school," she snaps.

"That ain't how it works, honey," Pops says, his voice calm. "You're running out of time, and you may not care about getting to school late, but you're going to make Lucas late to work, and it won't do. I washed some sweats. Why don't you go get those on? I'll pack up some breakfast for you to eat in the car."

She doesn't bother with an answer, just rolls her eyes and disappears from the kitchen. Pops and I exchange looks, but we both know better than to say anything when she comes back in sweatpants and takes the paper bowl Pops put her breakfast in.

"Let's go, Honeycrisp." I don't wince when I say it, but I should; she's going to hate it. I nicknamed her that when she was a toddler because she was so sweet. I've been trying to stop using the nickname, but old habits are hard to break.

"Ugh, stop calling me that. I don't even like apples."

Not so sweet now.

We get in my Explorer, and I turn on my service radio, letting it rest in the console between us. She's always liked listening to the police band. I'm never sure if it's a good idea or not. Maybe it's good that she knows what's really going on in town so she knows the kind of trouble you can find in Harvest Hollow. Maybe it'll make her anxious and neurotic, but given all the women I know who love gruesome true crime podcasts, I've erred on the side of letting her listen. Besides, 8 AM is not a popular time for crime.

The radio crackles as Brooklyn buckles in. "Sheriff, we got a 10-102 complaint. Manager at that new bar reported some graffiti this morning."

Jolie's place. I frown even as I press the button to answer. "I'll check it out before I come in."

"No need. Officer Avila is on it. Just wanted you to know since you asked."

I'd directed dispatch to contact me with any incidents related to Tequila Mockingbird. Hardin was stubborn—and worse when he drank. I'd expected he wasn't done tangling with Jolie, especially not since she'd backed him down in front of his friends.

I pull into the drop-off line at the elementary school. The line makes me want to jail at least seven people every morning, but I try never to let it show.

"Have a good day, Honeycr—" I break off at her glare and switch tracks faster than a bullet train. "That is, Brooklyn."

It doesn't improve her expression. If anything, she frowns more as she crosses her arms and trudges toward the school, drawing a long sigh from me as I watch.

I don't know what happened to sweet little Honeycrisp over the summer, but she left fourth grade with a smile and she's been turning up to fifth grade every day with a scowl since school started.

I carefully pull through the drop-off line to model good driving, then pull out of the neighborhood and head toward Maple. I want to see the damage to Jolie's place for myself before I head into the office.

As soon as I clap eyes on the bar, I've got a good news/bad news situation. Good news: I know exactly who spray-painted "Sullivan's" across her storefront in rust red letters. Bad news: I have to start work by having a chat with Shane Hardin, and there's no morning that can't be ruined by dealing with that turd bucket.

I call Becky, my admin, to let her know where I'm going and brace myself for my morning to go from tween to worse.

Chapter Seven

JOLIE

My phone rings around 9 AM, which means I've gotten six hours of sleep. That *should* be enough for me to not feel so grumpy when I answer it. I survived at the hedge fund on way less, fueled by caffeine and a fear of failure that drove me to work hours even a surgical intern would question.

But it's not enough. Because a certain sheriff occupied my thoughts for an extra hour of twisting and turning after I climbed into my bed. Does it even count as a bed if it's a mattress on the floor because the frame turned out to be backordered?

I grope for my cell and squint at the number. Maybe five people have this number, and all of them work at the bar except my property manager, so there's an eighty percent chance this has something to do with the Mockingbird.

Yeah, those are the brilliant math skills that would have made me a fortune if I'd stayed at Blue Slate and let my soul be sucked dry.

Not that I'm prone to drama. The woman who gets dumped by her boyfriend because his parents think she isn't good enough, so she runs away to buy the bar she hates most in the hometown she loathes so she can be exactly what his family thinks she is?

Who, me? Dramatic? Nah.

It's Ry. I mash buttons until the ringing stops. "What, Ry?"

"Good morning!" He's working so hard to be cheerful that I know something's wrong.

I sit up and blink into full wakefulness. "What's going on?"

"Everything is fine," he says. "Kind of."

I'm already cursing while I look around the room for pants. "Talk."

"We had a little vandalism," he says, the way you might say, "It's sprinkling outside." "Nothing that won't come off with some . . . soap?"

"Soap? What kind of vandalism are we talking?" I tuck the phone against my shoulder and rummage through my drawers for something to wear.

"Uh, graffiti?" There's a wince in his voice. "That comes off with soap, right?"

"Why are you asking me? I've spent exactly zero time as a hoodlum."

"Aren't you the hoodlum whisperer?" he asks in a not-so-veiled reference to Lucas Cole's appearance in the bar the other night.

"Wasn't then"—what an understatement—"and I'm not now. Be there in twenty." That's how long it takes to drive into town. I should have bought something closer, but that wouldn't have been hick enough to match my ex's perception.

Also, I sort of fell in love with my stupid house the second I saw it.

I end the call and look around for something to wear, but my wardrobe is either a closet full of business clothes or a dresser full of workout gear. I only have one setting: all out. Board room. Gym. If I'm not asleep, I'm grinding.

I slept in an oversized Duke T-shirt, so I grab a pair of leggings, jam my feet into my Nikes, and snatch my purse from the hook by my garage door. I use the four-way stop I missed last night as a ponytail-making pause, then drive the rest of the way to the Mockingbird in exactly fifteen minutes. I park in the lot behind the bar, which looks normal. Graffiti must be out front.

It's empty inside, dim light coming through the shuttered windows, but when I push open the front door, I walk right out to Ry and Lucas Cole.

"Hey, Jo," Ry says. Lucas tips his hat at me. His cowboy hat. The same one he wore Monday night when he came in, uninvited.

It's so stupid. We are not the Wild West, or the Deep South, or a Hollywood version of either. Hat tipping is not a thing in a town that gets tourist overflow from chichi ski resorts and granola-stuffed hippie hikers.

It's even more irritating that he looks good in that hat. And that uniform. Aren't they made of polyester? Isn't it supposed to be unflattering? But I'd watched him walk back to his patrol car in the dead of night—*all* the way back to it—because no one had given his backside the memo about polyester.

I'm petty. Not dead.

I'm also very annoyed with myself for finding Lucas attractive, so I ignore the hat tip and turn to look at the bar front. Drippy rust-colored letters spell out "Sullivans" across the wood, brick, and glass, a full twenty feet wide.

"Gee, Sheriff. I wonder who could have done this." I give Lucas a flat stare, and he nods.

"Yeah. Seems I owe someone a visit."

"Great. Let him know I'll send him the bill."

Lucas sighs. "He won't pay if we can't prove it was him."

"You think someone else besides the guy who was in here hollering about Sullivan's on Monday did this?" I ask.

"No. But common sense isn't proof. I'll have the shops with security cameras check their footage. There's a decent chance a couple of them caught at least some of this."

"What do we do in the meantime?" Ry asks. "Are we supposed to leave this as evidence for an investigation?"

"I got pictures," Lucas says. "Do me a favor and leave at least one of the shutters painted in case I need to match the paint."

"No." It's a knee-jerk reaction, but I don't want a single speck of the old bar's name on my new one.

"I'll need it for evidence," Lucas says. "If there's no security footage of him, then you'll need every other scrap of evidence you have to bring charges."

"You won't see it when the shutters are open," Ry tells me.

He's right. When the bar opens in a few hours, the shutters will be flipped and no one will see the spray paint, but I don't care. The first thing I did when I bought the place was order the contractor to remove the old name and send me pictures to prove he'd done it. I don't want a trace of it back.

"I don't care," I tell him. "I'm opening today, and I don't want a single customer walking past graffiti to get in here."

"What's going on?"

I turn to find Wayne Oakley coming up the sidewalk. It's too early on a weekday for much of Maple to be busy yet beyond the bank and the places that serve breakfast and coffee, but leave it to the nosiest man in Harvest Hollow to be out and about.

"Nothing, Wayne," Lucas says. "We've got it handled."

"Looks like you've had a graffiti incident," Wayne says.

"If you know, then why'd you ask?" I look at him without any effort to hide my contempt.

Lucas's eyebrows go up, Ry winces again, and Wayne Oakley takes a step back. It's very satisfying until he regroups and adjusts his belt over his paunchy middle.

"You must be the new owner," he says, extending a hand. "I'm Wayne Oakley, president of the Chamber of Commerce. Welcome to Harvest Hollow."

Does he not remember me? Because there is no way I'd forget the guy who forced the principal to investigate me for cheating because he couldn't believe I'd beaten out his daughter for valedictorian by a tenth of a point.

I look down at his hand then turn to Ry. "Call whoever you have to call." I walk into the bar and pull the door closed, but not before I hear Lucas's voice in low tones say, "I don't think she'll be joining the Chamber, Wayne." His amusement is clear.

"That was very—"

But I'll never get to hear the end of Wayne Oakley's sentence because the door closes with a bang. Tragic.

I head into my office to research spray paint removal, but I'm thinking about Wayne. Old Guard Oakley, as if being descended from the town founders made him better than the rest of the town. He'd taught his children the same snobbery.

So no, I won't shake the hand of the man whose daughter bullied me through high school, or the hand of anyone else who doesn't interest me.

I'm not here to make nice.

On Lucas's advice, Ry runs a couple blocks over to the hardware store to get the solvent he needs plus check on the rental price for a pressure washer. He promises to call in a couple of staff early to open for the afternoon while he takes care of the exterior, so I hit the coffee place nearby for the caffeine I didn't grab in my rush from my house this morning. I could get it at the Mockingbird, but it's always better when someone else makes it.

It's past 10:00 now, and their morning rush is over. Only one customer sits at a table and the women behind the counter are chatting as they get their sidework done. Like the bar, it mainly seems to be polishing water spots off glasses. It's a Sisyphean thing. One of them—Heather, according to her name tag—smiles at me. "What can I get for you?"

I smile back. The sheriff and chamber president might be surprised to know it, but in general, I'm good-natured. I'm not sure anyone would say I'm warm—not like Tina or Precious, who people just melt around. But I'm definitely not cold. I don't even have sharp edges.

Well. Not many.

I enjoy people and good conversations. It'd be downright stupid to go into the bar business if I didn't. And so long as none of the people who helped me find my sharp edges when I was younger don't come in, the Mockingbird will be a relaxing place to be.

I give Heather my order, and when she comes back with a hazelnut latte, I thank her, leave a generous tip, and take my coffee outside.

It's a ridiculous drink. Super sweet and way too indulgent. I might ruin Lucas and Wayne Oakley's perception of me if they knew I didn't drink my coffee black and acrid. But I love it, and I'll give up my hazelnut lattes when the world runs out of hazelnuts and milk.

The early fall day beckons me to wander down Maple instead of driving home to shower and armor up for the day, so I follow the impulse. The sky is Carolina blue, a color I can't bring myself to hate even as a Duke graduate, and the temperature tells me it'll be time to switch to sweaters in a week or so.

I mostly window-shop, noting a few stores I'd like to come back and explore later. Two blocks down, a thrift shop is advertising a "Get Women to Work" event, a clothing drive for professional wardrobe pieces, and I make a mental note. Toward the end of the business district where it changes to municipal buildings, the shops thin out and a familiar building takes shape, one I realize my feet have steered me toward on autopilot.

The Harvest Hollow Library.

I stop at the edge of the small, tidy lawn it sits on, and study the building that had sheltered me from so many things for much of my life here.

It's in a well-kept and stately renovated home that was willed to the town for use as a library in the early seventies, but the house itself dates back about a hundred years. It's Craftsman style, with a low-pitched angled roof, overhanging eaves, and a covered front porch, still holding the bin for after-hours book returns and a rolling cart with donated books for sale.

Do I want to go in? It looks so familiar and unchanged on the outside that the first happy sense of nostalgia I've had since arriving in town a week ago causes a twinge at the end of my nose, a warning of impending tears.

Another thing that might surprise Cole and Oakley: sometimes I'm sappy.

What if I go in and it's too different? What if it's "upgraded" with laminate floors and easy-clean counters? What if it doesn't smell the same? That would break my heart.

I walk past it, drinking the rest of my coffee as I debate with myself. And then I catch myself smiling. How did I not realize that I impulse bought a house four times bigger than I need because it reminds me of my favorite library?

Two minutes later, my empty coffee cup disposed of, I climb the front steps and smile again at the comfortable rockers and benches sitting on the porch for moms who want to sit in the shade and watch their kids play on the lawn.

The moment my foot touches the familiar oak floor inside, I freeze.

It's the same. It's all exactly the same, and the orange-scented furniture oil and the vanilla musk of all the books envelops me and shoves me back in time. I'm ten-year-old Jolie, slipping into the cozy library on a chilly November day, wanting somewhere warm to wait until the early dark fell so I didn't have to stay in our dirty apartment alone.

The sense memory rushes in with the force of a gut punch, and I give a tiny gasp, like it will equalize my internal pressure, and I can ground myself again in the present.

"May I help you?" asks a voice I know nearly as well as that smell. It's a pleasant voice, one that asked patient questions and gave even more patient answers.

Mrs. Herring.

I glance over to the circulation desk where she sits, ready to check out books to patrons.

"Just browsing," I say, and turn to the left, into the stacks. Mrs. Herring was one of my favorite people in Harvest Hollow. Most of my teachers were great, but school itself was sometimes hard because of other kids. But the library had always been the one truly safe space for me in town. Nothing bad ever happened here.

I want desperately to say hello, to tell her that her presence behind the front desk was a gift I didn't know I'd needed. She'd seemed so old to me then that I assumed she was retired, but she must only be in her late sixties now. I want to talk to her and find out how she's been. But at the moment, I feel about as tough as a newly hatched baby chick and just as bewildered by this sensory overload. I don't think I have it in me right this second to stand it if she doesn't remember me. I had one Mrs. Herring, but she's had dozens, even hundreds, of lonely Jolies over the years.

The library hasn't been open long. Less than half an hour, I think, and only a few people have come in so far. I wander the shelves in peace, smiling at the call numbers. The Dewey decimal system is one of the great loves of my life. I tend to fall in love with anything that imposes order on chaos.

It doesn't take long to wander the entire collection. The library is large for a Craftsman, but even with removing some of the interior walls, the space is limited. There's a small section near the front of the room by the windows with a handful of tables and chairs, just like when I was a kid. A few copies of the city and county newspapers sit on an accent table, and a low shelf of magazines runs along the wall below the windows.

The only other open spaces on the first floor are the public restrooms and the children's room with the kid books. The little remaining space is storage, I think. Upstairs, there are small study rooms. I would always invite classmates there if it was ever my turn to host a group project. No way would I have risked bringing them back to my apartment.

The paint on the walls looks as if it's been refreshed since my time here, and the tables show no wear, so they must be newer too. But the heavy wooden chairs are the same ones I used to sit in for hours, working my way through the stacks of books I'd tote over from the kid's room, and later, from the main fiction shelves.

I slip into one of the chairs and smooth my hand over the tabletop. All my irritation over the graffiti and the town officials has disappeared, and I close my eyes, taking in these familiar smells and sounds. I never expected Harvest Hollow to feel like home, and in the nine days I've been here, it hasn't. Until now.

"Jolie McGraw? Is that you?"

I open my eyes to smile at Mrs. Herring. She remembers.

"Hey, Mrs. Herring."

"My goodness, it's been a minute." Her keen brown eyes sweep over me, and I note the changes the last decade have wrought on her. Her deep brown skin doesn't show much evidence of aging, but her short hair shows more silver than before. Her red glasses still hang from a chain around her neck, and she's still wearing a cardigan. The librarian clichés end there, though.

She's slim, the kind of thin that you can only get from genes, and that short hair sits in a sassy cut that's stacked in the back and falls into perfectly formed curls toward the front, one almost but not quite daring to fall over her eye, the other tucked behind her ear. It's so chic, I kind of want to die.

Her cardigan is black and skims her figure to her waist, draping over a silky cream blouse with a loose floppy bow, and finished off with a pair of plain camel tweed trousers and ballet flats in a cheetah print.

Dang. If this is almost seventy, sign me up.

"How are you?" she asks when she finishes her mutual inspection. "And how long are you in town?"

"I'm doing well," I say. One feels both entirely comfortable with Mrs. Herring and as if one must use one's best grammar around her at the same time. "I'm back for good. I took over Sullivan's."

Her eyes brighten. "You're the owner of Tequila Mockingbird? Of course you would call it something clever. You were always one of my best-read patrons."

She's worked here for decades, I know, but she might be telling the truth. I was and still am a hardcore bookworm.

I stand and push my chair in. "I'll definitely be back. I need to reclaim my title."

Mrs. Herring smiles. "No one has ever taken it. Should we go get you a new library card?"

I grin. "Yes. Yes, we should."

Ten minutes later, I have a new library card in hand. It shows an illustration of the library on the front with the words "Passport to Magic" printed beneath it.

"Thank you, Mrs. Herring. I love it." I hold it up next to my face and give her a bright commercial grin like I'm advertising toothpaste. "I'll stop by later this week when I can block out some time to explore the shelves."

"Do you still read a bit of everything?" she asks.

"I read a lot of everything."

"Good. I'll set aside some books for you, and we'll see if you've already discovered them on your own."

"This is my kind of personal shopping," I tell her. "And if you find yourself further down Maple after closing anytime, stop in at the bar. We can gossip about the Thursday Murder Club folks over an adult beverage."

Her eyes twinkle. "I should have known you already discovered one of my favorite series."

I smile and leave with a wave, already looking forward to coming back, just like I did when I was a kid. But for the first time, my flashback to childhood is a good thing.

When I step outside, my smile widens. These Carolina skies aren't bad either. And my morning coffee was excellent.

This isn't how I thought my morning would go after witnessing the vandalism at the bar, but I lean into it, enjoying it even more when I think about how much it would tick off Shane Hardin if he could see me now.

The smile lasts until I clap eyes on the figure twenty yards down the sidewalk. It's the esteemed town sheriff again.

Then just like that, the smile is gone.

Chapter Eight

LUCAS

There aren't a lot of people who are neutral about an officer in uniform. I get lots of welcome looks. I get just as many scowls. So it shouldn't bother me when Jolie's face changes the second she sees me on the sidewalk, but it does. Maybe it's because in the instant before she sees me, she's smiling, something I've yet to see her do in the three times I've run into her so far.

In a way, it feels like more times than that because she's been on my mind so often. I owe her a better apology than "I won't give you a ticket."

"Jolie," I say. "You didn't have to come all the way down here for an update. I'm sorry I haven't had a chance to talk to Hardin yet. Had a bit of a detour."

That "detour" climbs out of my cruiser now. I'd gotten a call from school almost right after leaving Jolie's bar. It was the school nurse informing me that Brooklyn was complaining of a headache, and I needed to come get her.

"I was coming from the library, not to check on you," Jolie says as Brooklyn shuffles over to me on the sidewalk.

Right. Of course Jolie wasn't coming to talk to me.

Brooklyn joins me, her hood all the way up, a book pressed to her chest, her backpack hanging on one shoulder, but barely. She's so slouched it looks like it'll fall off any second, which means it could hit the concrete with her school-issued Chromebook inside. I want to tell her to hitch it up or put both straps on or straighten her shoulders, but lately, just breathing wrong with her can send her stomping into her room or make her cry. I decide not to risk it.

"Jolie, meet my detour. Brooklyn, Jolie used to tutor me in high school."

Brooklyn's eyes widen and dart from Jolie to me. "You were his teacher?"

"Tutor," I correct. "It means she helped me with math."

"He was bad at math?" Brooklyn asks Jolie.

Jolie's scowl disappeared when Brooklyn joined me, and now she looks uncertain. "Your dad was . . ."

"He's not my dad," Brooklyn says. It's an annoyed correction, and I get it. She has to make it often, but I'll still have to chat with her about her tone later. Great.

"I just wish I was her dad," I say, also used to this misunderstanding. "Brooklyn is my niece, and I get to raise her."

"Oh," Jolie says. "Okay."

I wonder if she knows anything about my brother, who is two years older than me. He had dropped out before she started at Harvest High, but our reputations had preceded both of us back then. Maybe she's already guessed why I'm Brooklyn's guardian now.

"Is that *Sea of Monsters*?" Jolie asks.

I blink, not sure what she's talking about. It definitely wasn't the next thing I expected out of her mouth. But Brooklyn shifts from standing slightly behind me to take a half step forward.

"You've read it?" she asks Jolie. Oh, books. Got it.

Jolie nods. "The whole series. Twice. Is it your favorite?"

"Yeah."

I listen to this with fascination. Brooklyn has gone from talkative to surly in the last few months, and this short exchange counts as a long conversation lately.

"You should try *Keepers of the Lost Cities* next," Jolie says.

"They're always checked out," Brooklyn answers.

"You can borrow mine."

My eyebrows shoot up. This is not the Jolie *I've* been dealing with for the last week or so. Brooklyn is surprised too. "You would loan them to me?"

"One at a time, but yes. If you're good at taking care of books. Are you?"

Brooklyn nods.

"Okay, then. Let me know when you're ready for the first one."

I wish Brooklyn would pull her hood down so Jolie could see her face better. Or just so I can. It's been a while since I've seen it without a scowl. But she only mumbles a thank you and falls quiet.

It stretches for a beat or two before I decide to break it. "Brooklyn here isn't feeling so well, so I picked her up from school. Brooklyn, go on in to the station. Becky will give you a place to work until Pops can get you." Her backpack has slipped a bit more, and I can't bite my tongue any longer. "Also, please put your backpack all the way on. It's going to fall off and bust your stuff."

Brooklyn makes a sound like a scoff. "It's fine, Uncle Lucas." She walks toward the station without adjusting her backpack or . . . no. "Walk" is not the word. It's more than a walk and not quite a stomp. As she reaches to open it, the backpack slips off her shoulder and hits the concrete with a thunk.

Jolie winces. I press my lips together and wait. Brooklyn stands there for about three seconds, frozen, then reaches down, snatches up the backpack to hold it against her chest like her book, and walks into the station without looking back.

I turn to Jolie. "Sorry about that. I guess that's another apology to throw on the pile. She's been tricky lately. Thanks for being nice to her."

Her eyes flash. "I'm not a monster, Lucas. I dislike *you*. I have no beef with your niece."

"Okay. I deserve that." I glance down the street toward her place, which I can't quite see from here. "Are you heading back? Could I walk you over and buy you a cup of coffee along the way to apologize? Cataloochee makes great coffee."

"I already got coffee this morning."

I'm not sure what to do with the return of her icy anger. In my job, I usually deal with people whose tempers are burning white hot. I rest my hands on my gun belt, already worn out from navigating the moods of the female of the species this morning. "Right. Got it. Hope your day goes better than it started. I'll let you know where I get with Hardin."

I only make it a few steps before she calls me.

"Sheriff."

I stop and turn.

"When you pulled me over last week, were you out that way because you live over there?"

"I do." I don't generally advertise where we live because there's plenty of former guests of the county jail who'd like to know. But it's not secret either, and whatever else Jolie is, she's not someone that I worry about knowing my address.

"With your dad?"

She's watching me, her eyes making small tracking movements like she's synthesizing the bits of info she's picked up and confirming her conclusions with my expression.

I shake my head. "Pops is my grandfather, Brooklyn's great-grandfather. But yes, we live with him. We moved in when I got custody of her."

"I live on White Pine." She pauses, then adds, "I need to go home and get ready for the day. I can drop Brooklyn off on my way."

That's unexpected. "You don't have to do that."

She looks at me like *Obviously.*

"I mean that it's nice of you to offer, but Pops will come get her soon. He's just on his morning walk, and he's opposed to cell phones. Besides, this is the third time in two weeks she's had me pick her up for a 'headache.' Probably do her some good to be bored in my office for a bit until he can come get her."

She glances toward the station. "You don't believe her about her headaches?"

I sigh. "That sounds bad, doesn't it?"

She shrugs. "Not if you're sure she's faking."

"It's kind of a new thing, but yeah. She is." My gut instinct is strong on this one. "Anyway, thanks again for the offer, but it's not urgent."

She nods and walks off, leaving me to wonder whether I've been extended an olive branch. Jolie McGraw had never been easy to read, which was probably why I worked so hard to upset her back in the day. But she's even more of a mystery now.

I watch her go until I realize my eyes are fixed on the view of her backside. Yeah, the sheriff can't be standing around ogling women. Better get in the office before I'm on the Harvest Hollow Happenings Instagram.

It's the bane of my existence. I can imagine the caption. *Sheriff keeps an eye on crime—if crime lives in the yoga pants of Sullivan's new owner.*

It's the worst—and I check it as religiously as the account's other eleven thousand followers. Whoever runs it has a way of capturing exactly the things you don't want it to.

But I still can't resist stealing one more glance Jolie's way before I head back into the station.

It'd be a crime not to.

Chapter Nine

JOLIE

I walk to my truck at a fast clip, a scowl back on my face, because my stone-cold heart went ever-so-slightly squishy when I found out Lucas Cole is a dad.

Sure, guardian, *legally*. But he's already doing way more for Brooklyn than my dad ever did for me. He's a parent, period.

I don't want my heart going even remotely squishy unless it's for my people. And I've already got one—Ry. That's more than some people get. Mrs. Herring flashes through my mind. Maybe two. But that's definitely as much people as anyone *needs*.

Ry is already working on the spray paint on the walls when I walk up.

"Fix your face, cuz," Ry says. "We'll have this cleaned up soon."

I smooth away the scowl. "Sorry. Ran into Lucas again."

"That's going to happen a lot when you both work on Maple," he says. "What'd he do to you this time?"

"He has a kid."

Ry looks surprised. "One, I did not know that. But two, why would that make you mad?"

"It's his niece. He's her guardian. And it makes him several percent less heinous."

He smiles. "High school was a long time ago. You've changed. Maybe he has too."

I consider Brooklyn's posture and attitude, then Lucas's barely disguised exasperation. It reminded me a lot of the few times he'd try to take his homework seriously before frustration crept into his face and then he did or said something rude. He had that same frustrated look today, although he'd done a good job of not dumping it on his niece.

"Maybe in some ways," I concede, but I'm still mulling that look of frustration. "But not so much in others."

Tina rounds the corner from employee parking. "I was promised loud machines if I came down early."

Ry grins. "Pressure washer is yours. We'll have to run it from the outside faucet straight through the bar, but then you can let it rip."

Tina rubs her hands. "Yesss. I used to work for my dad painting houses in the summer, and the pressure wash is the best part. So zen."

I shake my head, smiling now. Leave it to Tina to find the racket of a pressure washer soothing. Ry had recommended her for the server job. They were a year behind me in high school, so I hadn't known her well then, but his people instincts are good, and I'd liked her the minute I met her.

They go into the bar to set up the hose, and I glance back down the street toward the sheriff's building, thinking again about Brooklyn. Lucas is so much farther out of his depth than he realizes. I don't want to do him any favors, but this isn't about him. It's about Brooklyn.

I sigh and head back down the sidewalk, stepping into the station five minutes later.

"May I help you?" the woman at the reception desk asks. She's about twenty years older than me and has the soft lines of a mom who doesn't get much time for the gym. She's wearing very little makeup, and her eyes are watchful, but the faint lines near her mouth suggest she probably smiles a lot.

"Can you tell Lucas Cole that Jolie is here to see him?"

"May I ask what this is regarding?"

His absolute cluelessness about his niece. But I'm not going to put Brooklyn's business out there for everyone. "The vandalism to my bar this morning."

Her eyes widen. "You're the new owner?"

I nod.

She extends her hand for a shake. "Welcome to Harvest Hollow. I'm Becky Cuthbert. I'm sorry that happened. I promise, it's largely a safe city. The sheriff will make sure no one bugs you again."

"It's not his fault," I say. "And I grew up in Harvest Hollow. I know what it's like." The good *and* the bad. But she's right; crime here has always been pretty low.

"Hang tight and I'll let him know you're here." She picks up the handset for her phone and presses a button, says, "Jolie McGraw is asking to see you." She nods and hangs up, pressing something else that makes the heavy steel door to her left click open. "Come on back."

I shake my head. "I'd like to speak to him outside if that's all right. It'll only be a minute."

She nods and relays the message via phone again. "He'll be right out."

"Thanks." I step outside to wait. Becky doesn't look like she misses much, and I'd rather not be under her scrutiny. The last couple of days or so, I've been having this itchy feeling, like my skin doesn't fit right and I have to hitch it back into place.

I know it doesn't make sense, but I feel what I feel.

The station door opens and Lucas walks out. "Hey, Jolie. Did I forget something?"

Not *did you forget something.* It's hard to be annoyed with a guy who leads from a place of "maybe I'm wrong" while still somehow projecting complete competence.

"No, but I thought I should tell you I think I know what's behind your niece's headaches."

His eyes flare in surprise. "Okay. Shoot."

"How old is she? About ten? Eleven?"

"Ten," he confirms.

"And you said it's just you and your grandfather living with her?"

His eyebrows draw together. "Yes?"

"Does she by any chance wear a bra yet?"

"I . . . what?" He looks as confused as if I'd asked if *he* wears a bra.

Blerg. If it's awkward for me to bring it up, I can only imagine how hard it must be for Brooklyn. "When I was growing up, it was just me and my dad."

He nods. "I remember."

I wonder how much he remembers. There weren't too many people who hadn't heard about my dad and the infamous Harvest Festival crash when he ran the car he was driving on a suspended license into a candy apple booth. Destroyed the booth and broke the leg and two ribs of the one booth worker who couldn't jump out of the way fast enough.

"He didn't know anything about girls, less about tweens, and nothing about teenagers. There's a lot of stuff that goes on for girls that they don't always understand, and I had to learn most things the hard way. Internet searches at the library when I could get the public computer that was the most private. Books I wouldn't check out but I would read in the stacks every chance I got. My aunt finally noticed and talked me through some of the basics."

"Oh." Sheriff Lucas Cole looks absolutely dumbfounded for the first time. Ever. Including high school. Maybe "dumbfounded" is not the right word. Deer in headlights. Yeah. Clichés are clichés for a reason. Sometimes they're perfect. "But she's only ten."

"It's definitely puberty."

He flinches, and I press my lips together to hide a smile. I don't know why this is cute, but it is. "I guess I thought I had more time before wading into all of that."

I shake my head. "Sorry. The reckoning is here. Do you have a female relative she can talk to? An aunt or a cousin or something?"

He glances past me down the street, like he's suddenly going to find the Puberty Fairy floating our way to bestow knowledge on him, Brooklyn, or both. Then he looks over his shoulder toward the station. "Maybe Becky . . . ?"

He looks back at me like I'm going to have the right answer.

"Do they have a relationship like that? Talk together much?"

He hesitates. "No, not really. Brooklyn's not at the station all that often."

"Then it's probably awkward to both of them for Becky to suddenly bring it up. Even if she doesn't mind, Brooklyn will feel it."

He reaches up and scratches his beard. I would expect it to be wiry, but something about the way it moves makes me think it's actually soft against his fingers. "What would have helped you at her age?" he asks.

It's the right question. An insightful one, better than *What should I do?* I don't know specifically what would help Brooklyn because I don't know her well enough. But I can tell him what would have helped me at the same age. I think the sheriff of Harvest Hollow must spend a lot of time listening to podcasts about how to communicate better.

"A female role model, which like I said, I eventually got in my aunt. Sounds like you don't have any extra ones lying around?"

He shakes his head. "So I guess I talk to her myself. Any advice?"

I suck my teeth and consider this. "I know we're in a woke age where dads and dad types are supposed to be super comfortable talking about all this stuff with their girls. And if this is a long-term situation"—he nods to indicate yes—"then you'll have to get there. Sooner than not, it sounds like. But maybe I can help for right now." The words come out of me before I know I'm going to say them, but I don't take them back.

Seeing Brooklyn hunching in her sweatshirt that it's still too warm for, hiding the evidence of her body going haywire on her in a way no one may have taken the time to explain to her, it's familiar. Painfully familiar. I think about eleven-year-old Jolie, and I know I've got to help. If Brooklyn doesn't want me to, that's fine. But I have an idea for how to approach this in a way that won't mortify her.

"How's that?" Lucas asks.

"If she's just going home anyway, why don't you wait on having your grandfather come pick her up. Tell her you're sending her to my bar to hang out because it's quiet before opening, and I think Tina and I can talk her into doing some shopping where girl stuff can come up naturally. If you're okay with it, that is."

"You would do that for me?"

I give him a faint smile. "I would do that for her."

"Got it." He breathes a sigh of relief. "It's better than any idea I have, which is none."

I hand him my phone. "Put in your number, and I'll let you know when she gets there. Send her down in about ten minutes, so it feels more organic. It'll give me time to fill Tina in."

He taps some keys and hands it back. "I really appreciate this, Jolie."

I look past him to the station, like I can see Brooklyn hunched inside. "Like I said, I get it." I give him a nod and head back toward the Mockingbird. I don't look at my phone until I'm sure he's gone back into the station. He texted himself with the message "Jolie's number" and saved himself as "Lucas Who's Still Sorry About High School."

I admit it: it's kind of sweet.

Chapter Ten

JOLIE

The loud drone of the power washer reaches me before the bar comes into view. Great. The neighboring businesses are going to loooove that sound.

Tina is gunning the water at the section where Ry got the worst of the paint off already. He's farther down, where the overspray of the water won't get him. I walk up beside Tina and she grins at me. "It's fun, boss. You want a go?"

As I watch the faint traces of paint disappear beneath the blast of the water, I grin. It does look fun. "Yes, please."

She releases the trigger and hands it to me, speaking loudly to be heard over the motor. "Nothing to it. Just aim and pull. Careful because it has a kick."

The spray gun vibrates in my hand, barely coiled energy as it waits impatiently to be loosed to do its job. I brace my feet, aim, and pull the trigger. The force knocks me off-balance and the water pounds uselessly against the shallow eave over the spot I mean to get.

"You blind, cuz?" Ry calls. He's grinning. "No paint up there."

Tina grins too. "Warned you."

I have to laugh. I release the trigger and brace my feet before I let the water rip again, and it's extremely satisfying to watch more traces of paint disappear.

"Good job, Jo," Ry yells over the noise. "You pick up quick. I'm looking for someone to do some custodial work around here. Interested?"

I answer by turning the water on him, knowing he's too far away for it to do any damage beyond soaking him. His outraged yelp makes Tina laugh, and I keep the water flowing while I yell, "Dance, monkey, dance!"

"What's going on here?"

I release the trigger and turn to find a vaguely familiar-looking woman about my age standing there, looking confused.

"I'm the owner. Sorry about the noise. Doing a little cleanup."

She glances at the spray paint still remaining. Currently, my bar is named "ivans" because Apple Hat isn't a fan of apostrophes. "Heard about that. Thought I'd come over and see if I could help." She nods at the maroon awning across the street with "Domenico's" spelled out in gold cursive. "My family owns the jewelry store over there. I'll check our cameras and see if they caught anything."

"That would be great," I say. "I think the sheriff was going to send someone by to ask about it."

She nods. "He's on top of things. I actually came in a half hour early to open because he had Becky call me. That's his assistant."

"We met," I tell her. "I'm Jolie, by the way. I'd shake hands, but mine are damp at the moment."

"Jolie." She squints like she's trying to place me. "Wait, were you on the Harvest quiz bowl team in high school?"

"Yeah," I say slowly, studying her back, and then my memory clears. "You were on the Stony Peak team, right?"

"Sophie Keller," she says. "Or I am now. It was Domenico back then. Man, you smoked me in the district finals. I only felt better about losing to you when you won state. It's good to see you again."

"You too." I'm surprised to find I mean it, but while Sophie had been a fierce competitor, she'd never been mean. "I plan to get a trivia night going as soon as we get our feet under us. You'll have to come by."

"For a rematch?" she asks, arching her eyebrows.

I laugh. "Definitely. But I should warn you, I haven't lost a step."

Her eyes glint. "When I was in labor with my second kid, I had my husband test me with Trivial Pursuit cards to distract me from my contractions until they got my epidural in."

"You're on," I say. "For what it's worth, you were harder to beat than the guy at the state finals."

"That's it," she says. "I'm loyal to you forever now."

Tina snorts. "Y'all are some nerds."

"Ignore her," I advise Sophie. "She can wipe the floor with anyone in music or geography."

Tina shrugs. "Guilty."

"I love this!" Sophie gives a little clap. "When can we make this happen?"

I shake my head. "We're still getting our staff trained, and I'd have to hire the right emcee, so it could be a month at least."

"An emcee?" Sophie looks thoughtful. "Let me think if I know anyone. In the meantime, I'll go check our footage for you. Welcome to Maple Street."

"Thanks," I say.

She crosses the street, and I turn back to Tina. "Can you turn that off for a minute? Need to talk to you."

Tina grimaces. "Shouldn't have called you a nerd. My bad."

I shake my head. "Not about that."

I follow her over as she turns off the pressure washer, and suddenly the sounds of birds chirping, the soft hiss of tires on Maple, and distant conversations flood into its absence. "Want to be a puberty fairy with me?"

She gives me a sidelong look I can't decode, but she steps back and waves me into the Mockingbird ahead of her. "Say more."

I break it down for her quickly since Brooklyn could show any minute if Lucas talks her into it. Tina is already nodding as I finish. "I have three younger sisters," she says. "There isn't a version of this conversation I haven't had."

"Thanks, Tina. I think we have to ease into this kind of naturally. Any ideas?"

"Uh, yeah. A really good one. Let's go back outside." I follow her out as she calls to Ry, "Hey, boss. Come trade with your cousin."

"Why?" he and I say at the same time.

She fixes us both with a look. "You want my help or not?"

I sigh. "Yes." Then I walk toward Ry, who's heading my way. When we've switched places, I call, "Now what?"

Tina flips on the pressure washer and hands the nozzle to Ry. "Payback." Ry whoops and unleashes the water before I can even run two steps, and it hits me full in the back. I stop and turn, letting him get the rest of me, while I glare at both of them. Ry lets go of the trigger but doesn't look sorry in the least.

I walk back toward them as Tina flips off the motor again. "What did you do that for?"

"Looks to me like we need to go buy you a change of clothes when your little friend gets here, don't you think?"

With a glance down at my dripping shirt, I acknowledge she's right. "Evil genius."

"It's for the greater good," she says in a fake pious voice.

I've just wrung the worst of the water out when I spot a hunched figure in a hoodie standing on the sidewalk a few stores down. I smile and wave. "That's her," I say quietly to Tina, who nods.

Brooklyn gives me a small wave back. It lacks enthusiasm, but ten is rough, so I don't take it personally. I beckon for her to come over.

"Your uncle says you need a quiet space to work," I say when she reaches us. "We've got lots of tables to choose from if you don't mind hanging out with me and Tina."

"That's fine." Her voice is soft, like she doesn't want to put much energy into it. Or maybe more like she doesn't like it to draw any notice to her either. "You're . . ." She trails off and nods at my clothes.

"Soaking wet because my employees don't respect me?" I roll my eyes. "You're right. I need to go buy some new clothes really quick. You mind coming with us? I thought we could just walk a couple of blocks over to the Clothes Closet and find something cheap and fast."

She nods.

"You're good with that?"

Another nod.

"Great. Let's go. This is Tina, by the way. She's a server here, and I've known her since high school. And that's my cousin, Ry." He waves and gets a small nod.

We walk in the direction of the Clothes Closet, and I try to put Brooklyn at ease. For me, the best approach at that age would have been noninvasive questions that didn't ask me to do too much work. Nothing that sounded like it was trying to dig.

"Have you lived in Harvest Hollow long enough to know the stores well?" I ask.

Brooklyn takes a few seconds before she nods. "Two years."

"I grew up here, but I moved away for a long time. I haven't been back long, but a lot of things have changed. Is there anywhere you'd recommend besides the Clothes Closet? I'm going on what I remember."

Another pause. "No. That should be good."

This creates the first opening I can see. "School started not too long ago, right?"

She nods.

"Where did you do most of your back-to-school shopping?"

It's the wrong question. Her shoulders hunch. I shoot Tina a quick glance, unsure if I should wait Brooklyn out or change the subject.

Tina says, "My younger sisters all still like to shop at the Clothes Closet, but two of them are into thrifting. You into that?"

Brooklyn shakes her head. "I didn't get any clothes this year."

I stop dead on the sidewalk. "Did your uncle forget about back-to-school shopping?"

Brooklyn shakes her head fast. "No. He asked me a few times, but I didn't want anything."

"Oh, got it. Not so fun shopping with guys, huh?"

"It's not," Brooklyn says, and I want to cheer. She's taken a baby step. We're getting somewhere.

"I have an idea," I say. "Do you have a lot of schoolwork today?" She shakes her head. "No. We're not learning anything new yet."

My heart squeezes again. She's speaking at a normal volume, and she's saying words that are painfully familiar—the words of a bright girl who isn't being challenged by her work. I know the feeling well.

"What if we do some school clothes shopping now?" I ask. "I've got time."

"If my boss says I'm good, I'm good," Tina adds.

"You're good," I tell her.

"Shopping!" she cheers.

"I'll check with Lucas to make sure it's okay with him, but if he says it's fine, what do you think?" I ask Brooklyn.

She looks from me to Tina and back again. It's the first time she's met my eyes since we talked about books, and I notice that they're the same gray as her uncle's. Strong genes in that family. "I don't know?"

Her hesitation kills me. She's so afraid to ask for what she wants and needs, and I have to be so careful here to make sure this all feels safe and healthy.

"I get it if you're not into it," I tell her. "Don't worry. You won't hurt my feelings. But I grew up with my dad, and he was pretty checked out, so he never noticed if I needed stuff. And honestly, I would have felt weird asking him to take me shopping for underwear or whatever. Or even socks."

"Uncle Lucas isn't checked out," Brooklyn says, and her voice is clear and firm. "He's a really good uncle."

"That's good," Tina says. "I got seven uncles. Seven." She shakes her head like *Can you believe that?* "Anyway, one of them is a stinker, but the rest are pretty great."

"Uncle Lucas is pretty great," Brooklyn says.

"I believe it." Barely. I'm not going to criticize Lucas to his niece and tell her what absolute trash he was in high school. If he's good to her, then great. "In fact, I bet he probably set aside money for you to get school clothes, and he'll be happy to have you spend it. Would it be okay with you if I checked?"

Tina claps her hands. "Say yes, say yes, say yes."

Brooklyn smiles, even if it looks like she's smiling in spite of herself. "Okay."

I text Lucas.

JOLIE: Brooklyn says she'll do some school shopping with me and Tina. We have a budget?

LUCAS: Whatever she wants.

His answer is lightning quick, and I show it to Brooklyn. "Looks like we have a green light," I tell her.

"Yes!" Tina says. "Let's get you straightened out first, boss lady." She makes a gesture that sweeps from my head to my feet. "We don't really want to be seen out with a drowned rat. We have reputations to maintain."

I make a face at her, and Brooklyn makes a noise that might be a giggle. It warms my heart. If I had to guess, she doesn't laugh much. Tina and I go back and forth, teasing, the rest of the way to the store, while I text Lucas at the same time, making sure he knows Brooklyn is safe.

It's something I became more aware of and more angry about when I moved away from home and got older and wiser; with my dad's complete lack of supervision, I was very lucky nothing actively bad ever happened to me. I had to spend almost six months processing the fear a few years ago when it sank in how many times things could have gone sideways, where bad people with worse intentions could have gotten to me, because of his neglect.

But that didn't happen. I'm here and I'm fine. But I don't want Brooklyn to worry, and I'm sure Lucas has seen far too much in his job to rest easy.

JOLIE: Tina and I will be with her at all times, so you don't have to worry about leaving her alone with only one adult. I'll make it clear that you know we're buying her underwear and bras as part of her normal back-to-school stuff so she doesn't feel like there's any secret keeping.

I'd volunteered at a tutoring center near my condo on Saturday mornings for a long time, and the training was extremely thorough in defining appropriate boundaries with the kids. Not asking them to keep secrets from their parents is a major one.

LUCAS: Thanks, and I trust you, but I'll verify. She's got her location app on. Expect to see a few of my deputies who know Brooklyn stopping for a friendly hello every thirty minutes.

I send him a thumbs up and mentally reward him some points. I'm not sure what they're for. Brownie points? Good guy points? Maybe I'm just restoring some of the many, many human points he lost in high school.

Either way, Lucas Cole is on the scoreboard, and in Jolie Mc-Graw's world, that's not nothing.

An hour later, I'm in the first pair of jeans I've bought in five years, wearing a black T-shirt that was all I would agree to from the ten things Tina pulled off the rack, and my hair has dried enough for me to graduate from drowned rat status. We've also had two friendly run-ins with deputies as we've gone from store to store, each saying "hey" to Brooklyn, like they're surprised to run into her on their various made-up errands.

Best of all, by the time we walk into the third store, Brooklyn's hood is down, and when we finally head back to the Mockingbird, she has two shopping bags full of clothes.

Tina the freaking magical fairy godmother made it smooth as French silk pie; we walked past the bra and underwear section and she grabbed two packs of socks from the rack. "Size seven?" she asked Brooklyn. Brooklyn nodded and Tina tossed them in the cart.

Tina grabbed two packs of cotton briefs. "Girl's medium?" she asked like she was barely paying attention to the answer. Brooklyn had nodded again. "Shirts medium too?" Tina asked. Another nod. And just like that, Tina pulled three training bras in neutral colors and tossed them in the basket. "You good on pajamas?"

It was that easy. Then we pulled a bunch of other clothes and sent Brooklyn into the fitting room to try them on, and as Tina would collect anything Brooklyn rejected, we began to hone in on her style. Turns out that Brooklyn is an athleisure girl with a preference for soft neutral colors who doesn't like words anywhere on her clothes, but if there's a butterfly, that's a bonus.

We're heading back to the Mockingbird with a pretty good wardrobe for the kiddo without any discernible cringing from Brooklyn.

And her hood never went back up.

Back at the bar, I set Brooklyn's bags in the office, then sweep my hand to encompass the entire place. "We're not opening for lunches for a while yet, so you've got plenty of workspace. Any table you want."

She walks over to a booth and turns to me with a questioning look. Not a surprise that she would choose somewhere small and burrow-like. It's what I used to do in the library.

I nod. "Good choice. I'll let Lucas know you're back. Maybe your grandfather is ready to come pick you up."

"Okay. And he's my great-grandpa." She slides her backpack off and slips into the bench to set it beside her. "Thank you, Miss Jolie," she says softly.

For a split second, my throat closes up, a knot forming until I force it down with a swallow. "Of course, Brooklyn. I get it. Hang out as long as you want. I need to get something from my office, but let any of us know if you need anything."

I smile and hurry to my office, closing the door quietly and leaning against it. What I need is a deep breath to ease the ache in my chest. I don't know what it is, exactly. I'm trying to pin it down because I don't like any feeling I can't explain. The closest comparison I can come up with is that it reminds me of the feeling

I get every time I see one of those videos on social media of soldiers coming home to surprise their families.

What the actual heck?

Just then, I recognize the music Ry is playing on the bar's PA system now that the worst of the outside is cleaned up. Elvis. I listen for a few bars. It's "Love Me Tender," and the word catches my attention.

Tenderness. I'm feeling tenderness.

It's new, and I'm not sure I like it.

But for Brooklyn and Brooklyn only, I'll allow it.

Chapter Eleven

LUCAS

I worked for the sheriff's department for eight years before I ran for sheriff. I wasn't ignorant of the challenges I'd face in my job. Not from criminals. Not even from dealing with people making a single poor choice that lands them in my place of work. But none of that—not one single bit of it—prepared me for the single greatest aggravation of my career to date: baby dolls.

Yeah. Big glass eyes, frilly dresses. Those dolls. The ones Beryl Griggs had told me about first and I had dismissed. I'd found that report about as credible as her claim last year that the Silver Sneakers morning walking group was an organized band of porch pirates.

They weren't.

Beryl had gotten her girdle in a twist because Barbara Lee's grandson was always parking in front of Beryl's house when he came to visit his grandmother across the street. Yes, he parked there on purpose because it aggravated Beryl, who he called a "hateful old crow" when she'd called the sheriff's office on him. But Barbara Lee's grandson wasn't breaking any laws, and Barbara Lee was even less inclined to persuade him to park elsewhere after Beryl's call to our office.

Anyway.

We get real criminals too. The usual stuff you find in any city our size. And we get tourists in here partaking too much of the local fermented goods and acting a fool, so we have to go keep the peace by giving them a night of hospitality in one of our cells.

But Beryl Griggs has generated an astonishing amount of wild goose chases with her outlandish claims.

So no. I did not take her initial doll warnings seriously.

But as Becky hands me her phone to look at Harvest Hollow Happenings, I scroll through the posts and concede that Harvest Hollow may, in fact, have a doll problem.

Which means I now have a doll problem. I sigh and hand back Becky's phone. "Explain this to me again."

"These dolls started showing up a week ago. The first one was on a porch over on Delancey. The dad was leaving to go to work when he found a doll." She scrolls and shows me a picture of a doll with smooth brown hair and big brown eyes. These are dolls that look like little girls, not babies. It's dressed kind of old-fashioned. I don't know my fashion eras, but I'd say it's not an outfit from this century or the last.

"They didn't think too much about it until a few days later when someone else in their daughter's class found a doll on her porch. She brought it in for show and tell." Becky shows me the doll in question, a blonde doll with green eyes. "Kid who got the first doll is in the same class. She mentions to her parents that her friend got one too. Parents think it's weird and call second friend's parents. Same situation. Appeared on their front doorstep one morning. No note."

"Tell me how it gets to crisis level," I say. Because that's where we are. Becky has fielded six phone calls about it this morning and put the mayor through to tell me that it was going on this week's city council agenda and "the people" were demanding to know how my department would be dealing with these threats. That's the actual word he used to describe dolls appearing on people's porches. "Threats."

"So the parents get on Happenings and ask if anyone else has received them. That's when even I have to admit it gets creepy," Becky says, almost apologetically. "Turns out it's not entirely random. So far, six girls have received the dolls over the last two weeks. The youngest girl is seven. The oldest is twelve. They don't always appear on the front porch but they do always appear without a note. And, boss . . ." She draws a deep breath. "Each doll looks like the girl it's left for."

Okay. It's a little weird. "Doorbell footage?" There's always doorbell footage. It's a blessing and a curse for us. Sometimes it truly does help us find our suspects. But it also turns regular people into Harvest Hollow CSI, and they have a tendency to overestimate both their skill *and* their authority to get in the middle of things.

She shakes her head. "Three of the families have them, but they all checked their video out of curiosity, and none of them saw who left it. At those houses, the person left the doll on the hood of a car."

"None of the neighbors' cameras picked up anything?"

"One of them caught footage of someone leaving one of the dolls on a car, but it's too dark to make out much. Gender, race, nothing. Just someone shadowy walking over to the car then leaving again. Here."

She plays me the video that the neighbor sent to Happenings. Skimming the nearly three hundred comments below it tells me they're either people asserting their theory of the "Doll Bandit" as gospel fact or demanding that SOMETHING BE DONE, generally in all caps and usually with at least one word in the sentence misspelled.

I lean back in my chair and stare at the ceiling for several moments before I straighten and shake my head at Becky. "How dumb am I that I've been putting all my time into planning crowd control for the Harvest Festival that I didn't even put 'serial doll leaver' on my September bingo card?"

She shakes her head. "I know. But honestly, it kind of skeeves me out."

"Who's on this?" I ask.

"Slocum."

I nod. "Tell her to come find me when she gets back to the station." Slocum will do fine. I just need to be briefed on anything

Becky might have missed—an unlikely occurrence—before I go to the city council meeting in two nights.

Becky heads back to the front desk, and I check my cell to see if I've gotten any texts from Jolie. I know they've headed back to her bar at this point because my deputies have reported back. They've said Brooklyn seems to be enjoying herself, but the reports are otherwise thin on details.

Should I text Jolie to check in? She's gone above and beyond in making sure I have no reason to doubt her judgment or motives concerning Brooklyn. Unnecessary, since a big part of my job is being a good judge of character, and I have the advantage of knowing her from high school. Jolie—however much she may have changed in some ways—still has a steadiness running beneath her now-spiky edges. It's the kind of steadiness Pops would say makes someone "good people." So, unnecessary but appreciated.

I'm still debating when she texts me herself.

JOLIE: Mission accomplished. Wardrobe acquired. Brooklyn seems good. Bought myself a dress on your dime as tax.

I don't know if she's being serious or not, but if Brooklyn chose clothes and she "seems good," Jolie could buy herself ten dresses on my dime and I'd offer to buy her another one. Another dozen.

LUCAS: Should I send my grandfather over to pick her up?

JOLIE: Happy to let her hang out here, but she probably needs downtime from so many new people today.

Perceptive again.

It's not a surprise. I'd sensed that about her when she was tutoring me, that she could read me better than I wanted to be read. It was a lot of why I'd lashed out, I think. I see it all the time. Look too closely at someone who doesn't want to be seen, and it provokes them.

I let Jolie know that Pops will be by soon for Brooklyn, and I call him to give him the green light.

Then I sit back and ponder the two great mysteries the day has brought me: the "Doll Bandit" and Jolie. I'll need a lot more information to get much further with either of them.

Chapter Twelve

JOLIE

When Lucas's grandpa comes in to get Brooklyn, he thanks me for passing time with her while he was out.

"Not a problem," I tell him. He's got to be at least eighty, and the stoop of his shoulders shows it, but he moves with a firm step and meets my eye with a steady gaze. "She helped me pick a dress. And we talked about books."

"Can I go to the library after school tomorrow?" Brooklyn asks. "Jolie gave me some new ideas for books."

"Sure can," he says. "Miss Jolie, my grandson tells me you live out our way?"

"I bought a place on White Pine," I tell him.

He nods. "I know it. Pass it every morning on my walk. Nice place. Needs a dog."

I shake my head. "I'm not really an animal person."

He narrows his eyes and gives me a long look. "Nope, you are. Shiba Inu."

I blink at him. "Sorry?"

He shrugs. "I know these things."

Brooklyn nods. "He does. He says I'm a cat person, but Uncle Lucas is allergic."

I don't know why it strikes me as funny that Lucas has allergies. He seems too cool for allergies. As if allergies care about your job title or emotional maturity. But I don't smile. "Thank you for coming to get her, Mr. Cole. I could have walked her back to the station though."

"Call me Mr. John," he says. "And it's no trouble. Brooklyn and I do all right together."

She nods. "We're going to get Peanut Nutters on the way home. It's our favorite."

Mr. John gives her a fake scowl. "Now did I say we were going to do that?"

"No, but we will. Kind of how Uncle Lucas always says *Little House on the Prairie* is so boring, but then he watches it with me every time I put it on."

Oh no. She's given me another heart pang, one that strikes right at the patched-over part that shut Lucas out in high school. Can't have that.

"I better get back to work," I tell them. "Lots to be done before we open tonight."

Mr. John takes the cue and leads Brooklyn out, nodding at me once before the door closes behind him. It's a nod I've seen a lot in my life, the nod of an adult who is granting approval for a job well done. I got it from teachers, then professors, then managers. It's always satisfying, but there's something about Mr. John's nod that also makes me feel . . . warm?

What is happening?

Irritated by the syrupy feelings trying to slip around inside me, I turn toward my office, which is when I catch Tina watching me as she checks the candles in each tabletop hurricane glass. She's wearing a smirk.

"What?" I demand.

"Nothing, boss."

"Say whatever you need to say," I tell her.

"Nothing to say," she says, "except that you're not tough."

This makes me grumpy. "Let's see if you feel the same way when I get my hands on Apple Hat and his friends."

She grins. "I'm living for it."

Chapter Thirteen

LUCAS

Brooklyn is her old self.

It's a miracle.

She was in a good mood when I got home Friday. We didn't talk about how she'd miraculously "healed" enough to go shopping. I didn't press my luck by following up on her "fine" when I asked how it had gone. Lately, every conversation is a minefield, and I never know what will set her off. But she stayed mellow through dinner.

We had a non-grumpy weekend.

And then . . .

Then she got up this morning for school on time. No complaints.

She comes to the table in jeans and a T-shirt. No oversized hoodie in sight. Pops and I exchange looks. We hadn't discussed whether we should bring up the bra thing, but we seem to be reaching a mutual decision to keep our traps shut. If Brooklyn hadn't been comfortable enough to bring it up with us in the first place, I'm fairly sure she won't welcome a conversation now.

She sits, eats her breakfast, and comes out to the car with me without any nagging. "Can I walk to the library after school today and have Pops get me there?" she asks.

"Sure." Brooklyn has pretty decent common sense. There's no danger in letting her walk from the school to the library. "Looking for anything in particular?"

"*Keeper of the Lost Cities*," she says.

The book she and Jolie had discussed. "Would I like it?" I ask. "Doubt it."

"Why not?"

She grunts. Danger sign. "It's not about World War II."

I chuckle. "Fair enough."

We ride in easy quiet the rest of the way to school. When she climbs out in the carpool line, she gives me a small wave before hitching her backpack up and walking to her morning lineup.

Even the drop-off line can't defeat my good mood this morning. Normally, I'm white knuckling with my teeth bared. I'd already figured out the most important rule of drop-off by the second day of school last year: if your kid isn't old enough to get themselves out of a vehicle while also hanging on to all the assorted crap you've sent them with, you do not belong in the drop-off line. Parents who *get out* to hug their little darlings should be charged as public nuisances and prosecuted to the fullest extent of the law.

But like I said, today, not even the drop-off line can defeat me. Not even when the mom in front of me gets out to walk her kid over to the campus supervisor, hugs said child, and watches until the supervisor walks her precious cargo to his line before she gets back into her Porsche Cayenne.

I'm still smiling when I turn out of the parking lot. Jolie worked a miracle, and the more I think about it as I turn on to Maple, the more I feel like I should thank her for it. When I walk into the station, I stop at Becky's desk. "Becky, can you call over to Blooms and have them deliver an arrangement of thank you flowers to Jolie McGraw? Send them to the Tequila Mockingbird. Use my personal credit card."

"Sure, boss." But she's not done. I've barely started toward my office when she says, "But is that the right move?"

I turn back to her. "A thank you?"

"No, sending over flowers. This is for helping with Brooklyn, right?"

"It is."

"That's a different favor than buying tickets to the law enforcement gala. More . . . personal." She nods, satisfied with her word choice.

"What are you suggesting?"

"Personal favor deserves a personal thank you. Not a note, and not at her business."

I frown to hide how much I like this suggestion. This suggestion that asks me to do what I wanted to do anyway. "Yeah?"

"Definitely."

I hesitate just to sell it, the idea that I'm not ready to drive over to Jolie McGraw's house right this second. "All right. But send me Avila's report on the spray paint investigation so I can update her."

"Update her." Becky nods. "Good idea."

Ten minutes later, an email pops up with the subject line "Update for Jolie."

Jolie. Not J. McGraw or even McGraw. Becky must have really taken to Jolie. I open it, skim through Avila's notes, which don't say anything new, and send it to print. Then I call Avila and tell him I'm going out to the lumberyard myself in the morning to talk to Hardin. He's been "down sick" both times Avila went by his home.

It feels good to be doing something for Jolie.

❦

I wouldn't normally show up at a person's place of work; that's the kind of thing that starts rumors or worries bosses about who's in their employ. But since I'm confident Shane is our guy, I don't really care if it creates friction at work. He needs to be made uncomfortable to remind him that he doesn't have free rein in the Hollow.

I don't bother with the public entrance to Kenlan Lumber. Instead, I pull around straight to the back where the guys are manhandling the freight or cutting wood down to standard beam sizes. I love it back here. The smell of sawdust always reminds me of newness, of something about to be made. Makes me wish I'd learned to work wood. Pops knows how. I'll make sure he teaches Brooklyn the way I wish I would have learned when I was her age.

I park and climb down from the Explorer, earning a few wary glances as my boots hit the dirt. Even people with clear consciences do this sometimes—look at me like they're nervous that I'm there for them. I get it. I remember the days before I wore the badge.

One of the men walks over to me, his clipboard indicating he might be a supervisor.

"Help you?"

I smile. "Looking for one of your employees who's been hard to get hold of. Shane Hardin?"

A slight change flickers in his expression, then it settles back to normal. Which is to say guarded. "He in trouble?"

"Not at the moment."

The man considers this for a moment then nods and pulls a radio from his belt and speaks into it. "Roland, I'm sending back a visitor for Hardin. Give him ten on the clock." He raises his eyebrows at me as if to ask whether that's enough time. I nod. He points to the open warehouse door. "Straight back and to the right. You'll see him."

"Thank you," I tell him, and head in the direction he indicated. I don't know if this guy realizes I'm the sheriff and not a deputy. Probably not. It's already going to be a big deal that a uniformed officer is at Hardin's jobsite; if they knew I'm the actual sheriff, the speculation would fly even faster. It's unusual for the sheriff to get involved at this level in a community our size. But since I was the one who was at the Mockingbird the night of his attempted intimidation, I take it kind of personally.

I don't feel bad about strolling through Hardin's jobsite though. Shane Hardin had his chance to have this conversation out of sight of God and everyone, and he ducked it, so he gets what he gets.

Voices sound up ahead, the gruff voices of men at work, and when I round the corner, heads turn and the talking stops. All except for a single succinct curse from none other than Shane Hardin.

"Shane," I say, nodding at him.

"Take ten," another guy tells him.

"Speak to you over here?" I jerk my head to the opposite corner of the warehouse, which is full of lumber odds and ends but empty of workers.

He doesn't say anything, but he heads that direction.

"You tagged the new bar on Maple," I say when we're out of earshot of the others.

He scoffs. "Says who?"

I hook my fingers in my belt like every cop you've ever seen on every TV show, but hey—our tactical belts bristle with so many essentials that they make for good armrests. It helps that it telegraphs "peak law enforcement." I take a slow look around the warehouse before resting my eyes on Shane Hardin again.

"Notice y'all use rust-colored spray paint to label the wood in here." Several stacks are sprayed with identifying lot numbers on the sides since they'll be painted over and covered up in different projects. "How good do you think the chances are that the empty cans I saw out in the lumberyard will be an exact match for the paint on the bar's exterior?"

"You ain't wasting department resources on getting those matched," he says. He's right. "And even if they matched, that's circumstantial. Can't prove I was there."

"Sure," I say, like this doesn't bother me, because it doesn't. This job requires an extremely long fuse, and he's not even close to lighting it. "Not with the paint. But Domenico's across the street did us a favor and pulled their security footage from that night. Didn't have to request a warrant, even. I enjoyed watching the replay. Suspects don't usually make it so easy for us. Neighborly, don't you think? Of the store," I add. "And the suspect, now that I think about it."

Shane scowls, but his eyes shift to the side for a single fraction of a second. I've got him running scared. I'll leave out the part where the footage was too dim to make out anything with certainty.

I keep my pleasant smile in place but stare him right in the eye. "The owner got it cleaned up too fast for me to haul you down there and make you do it, but that kind of luck is only going to go your way once. You feel me?"

Shane crosses his arms and refuses to answer, staring at me from sullen, half-closed eyes.

"That's what I thought," I say. "Have a good day, Hardin." I wave at his supervisor, who is pretending not to watch this all go down, and stroll out as relaxed as I came in. "Thank you," I call to the boss in the yard. "Appreciate you."

He nods, but their tension won't ease until the second my cruiser disappears from their property. Mine will too. He's handled, and I can't wait to tell Jolie I took care of it for her.

Chapter Fourteen

LUCAS

From the lumberyard, I head over to a small café that's closer to our side of town—mine and Jolie's—than my usual spot near the station. I grab her a coffee, black, with cream and sugar for her to add as she pleases. I even throw in a fresh muffin at the last minute.

I get to her house ten minutes later. I knew exactly which one she was talking about. It's a newer home but it has that cozy feeling like the library. It's the kind of house that looks like it's made for relaxing. Like you wouldn't host fancy dinners there, but friends could drop by for barbecue and to watch a game anytime.

It's the kind of place I'd pick for myself if we ever moved out of Pops's, but I hope he's around for a lot longer. I'm not ready to handle Brooklyn by myself, but also, he and I . . . we're figuring each other out. We're at an okay place, one that gets more comfortable the longer we spend time around each other.

The garage is behind the house, so I can't tell if Jolie is home or not, and since it's morning, there are no lights on to give me clues. But I take a chance that she's adopted more of a swing schedule to suit the bar, and I park in her driveway and ring her front doorbell. It's a camera one—not necessary outside of town, but smart for a woman living alone—so I make sure she can see my face.

A few days ago, I'm sure that would have given her reason enough to ignore the door, but I think we're at a point where she'll answer if she's here. Sure enough, I hear her fumble with locks. More than one. Good. Then she opens the door, looking

THE FALL BACK PLAN

slightly rumpled, and it's kind of . . . adorable. It's not a word I use
often, but at the moment, she reminds me of a kitten that adopted
the station for a while. She'd lurk around the auto bay, hissing or
darting away from anyone who tried to go near her. But if you
found her curled up sleeping in a patch of sun somewhere, she'd
let you pick her up and pet her, blinking at you sleepily until she
woke up enough to swat and demand to be set down. I might have
done that several times even though it made my eyes itch.

Jolie, the sleepy kitty. She'd kill me if she knew I was thinking of
her that way.

"Hey," she says, blinking, and I suppress a smile. "Why are you
here so early, and why are you looking at me like you're trying not
to laugh in church?" Her hand goes up to touch her hair like she's
worried she'll find something in it.

I hold out the white bakery bag and the coffee. "I came to say
thank you. Brooklyn got up and went to school this morning on
time, no complaints."

She takes my offerings then looks confused as to how she ended
up with them in her hands.

"I don't know how you take your coffee, so there's sugar and
cream in there too."

She looks from the cup in her hand to me then shifts. "Would
you like to come in?" The last word disappears into a yawn, but
since she's already turning into the house, I follow her. She's wearing jeans and the view is excellent. I wonder if she got dressed just
to get the door.

I glance around the house as she leads me to her kitchen. It's all
upgraded interior trims and new paint, but the walls are bare of art,
and her furniture is plain too. No throw pillows or blankets. It all
looks new.

The dining room space is empty, but the kitchen has a large
island with a breakfast bar, and she pulls out a stool. She nods to
the end of the island like I should do the same, so I do. I watch as
she digs into the bag and pulls out a muffin. Another blink, then

she sets it on the counter. Back into the bag for the cream and sugar, all of which goes into her coffee.

I hide yet another smile, but she catches me this time.

"You thought I took it black." It's not a question.

"I did," I agree.

She shrugs and settles in for her first sip. I give her a minute. After a couple more swallows, she sighs and stretches. It's fascinating. It's like watching a butterfly emerge from its cocoon in a time lapse as she wakes up before my eyes.

"This is good," she says.

"Not as good as Cataloochee, but it's okay."

"Thank you for bringing it."

"Not sure it was a good way to say thank you, seeing as it seems like I woke you up."

She shakes her head. "I was awake. Just wasn't up."

"Then I'm sorry to drag you out of bed sooner than you meant to leave it."

She waves her hand like she's dismissing the concern and takes another drink of her coffee. When she sets it down, she gives me a much more alert look than I got at her front door. "You are completely different from high school."

I flex a bicep. "Thanks. I work out."

She snorts. "That's not what I mean, and you know it. High school you would never have said thank you or sorry or brought me coffee for any reason."

I knew what she'd meant. "High school me was broken and angry all the time. And high school me took a lot of that out on you. Have I said I'm sorry for that yet?"

"Yes."

"Not enough."

This time she makes a sweeping motion with her arm, as if to say the stage is mine, and eyes me over the rim of her cup as she drinks more of her coffee.

THE FALL BACK PLAN

"It surprises me that you're going to let me apologize." It's not a challenge, just curiosity. "Most people would say it's fine and wave it off."

One of her shoulders rises and falls. "I can do that if you want me to."

I shake my head. "No. I really do want to apologize, but you tend to zag where other people zig."

"Zig a zig ah." Her face is deadpan.

"Did you just quote the Spice Girls?"

"Felt appropriate."

I laugh. I can't help it. I'm learning that Jolie's sense of humor is so dry you'll miss it if you aren't paying attention. "You're right. Zig a zig ah."

She holds up her coffee cup in a silent toast. "Can I get you anything? I don't have dishes yet, but I keep packaged stuff in the fridge."

"I'm good," I tell her.

"Then please, don't let me keep you from your apology."

I smile again, something she makes me do more times in a minute than anyone else has in a long while. But I also draw a quiet breath before I start. "So I was broken and angry in high school."

"Same," she says, nodding for me to continue.

"My dad wasn't great. Short tempered. Hard time holding down a job. Knocked my older brother around sometimes. Didn't set many limits, and I wasn't a naturally disciplined kid. Didn't sleep enough. Ran around with my brother because he could get stuff. Mostly showed up at school because my dad got mad if the truant officer came. Didn't care if I went. He just didn't want to be bothered about it. I still missed too much. Too much to fill in the gaps. It started catching up to me in tenth grade, mainly in math and science." I stare down at my hands, remembering the feeling of defeat I'd feel the second I would turn down the hall leading to all the math classrooms.

"I failed algebra twice, and by the time I was a senior, I was taking geometry for the second time. I felt so stupid having to be tutored by someone two grades behind me. I figured if I acted like I didn't care, no one would see how humiliating it was."

She sets her coffee cup down, her eyes fixed on mine now. I have her full attention. She nods for me to continue.

"That day I walked out on you in the library ended up being my last day of school."

"I wondered," she says. "When you didn't show up for our next few tutoring sessions, I thought maybe that's what happened. Since I never saw you in school besides tutoring, it was hard to tell if you were only blowing me off or everything off. But it was so stressful tutoring you that I didn't want to follow up on it."

"I really am so—"

She holds up a hand to stop me. "Don't. You don't need to feel bad again. That's not why I brought it up. I'm putting it together, that's all."

I nod and continue. "I dropped out and kicked around for a year working jobs I hated. Manual labor stuff that left me bored out of my mind. Too much time to think. I decided to get my GED and try community college, see if I could get a better job. My brother was already on probation for burglary by then, and I knew I didn't want to go down that road. So I didn't. I went the other way. Got my associate's degree, then a bachelor's in criminal justice."

She's studying me with interest now, and I'm so glad it's not pity.

"Anyway, I wanted you to know. It's not an excuse. I just wanted to be clear that the way I treated you was never about you. It was about how crappy everything was at home. I remember exactly what a punk I was." The attitude. The insults about everything from her looks to her personality. "You didn't deserve it."

"Heard and accepted." She drinks more coffee and her eyes glaze over like her mind has wandered somewhere. She gives her head a small shake after a few moments and focuses on me. "Thank you for that."

"Sure." I wonder what she thought about in her short absence. I knew from tutoring that she had lightning-quick processing speed. Her mind could have wandered a million places in the space of those breaths. I'd love to know if it had wandered to me. I nod at the muffin, still sitting untouched. "Not a fan?"

She eyes it, then sets her cup down and straightens her shoulders. "Blueberry muffin." She stops, and I wait, my curiosity sharpening.

She clears her throat. "My dad was a drunk." She stops and presses her lips together. "An alcoholic," she says a moment later. It has the sound of a correction that's been practiced many, many times. "You heard about him crashing at the festival?"

I nod.

"I had to fend for myself all the time. Groceries weren't a thing at our house. I got free lunch at school, but other meals . . ." She shakes her head. "I learned to go through his pockets for loose change when he was passed out, and I figured out where to buy the cheapest food in town. The Minit Mart on Juban would sell old baked goods for half price on a shelf near the back."

Understanding dawns. "They had a lot of muffins?"

"Blueberry, specifically. Blueberry muffins taste like poverty to me."

I rest my forearms on the counter. "For me, it's spaghetti with cheap sauce. Don't think I could ever eat it again."

She nods. This isn't the first time this has happened to me, this bonding over a shared poverty experience. I'd bet she also saved food from her free school lunch in case nothing materialized for dinner. And there was the constant stress of the weekend, eating cold cereal for every meal, which was still better than the too-frequent weekends when there was nothing to eat by Sunday night.

It's been useful in helping me understand some of the people I work with on calls, but I don't like dwelling on my own memories of those times.

I straighten. "Look at us now though. Top law dog"—I point to my chest, then to her—"and fancy new bar owner."

She smiles. It's small but genuine. "Enough of all that. Thank you for the coffee and the apology. I promise the muffin thing isn't personal." She slides from her stool, and I take the hint and stand too. "Let me let you go. I know you have to work."

"Actually, I've got something on that for you," I say.

She tilts her head, an invitation to continue.

"I spoke with Shane Hardin this morning. The Domenico's footage isn't clear enough to nail him outright, but I stopped at his work and pointed to some interesting coincidences that are going to go against him if he causes any more trouble. I can push it if you want. He's a known quantity, and I can get the charges, but I'm not sure they'll stick."

She's shaking her head before I finish. "No. It's okay. The mess is cleaned up, and I'm over it."

"You sure?"

"Positive."

"All right. Back to the station for me then." I take a step to leave at the same time she takes a step toward me. Suddenly we're in each other's space, not even an arm's length between us. She's barefoot, and it makes me realize how slight she is without her usual high heels for armor. She couldn't even rest her chin on my shoulder if we—

Uh, no. If we nothing.

But I don't step back, and neither does she. After about two seconds, she looks up at me through her lashes, and her eyes flick down to my mouth before dropping. A small burst of adrenaline hits my bloodstream, but she steps back. Disappointment chases the adrenaline, but that's stupid. My body tried to prime for something that isn't going to happen. My brain knows better.

She turns to lead me out. "Thanks for the coffee and the update," she says as she opens the door and gives me space to exit.

"No problem. I promise not to apologize again."

Another smile. Still small but still genuine. "I appreciate that."

Then, like an *idiot*, I kind of . . . tip my hat to her. *Again.* Just...what? What old-timey cowboy has taken possession of my body and made me do that? But I keep a straight face and walk toward my vehicle at a businesslike pace.

I chance a look toward the door once I start the engine, and she's still there, leaning against it, looking my way. But once again, I'm not sure she's actually seeing *me*.

I'd give a lot to know what goes on in that head of hers.

Chapter Fifteen

JOLIE

It has been a strange few days.

I'm sitting in my office at the bar, staring at a bulletin board with the business cards of local vendors on it, not really seeing them. I've caught myself doing that several times in the last day or so.

Lucas's visit yesterday morning still has me . . .

I don't know. I don't know how I feel. When I don't know how to feel, I tell myself how to feel and then I feel that.

But that's not working this time.

He caught me so off guard. Every part of his visit did. From finding him on my doorstep at all, to the muffin that suddenly dragged me back to childhood, to his apology.

I meant what I told him yesterday: I appreciate the apology.

But I also feel like . . . like one of the ropes on my moorings broke, and I'm ever-so-slightly adrift. Lucas Cole was one of the people I'd meant to put in his place if our paths ever crossed again, but to stick with the boat metaphor, his apology has taken the wind from my sails.

Some of it, anyway.

Leaving Chicago was a function of my failures there. The engagement that never happened. The job burnout that I couldn't outwork. But I'd come back to town looking like a success to the people whose contempt had motivated me through high school and beyond. I'd made enough money to buy the things that would impress them.

I'd worked hard for that money because I'd wanted to show them all up. To prove that if they looked down on me for my address and my thrifted clothes, I could outmatch them on all of it. It hadn't mattered to me if they ever knew about it; it had been enough to know myself. Until Phillip Freaking Horsley.

Even thinking his name irritates me, and I don't like bringing my bad moods with me to work. Time to head this one off.

I walk out of my office and glance over at Ry, who's interviewing a job applicant at one of our dinner tables. We've been open three weeks now, and business is increasing by about thirty percent a week, so we need more servers. Social media is working. People love being the first to try a new place, and the ones who have some pull on platforms like Instagram are fairly easy to spot and comp for drinks. It's the way they dress, do their hair, and then don't look at all embarrassed about doing a bunch of pictures with different poses. Taking one picture in a crowd makes me feel self-conscious. The pros don't care.

I won't necessarily pay for influencer partnerships, but I'm happy to send them complimentary drinks if it keeps them posting about the Mockingbird. Based on the steady increase in business, it's working. And I like that it feels more organic than sponsored posts.

It's time to start creating a sense of community here. Bars live and die by repeat business. I need to give customers a reason to keep coming back. While we aren't a sports bar, I will make sure we have at least one sport-focused night a week. Like maybe showing the Appies away games aired by the local station? And possibly Panthers games in the fall since it's too far for anyone but the most hardcore Harvest Hollow fans to drive to games.

Trivia is the first thing I want to start up though. It'll do more to set the tone for the kind of place we are.

I slip behind the bar and start refilling the napkins and straws. Normally, that's a server job, but it's helpful to keep my hands busy while I think. I've mulled different trivia formats, and it's one of the few leisure time activities I've made time for since college, so

I've got preferences. I've played when it's done with phone apps similar to Kahoot!, with the scores broadcast on a screen. That's nice because people can play against anyone else in the bar who's logged in. I've done it where the competition is just among people sharing a table, but people sharing a table already have a sense of community with each other.

Like I told Sophie, hosted is the way to go. The way Alex Trebek added a snap to *Jeopardy!* and the difficulty of finding hosts good enough to replace him show how much of a difference the right personality can make. With the right person on the right night, Tequila Mockingbird could become a must-do experience as friends and coworkers form teams and compete week after week.

As if thinking of her conjures her, the front door opens and Sophie walks in, scanning until she spots me behind the bar. "Hey," she says. "I wondered if you had a quick minute to chat."

I nod at the bar. "Pull up a stool. Can I get you something to drink?"

"I'll take a Coke if it's no trouble."

"None at all. I've got anything you normally mix with alcohol."

She grins. "How about a Shirley Temple then?"

"You got it. What's up?" I pull a glass and scoop in some ice, then fill it with Sprite while I reach for the grenadine.

"I can't stop thinking about the trivia night you were talking about. When do you think you'll start those?"

I eye her in silence until the glass fills. "Funny you mention it. I was just figuring that out when you walked in."

Her expression brightens. "I want to host it."

Her words come out in a rush, and I pause for a second, unpacking them. "You want to host?"

"I do. And I'd be really good at it too. I know I would."

She's been a good business neighbor, so I'm open to considering it. "I'm not totally sure of the details, but it would only be one night a week. Maybe even only once a month at first."

"That's fine," she says. "But my husband has his travel softball team, and I need an outlet too. I've been doing macrame at home, but ever since you mentioned it, I keep thinking about how I need time out of my house that's not just the store. Something that's *fun*."

"You don't want to just compete?" I ask.

She shakes her head. "No. To be honest, I doubt anyone can beat me."

That wins a small laugh from me. "I get it."

"For me, it'll be fun just to be there facilitating it, getting the answers correct in my head. It's enough for me to know I'm winning." She grins and adds, "I don't need to demoralize everyone else."

I slide her drink to her, complete with a twist of lime and a cherry on top. "You're that confident?"

A shrug. A *cocky* shrug. "Gotta stay sharp somehow."

I like her. But that doesn't mean she'll make a good host. It does mean that I want to give her a shot. "Care to put that to the test?"

Her eyebrow goes up. "What are you thinking?"

I glance over to Ry, who has just finished with the applicant he'd been interviewing. "How about you and I go head-to-head, best of twenty?"

"Challenge accepted. Format?"

Ry walks the applicant to the door, and as the guy walks out, Mary Louise walks in.

"Hey," I say to her. She answers with a nod that includes Sophie. "Would you be willing to run down to Church of Play and pick up a game of Trivial Pursuit?"

Shrug. "Sure, Jo."

"Thanks." I open the register and hand her some cash. "Text me with which editions they have."

"There's more than one?"

Mary Louise's question makes Sophie laugh, but not in a mean way. "So many more," Sophie tells her. "There is so much useless knowledge in the world."

Mary Louise shakes her head, clearly wondering how many editions of *Trivial Pursuit* any one society would need, but less than ten minutes later, she's on her way back with our selection from the four options the game store two blocks over had to offer. Sophie and I agreed to the *Totally 80s* edition, a challenge since neither of us was even born yet.

Several minutes later, she and I are seated at tables next to each other, each with a call bell, the ones we use at the bar when a patron can't get Ry's attention. Ry is standing in front of us, Mary Louise beside him.

She's looking doubtful about the situation, and Ry is already shaking his head. "The second one of you chooses geography, the odds of me pronouncing the place names correctly drops to half."

"You'll be fine," I tell him. "There's no geography in this edition. And we can get anything else you mangle from the context clues."

"Yep." Sophie's eyes are sparkling, reflecting the excitement I feel for our match.

This feels like . . . fun? I barely remember the last time I had any that didn't involve drenching Ry with a pressure washer.

"Okay, Mary Louise will decide who rang first," Ry says. "Tie goes to whoever got the last question right. You can't pick the same category two turns in a row. First one to answer twenty correctly wins. Ready?"

We both give him a short nod then smile at each other. We're acting like we're at a starting line waiting for the pistol to crack.

"First category is music," he says. "What group got a spot on the charts with a cover of the song 'La Bamba'?"

Our bells chime at the same time, and Mary Louise groans. Ry shakes his head. "Getting caught in a nerd showdown was not on my to-do list today. All right, Jo. You go since you're my boss."

I smile at Sophie. "Take it if you know it."

"Los Lobos." No hesitation, and she's correct. "I pick headlines."

And we're off. It's a neck and neck battle, and we're tied at sixteen when I miss which boxer had the nickname "Marvelous." It's Marvin Hagler, a person I did not know existed until this question, and Sophie pulls ahead by answering a question about the name of the filly who won the 1988 Kentucky Derby.

"Winning Colors is my enemy now," I say, glowering. It only makes Sophie laugh. "Movies," I say, trying to claw my way back to a tie in my strongest category.

Ry is halfway through a question about Alan Rickman when the front door of the bar flies open. I don't even have to turn to guess who would shove it with that much force, but I do. Sure enough, it's Bad Apple Shane.

I start to rise, but Mary Louise is already on the move, and she presses her hand against my shoulder to keep me down. "I got this," she says. We turn to watch.

She walks over to intercept Shane, stopping in front of him, her arms folded. I don't hear what she says to him, and that's part of why Mary Louise is perfect for this job. She'll try to defuse before anything else. She's not talking big and forcing Shane to save face.

Unfortunately, it doesn't work. Shane's chest puffs out, and he shoots a hard look past her to me.

I get up so I can keep an eye on him from straight on, keeping my movements as casual as possible. Sophie follows suit, leaning on the table, but I sense the tension in her; she's ready to move if she needs to.

"Tell that trifling—" Shane starts, using a term I don't much care for.

"I'm right here," I say. "Tell me yourself."

Mary Louise's shoulders tense. She doesn't like that I'm getting involved, but I have to calculate the risk here. If I let her handle him completely, the evidence up to this point suggests that he'll turn up again sooner than later. Especially if a visit from the sheriff hasn't done the trick. But his buddies aren't here. That could mean he was furious enough to come here without them, but it could also mean a chance to let him get whatever is bothering him off his chest, so he'll drop it without having to put on a show for them.

Ugh. Toxic masculinity. Give me a Ry any day. Or . . . a Lucas.

"It's okay, Mary Louise. I'm not in danger with all of you here. What do you need to say to me, Shane?" I'm not using his name to be polite. I'm using it to remind him that I know exactly who he is.

"You sic the sheriff on me?" he demands.

"Nope."

He pauses like he's waiting for me to say more. Good luck. I don't owe him explanations.

"You better not have," he says.

"The sheriff does what the sheriff wants to do," I tell him. "I'm not in charge of his investigations."

"Yeah, well, he better not bother me again." It's the tough-guy bluster.

"You should probably tell him that," I say. I watch his face grow slightly redder. That's a lot of anger trying to find its way out, and a matching anger is surging inside me. I'm caught between warring impulses. As a kid, I learned how to placate my dad to avoid most of his eruptions. I did the same thing with the mean kids at school, becoming invisible whenever I could, trying to do everything perfectly so if I caught anyone's notice, there was nothing to criticize.

It had taken a long time, but as a woman in a very testosterone-driven office, I'd learned to assert myself more. At first, it was setting boundaries around how I would let them speak to me, or not letting them get away with taking credit for my work. Over time, I'd learned that the best defense was a good offense. They learned not to push me if they didn't want the smoke.

I hate that my stronger instinct is to placate Shane and get him out of here without incident. But pushing back on Shane right now will only antagonize him.

I force myself to take a quiet, calm breath through my nose, then another. I slide my hands into my pockets so Shane won't see me clench them so hard that my nails bite into my palms.

I don't know what to do here, so I tell him that. "You've taken this bar buyout pretty personally, and believe it or not, I get that. It's personal for me too. It's none of your business why, same as your reasons are none of mine. But for me, I bought it to get rid of all the bad vibes. I'm turning it into something good. If your goal is to stop that, you're doing a pretty decent job. I don't know what to do with you right now to solve the problem. I can have Mary Louise see you out"—he tenses—"but you'd be back, wouldn't you?"

He lifts his chin. It's a silent but clear "Yes."

"I need you not to come back if you're going to be mad every time. What do we do about that?"

He says nothing for a long moment. Then something in his face shifts. The color evens out, but his jaw grows harder.

And then he reaches behind him for his waistband in a move we've all seen too many times in movies to mistake: he's going for his gun.

Chapter Sixteen

LUCAS

I want to see Jolie.

I have no legitimate reason to see Jolie. But this has to be a solvable problem.

I need an excuse to stop by, one that she won't see right through. I'm not a shy guy. I know how to ask out a woman. But Jolie and I have a history. A bad one. We're turning a corner, but I have no idea how she'd take it if I dropped in or called her up and asked her out on a date.

I drum my fingers on my desk, but nothing comes to me. That's not good, since I'm spending as much mental energy on inventing excuses to see her as I am on our Doll Bandit. That's what the Happenings detectives have named it.

The intercom on my desk phone beeps and Becky's voice comes through, sounding tense. "Boss, you better get to the Mockingbird. Sophie Keller texted me they've got trouble."

I'm on my feet immediately. It's only 2:00 and they're not open for lunches yet. I curse, because it's a good bet the trouble is Shane, which means this is my fault. He got riled instead of scared. I charge out of the office and call to Becky, "On it." I'm out the rear exit before she can even acknowledge hearing me.

At this point, I could get to Jolie faster on foot, but it tends to panic people when they see the sheriff running, so I hop in my vehicle and tear out of our lot, already on the radio to see who's patrolling closest to the bar, giving orders to meet me for backup but not to run lights and sirens.

By the time I'm out of my vehicle and striding toward the entrance three minutes later, I've got one deputy stationed at the back door and another one waiting for me at the front. I nod at him. "Be ready."

I open the front door, braced for anything. Years of experience have taught me to assess a situation in microseconds, but I'm still not prepared for what I walk into.

Ry is diving toward Shane as Mary Louise tackles him from behind. Jolie—her face frozen and blank—is rushing toward Sophie, who wears a look of pure fear. Jolie hooks Sophie around the waist and tows her backward.

I don't know what exactly is happening, but I know Shane is the source, so I pull out my taser and race toward Mary Louise to help.

She's got him on the ground now in an arm bar, and he's trying to yell something, but his face is pressed against the wooden flooring, and I can't hear him over Sophie's shriek of, "Gun!"

He's kicking, trying to buck Mary Louise, so I subdue his legs, reducing his leverage. "Stop resisting," I tell him.

"Mn hung," he mumbles into the floor.

"What?" Mary Louise asks, her voice flat and cold.

"Mno nguhn!"

My blood pressure drops. "He said no gun."

"Yesh," Shane says. It's a very emphatic *yes*.

Mary Louise doesn't let him go, but she gives me a quick glance over her shoulder. "I'm going to check."

I nod. "I got him. Hardin, if there's no gun, calm down and we won't have a problem."

He stops contorting. Mary Louise does a quick sweep across his lower back, frowns, and slips something from his waistband, then holds it up. "Flask."

"I'm going to do a quick search to make sure you're not carrying anything else we need to worry about," I inform him. He makes a grunt that sounds like agreement.

I do a fast pat down of both legs, but he's not concealing anything. We let him up after I give Mary Louise an all-clear nod.

He pushes himself to his feet and brushes off his front. Jolie has Sophie halfway to her office, but they both stop and turn.

"I don't have a gun," Shane repeats.

"You deserved a takedown," Mary Louise says.

He nods. "Fair." He looks toward Jolie. "Can I talk to you in private?"

"No." That's Mary Louise, me, and Ry in unison.

"Yes," Jolie says. "But out here, so they'll feel better. Let's take that booth." She points and he heads toward it. She squeezes Sophie's arm. "Are you okay?"

Sophie has her hand pressed against her heart. "Yeah, fine."

"We can finish our discussion in a bit if you're up for it."

"I think I'll head back to my shop," she says. "Trivia ended up being way more action packed than I expected. I need a breather."

Jolie smiles at her. "You're hired."

"But you didn't see me host anything yet." Sophie sounds surprised.

"You just made a joke thirty seconds after we thought we were dealing with an active shooter. You'll do fine under pressure," Jolie says.

"Even though I screamed?"

"Shows you were into the moment," Ry says, and Jolie points at him. "Yeah. That."

"I'm inclined to agree that they should hire you for anything, even though nobody asked for my two cents," I add.

"Sweet," Sophie says. "I'll come chat with you about the details tomorrow?"

"Sounds good." Jolie waves as she heads for the exit then joins Shane at the booth.

Mary Louise and I exchange glances. She doesn't look thrilled.

"If she thinks I'm letting him out of my sight before he's off the premises, she's crazy," I say.

Mary Louise nods. That's it. Just a single nod.

"Mary Louise, come work for me."

One half of her mouth goes up. This is not the first time I've asked.

"No, Sheriff."

"Why not?"

"I set my own hours. And Becky talks too much."

I give a soft laugh so we don't interrupt the pair we're watching so closely. "She does, but she's a sweetheart, and she's good at her job."

"She is, but she's married to my cousin. I get enough of her at holidays."

I didn't know that, but it doesn't surprise me. Harvest Hollow is the kind of place where people like to stay, and there are lots of family trees with sprawling roots thick with cousins, usually grouped in the same sections of the city. Lots of Moores on this side of town. Lots of Shelbys on the other side. That kind of thing. I once accidentally went on a date with a second cousin.

The normalcy of the conversation is doing a lot to restore my equilibrium. There is nothing in Shane's body language to suggest that he's going to make a move Mary Louise and I won't like, and Jolie's says she's not on alert.

Even as I quietly give the order into the radio for my deputies at the exits to stand down, I stay right where I am.

I'm not letting anything happen to Jolie on my watch.

Chapter Seventeen

JOLIE

"What do you need, Shane?" I keep my voice low so Mary Louise and Lucas can't hear since neither of them is about to take their eyes off us.

"I won't do nothing to you," he says, looking over at them.

"I believe you, but can you blame them if they don't trust you?"

"Guess not." He turns back to me. "Sullivan's is the reason I quit carrying this." He hands the flask to me. "Give it a shake."

I do. There's a slosh.

"Used to be that I'd stop by Sullivan's every day after work. I'd drink one whiskey. Had a deal with Janice. If I quit carrying my flask and kept it to one drink a day, on Fridays she'd pour me two with the second one free for good behavior. Sounds stupid, but it worked. A week after she shut the bar, I took my flask out again. It's such a habit that when Mary Louise tackled me, I was reaching back to touch it like it's a security blanket. Had to know it was there to help with the stress." He sits back, finished with his story, like he expects me to fill in the blanks.

And I do. He's got a drinking problem, but unlike my dad, he's tried to handle it. Janice tried to help him in her own misguided way. He's lost that support, and now he's drinking too much again.

I hear we're supposed to be understanding of alcoholism. That addiction isn't a person's fault. That there's science or genes or something behind it. We're supposed to have compassion and treat it like an illness.

That's not me. Maybe one day I will not feel an icy rage every time I think about how my dad chose liquor over me for every single day of my childhood. But that compassion? I have only enough for my kid self. That scared little girl who got me to here. My dad? No. None for him.

"Why are you telling me this?" My dad would never admit to a problem, even when he couldn't stand up straight. Even when my shoulders and spine ached from trying to get him home from Sullivan's, all his weight on me as I held him up and tried to guide him down the sidewalk.

"Having the sheriff show up at your workplace is something of a wakeup call," he says. "He can't do that again. I can't get fired."

"I told you I didn't send him."

"I know." He looks at me from tired eyes, like he's weighing out a decision. He's not that much older than me, I realize. He's probably not even forty yet. Physical labor has got him moving like an older man. "Me and my lady have been good for a couple of years, but we're starting to fight again. That's mostly on me, and if I lose my job, she won't tolerate it."

It's his fault, and I can see in the defeat on his face that he knows it. "Not sure what I can do about that if I keep getting graffiti or disruptive visits, Shane. Help me set those worries aside."

"I knew when I dug that flask out of my shed that I was messing up. I know it sounds stupid that a bar was all that stood between me and trouble, but that's how it was. Coming here, I always knew I could have one drink. But I also knew I couldn't have more than one drink. And that was enough to keep me from buying a bottle of Jack and bringing it home."

I study Shane. I may not understand his need to drink, but I can respect his effort not to. "I'd cut you the same deal," I tell him. His eyebrows go up. "One drink a day and a free one on Fridays, but I have two conditions. One, you never make me regret it."

He nods. "Okay."

"Follow me for the second condition." We slide out, and I call, "We're fine," to my bodyguards. "Just getting him something." I lead him down the hall to the restrooms. I reach inside the door of the ladies' room and pluck a pamphlet from the holder on the wall to hand to him. "If you decide you want more help, that's a good place to start."

He takes it and reads the title aloud. "'The Mountain Man's Guide to Curbing Your Drinking.' Is this for real?"

"As real as Mary Louise's tackling skills." I give a small laugh when he winces. "I don't want to profit off anyone's misery. We don't overserve, and we'd be glad to lose a customer if it meant they're getting help for a problem. I looked at a bunch of different materials, but this seems the most common sense, and the title most likely to interest people."

"It's a weird thing to put in a bar." He turns it over, skimming the back. "All right. Can't promise I'll do anything but read it."

"Good enough for now. There's a regular meeting for people trying to quit in the St. John's Episcopal rec room a block over. Every so often, I'm going to ask you if you're ready to get some help. Keep that pamphlet and answer me without starting anything when I ask. I'll accept a no until you're ready to say yes. That's the second condition. Can you live with that?"

He tucks the pamphlet into his back pocket. "I can."

"Then we have a deal." I walk him back to the main floor where Ry, Mary Louise, and Lucas are waiting. "Shane, will you solemnly swear in front of the witnesses most likely to lay you out if you don't, that you and I are done with mutually assured destruction?"

He shakes his head. "You are one odd chick, but yeah. I swear."

"I'll tell Ry about our deal. Mary Louise will see you out."

"I can do it," Lucas says.

I nod to Mary Louise that I'm fine with this, and Lucas jerks his head toward the rear exit. "Let's go that way so we don't set the whole block speculating about what happened."

Shane doesn't say anything, but his shoulders relax a bit more as he follows Lucas.

Soon it's just me, Mary Louise, and Ry. "You're my heroes," I tell them. "But Mary Louise, why were you even in here so early? We'd have been in trouble without you."

"Told Ry I'd sit in on his interview with a security applicant."

Ry glances at his watch. "He'll be here in another ten minutes. Glad he missed that whole mess."

Mary Louise gives us a fleeting smile. "Don't know. Might have made our decision easy either way."

"I think I like demonstration interviews better for trivia hosts than for security," I say. "Find us someone as good as you, okay?"

"Can't be done." She says it like she's informing us the sun rises in the morning.

"You're right. How about almost as good?"

"On it, boss."

"I'm going to go do some paperwork to settle my nerves." As I turn toward the office, I hear Mary Louise asking Ry to repeat what I just said.

"You heard her. Math relaxes her."

I close my office door on the sound of her bafflement with a smile. It fades as I drop into my office chair and rest my head on my desk, an adrenaline crash sweeping through my system. My heartbeat accelerates, and my hands shake so badly that I clasp them together and hold them between my knees to steady them. I draw deep breaths and try to settle my racing thoughts.

"There was never any danger," I tell myself. Then I repeat the phrase over and over in my head, trying to convince my nerves that I'm telling the truth.

A knock on the office door startles me into a jump as Lucas opens it and pokes his head in. The faint lines around his eyes crease. "I was going to ask if you're okay, but I guess not."

I shove my hand through my hair, not caring if I mess it up. "I will be. My mind suddenly wants to play 'what if.' It's stupid. Nothing happened."

A look I can't interpret crosses his face. Worry? Anger? I might have known him a long time, but every time I'm with him, I'm realizing I don't know him well. It's the onion thing. I see past one layer, and there's another one. Not in a "keep out" way. In a "there's a lot to discover" way.

If Phillip hadn't bankrupted me emotionally, I might find those layers intriguing. But I have nothing but a few pockets of spare time to offer right now, and Lucas is basically a single dad. I don't think single dads are casual daters. I don't get the sense from Lucas that he's that type, anyway. I get solid vibes. Roots kind of vibes.

I can't help with Brooklyn and be involved with Lucas. We won't work, and then who's there for Brooklyn? Because I'm going to be important to her. I can feel it in a way I can't explain but that I also can't deny.

I shake my head. No. My emotional energy can go to her. She needs it more, anyway.

"No what?" Lucas asks. "I didn't ask a question."

"Sorry. No, I'm not okay. Yes, I will be."

"It's okay to not be okay," he says. "I've got ten years on this job, and that still shook me when I walked in. That's with a gun on my hip, combat training, and a deputy backing me up at each entrance."

"You were scared?" That kind of does make me feel better.

He shuts the office door behind him and leans against it. "Yeah. I was."

His tone is hard to decipher, and despite everything I just told myself about not getting into anything with him, I want to be better at this. Better at reading him.

"I'm sorry you were scared, but it makes me feel like less of a wimp."

He rests his head against the door and scans my face. I'm not sure what he's looking for, and the longer he looks, the more naked I feel. Inside, I mean. Is that even a thing? Being naked inside?

"Jolie." He hesitates. "I've been in scarier situations and not felt half as much fear."

My stomach sours slightly at the idea of him being in more dangerous situations, and my mind races to find the meaning behind the rest of his words. He's saying he was more scared because it was me. And he'd only be saying that if . . .

But no. A loaded moment in my kitchen yesterday morning because he brought me coffee isn't evidence to assume he suddenly has feelings enough to worry about my safety. He has to mean it's because knowing someone in a scary situation makes it worse for him. That makes way more sense, and I'm glad I realized that before jumping to an embarrassing conclusion.

I lean back in my chair, forcing my body to look relaxed. "Thanks for reassuring me. I feel better."

A pause, then he nods. "Sure. Whatever you said to Shane worked. I truly don't believe he'll cause you trouble again."

"Agreed." I stand and regret it immediately. For one, my knees aren't all the way steady yet. For another, it puts me much closer to Lucas than I meant to be. I can't step back in this small office without making it obvious that I'm retreating. "I better get out there and show my face so Mary Louise and Ry don't worry."

He straightens and turns to open the door.

The fact that the view is as good going as it is coming doesn't matter.

It doesn't.

It's my new mantra.

Because despite all the conclusions I've reached about my emotional availability and my priorities in the last five minutes, some maverick part of my brain is trying to make me go rogue.

I don't have room in my heart for Lucas Cole right now, and it better get the message—*quick.*

Chapter Eighteen

JOLIE

I thought the worst part of my day would be the split second I thought Shane Hardin was pulling a gun on me.

Believe it or not, I'm wrong.

We've got a decent crowd for a Wednesday night. For the last week, I've been leaving closer to 11:00, when the crowds thin. Right now, it's 7:30, and it's hopping. A group of women my age have come in, about twelve of them, most of them flashing wedding rings. They've got Tina and Precious running hard, and from what Precious says, they've come over after the PTA meeting at one of the elementary schools. Not Brooklyn's.

And right in the middle of them sits Sloane Oakley. Or whatever her married name is. She looks the same as ever: the kind of pretty money can buy. Perfect, subtle highlights. Well-practiced makeup, not too heavy. Tastefully dressed in riding boots, a plaid pencil skirt, and an expensive-looking sweater.

My stomach clenches, and I remind myself that these days, I'm also the kind of pretty that money can buy, and there's nothing for her to pick on. Maybe she wouldn't if she could. Maybe she's changed, even if her position as the nucleus of this group of women makes me doubt it.

Sometime in the weeks since opening the Mockingbird, I lost the fire in my belly for payback. But I don't know if I'll ever stamp out Teenager Jolie, who at least wants all her bullies to know that she's done well.

I watch them for several minutes from across the bar after they take their seats, staying at my corner table and keeping an eye on them. But subtly. I don't want any of them to turn around and catch me gawking.

What I *should* feel is satisfaction that so many women with disposable income are in here ordering our boutique cocktails and glasses of our nicer wines. I slip into the office after they order their first round of drinks, and the sales number makes me smile.

But what I mostly feel is . . . young? A need to stay unnoticed, just like I did whenever I could in high school. I want to keep an eye on them, so I know exactly where to be to avoid them.

I force myself to resist the instinct, just like I had to do a few hours ago with Shane. When they start ordering their second drinks, I'm so twitchy inside that I can't take it anymore. "You are not this person. You outgrew her. Thank her for the job she did and be the Jolie you are now." I say this aloud but quietly. *I* need to hear it; no one else does.

Tonight, I'm wearing a black sleeveless sheath, fitted and de-signed to wear under suit jackets, but it works well as a dress on its own. I'm also wearing boots because they're one of the best things about fall. I may not be a pumpkin spice latte fan, but every other stereotype about girls and fall? Definitely me.

I draw a steadying breath and head over to the bar to join Ry. The women are seated at tables near it. I want to prove to myself that I can be in their vicinity and not wilt. Or regress. I walk past them. They're on my left, and I smile at the table to my right. *I'm doing this. I've got this. I'm a bona fide grown up.*

"Gappy?"

It's Sloane's voice. I'd know it anywhere. Sweet as an Oakley apple, but where other people might hear mischief in it, I know it's the rot of meanness.

For a second, I falter. But that's not my name, so I ignore her and join and Ry behind the bar. "Hey," I say, as he's muddling mint leaves for a mojito. "Numbers are looking good. How about I handle the wine and beer?"

"Sure, cuz."

"Gappy."

I look up to find Sloane standing right in front of me. "Sorry, who?"

She smiles like *Isn't this so fun?* "It *is* you. I knew it. Sloane Oakley-Hunsaker. We went to school together."

I want to say something devastatingly cool here, but my blood is pounding in my ears, and I can't hear myself think.

Ry says, "That's not her name."

Sloane gives a silvery laugh. "Of course not, duh. It's just a fun nickname. Although between friends, it looks like you got some work done. More power to you, sweetie."

It's the "sweetie" that does it, that jolts me out of my ear-buzzing paralysis. She says it like she's speaking to the help, or someone much younger.

"It's Jolie," I tell her. "Next time you forget, you can check the Harvest High Wall of Fame. It's inscribed on the valedictorian plaque, right above yours."

Her eyes narrow for a split second. "That's right, you did get that title." She glances around. "Doesn't look like it did you much good if you're working as a bartender."

"Bar owner," Ry snaps, and I shake my head at him to let him know I have this.

"Don't feel bad for the mistake," I tell Sloane. "It's probably hard for people who never leave this town to catch the vision of the ones who do."

"I left," she sputters. "I went to UNC and got a degree in computer science. What did you ever do?"

I rest my arms on the bar and lean toward her, so I don't have to talk over the music. "I majored in finance and made more money than I'll ever need in Chicago." I make a lazy wave to encompass the bar. "Decided I'd start a new empire. Welcome to home base."

I've decided no such thing, but it doesn't matter in my quest to put Sloane in her place. Every time I can tell I've gotten under her skin, my footing feels that much more sure, and I have the advantage now.

I want to keep belittling and undermining her the way she did to me for so long, but I won't. It means becoming like her, and though Sloane would be shocked to hear it, I never wanted to be like her. I just wanted her to leave me alone. We're having the moment I'd always wanted: me standing before her in all my success, and her having a hard time believing it.

It's almost enough. Almost. I place a wine glass in front of her and turn to consider our wines before choosing a pinot noir and pouring it for her.

"Enjoy this on the house," I tell her. "Then leave. And don't come back."

Her mouth drops slightly open, and even in the soft lighting, I can see her cheeks reddening. There's a chuff from Ry—the sound of him fighting a laugh.

Sloane looks mad, not hurt. Her face says "Who do you think you are?" even if her mouth hasn't found the words yet.

"You're going to catch gnats," I tell her. It's the same thing she said to me when she'd pulled the flower wreath off my mortarboard at graduation. I hadn't been able to afford a custom wreath like a lot of the girls got from the local florists with their favorite flowers, but I'd made my own so my graduation cap wouldn't look so bare. It had been simple, made from wildflowers that grew on the undeveloped property behind our apartment complex, but I'd liked it.

"Oh, sweetie," she'd said, "I can't let you go out there looking so homemade." And she'd pulled it off my cap while we milled around, waiting to be organized for our procession onto the football field. It had caused the bobby pins securing my cap to pull hard at my hair. "Close your mouth or you're going to catch gnats," she'd snapped.

My eyes had smarted, and a few minutes later, I'd had to lead the procession with Sloane right behind me, her waving like the homecoming queen she'd been in October, me hoping everyone thought my eyes were watering from graduation sentimentality and not Sloane's straight-up meanness.

Her mouth snaps closed and her eyes tell me she knows exactly why I said it.

I nod at her glass. "It's one of our best wines. Enjoy. But over there with your little friends."

She sits there for a couple of seconds before she picks up the glass with a fake smile. "So interesting how some people let money change them."

"So interesting how some people don't ever change. Bye, Sloane."

There's nothing left for her to do but gather her tattered dignity and return to her friends.

Ry moves closer to me so the customers at the bar can't hear us. "That was almost everything I wanted it to be. It could only have been better if you'd said it in front of her friends." He holds up his hand for a high five, which I give him. "You're not going to regret it now and wish you were nicer, are you?"

I snort. "No. That was completely satisfying."

"That's my girl," he says.

"Go earn your tips," I say, grinning at him. "I'm going to run the numbers one more time, and then I think I'll head home early."

"Good plan."

In my office, the door closed safely behind me, my smile wobbles and disappears. I'm not at all sorry I told off Sloane. But that moment of paralysis when she first confronted me scares me because I'd felt a flash of fear. It was the old fear of never knowing what I could do to protect myself from her, and I haven't felt that kind of vulnerability—the fear of being pushed around—in a long, long time. Years.

There's a crack in my armor, and Lucas Cole is the reason why.

If the armor is thinning, I need to build thicker walls. I still have a few scores to settle, and Lucas Cole can't be my weakness, so I'd better make my walls strong enough to keep him out.

Chapter Nineteen

LUCAS

Three times over the next week, Becky comes back to my office with books that Jolie dropped by for Brooklyn. After the first time, I tell Becky to call me next time Jolie comes in.

"She definitely did not seem like she wanted me to do that," Becky answers. "But I'll make it happen, boss."

The next time, Jolie tells Becky she's in a hurry so not to call me. The third time, Jolie sends the books over with one of her servers instead of coming in herself.

Every day, more than the day before, I wake up wanting to talk to Jolie again. About anything, really. Brooklyn and books. How she's still leaving the house without a complaint every morning. How it's been a week and she hasn't called home sick.

About her bar, or the weather, or how the Appies are doing this season. Just anything. I want to talk to her about anything.

But when I stop by the Mockingbird the next afternoon, Ry is outside with a tech from a security company who's installing a camera alarm system, and he says Jolie is interviewing a chef and it's not a good time.

The next two times I drop by, Ry tells me Jolie isn't there, but the first time, I suspect she sees me coming on the security system and tells him to say she's out. The second time, I'm positive that's what happened because I spot her truck parked behind the bar.

I don't want to drop by her house again because that's a tricky thing to do when you're the sheriff and you haven't been invited, even in your unofficial capacity. It wouldn't change the fact that I'd be pulling up to her house in a department vehicle.

At some point, I begin to wonder if I'm stalking her. Am I like the deluded guys we have to talk to sometimes, the ones who are convinced the woman they're obsessed with wants to talk to them, that her call to us is simply a misunderstanding?

I do not want to be that guy.

I stop dropping by the bar.

But every day, I still wake up wanting to talk to Jolie.

Chapter Twenty

JOLIE

"Momentum."

Ry looks up at me from the schedule rough draft he's working on while Precious slices limes for the bar. "Momentum? Is that a new cocktail? Let me guess: vodka plus some weird energy drink?"

I shake my head. "No. Momentum. We have it. Can you feel it? It's gathering. Everything is coming together at the right time. Precious, did your aunt tell you that she accepted the offer to be our new chef yesterday?"

Precious claps her hands and squeaks. "Oh, my gosh, that's awesome. You won't be sorry. She's just needed a chance to shine."

"She'll be perfect," I tell her. Her aunt, Bonnie, is past fifty, and for the last ten years, she's worked as a sous chef in two different local restaurants. She applied to be the chef here, and she's excited to put together a gastropub menu for our steady evening business, eventually expanding into a full lunch menu. She'd made it clear that she could do more than either of the kitchens she'd worked in had let her do, and she'd almost cried when I called to offer her the position.

"It's going to be so good," Precious says. "You're going to be so happy."

Happy. It's an interesting word choice, and I mull over it as I head into my office. Happiness has never been my goal, and I'm not sure I've ever thought about that before. Security, yes. Stability, yes. Any and all avoidance of chaos, definitely yes. The last word with the people who expected me to fail when I was here? Yes, yes, yes.

Maybe those are the things that add up to happiness, even if I haven't put it to myself that way.

I sit at my desk, but I don't log into the computer, instead staring at the dark screen, my mind busy but unfocused. It's . . . noisy. Inside my head, not the bar, which hasn't opened for the afternoon yet.

I'm not used to this kind of restlessness, and I'm not sure what to do about it, but I go back onto the floor. "I'm taking a walk," I announce.

Precious and Ry both nod, and I pause, not sure what to do next. It's one thing to leave for the bank or to pick something up somewhere. But just to go on a walk? When they keep at their tasks without comment, I head out of the front exit and find myself turning right on the sidewalk. Toward the sheriff's station. Except that's definitely not why I'm walking that way. I'm going to the...

Library. That's where I want to be. I want the soothing effect of the library, where I can walk in and let the Dewey decimal system soothe me. That's the perfect antidote for a noisy mind. A quiet library.

I'm careful to look away from the sheriff's station as I pass, and when my unruly brain tries to wonder if he's in there and what he might be doing, I force myself to think of something else. Like whether I need to talk to our brewer in Asheville about adding another IPA to our lineup. Or maybe a lager?

Mrs. Herring smiles at me from the front desk when I walk in. "Hello, Jolie. I admit I expected to see you before now. It's not like you to go so long between library visits."

I haven't been in since that first day, and already I feel it working its magic on me. "Hey, Mrs. Herring. Needed to give myself a break, and my feet carried me here."

She chuckles. "Smart feet. Looking for anything in particular today?"

It's a little after 2:00. Schools will let out in an hour, and we'll open. It's not a coincidence. We're building a steady repeat business of different teacher groups coming in after work for a drink almost every day of the week. When we open the kitchen, we'll get even busier because we can turn it into a happy hour with half-price appetizers.

"Order in chaos?" I say. "Some people have Zen gardens or meditation apps."

She nods in understanding. "And you've always had the library."

Always. I consider that then smile. "I guess I always have."

"Would it interrupt your peace and quiet too much if I ask you to catch me up on what you've been up to since you left Harvest Hollow? You can pull up a chair, and we'll have a nice visit." She points to the empty chair tucked beneath the counter next to her.

My eyes get big. "Wait, like sit behind the checkout desk? Am I allowed?"

"You are if you're invited. Come on around." She meets me at the side door and welcomes me in.

I take my seat and survey the library from this angle. "It looks totally different. I feel like I snuck into a restricted section or something."

Mrs. Herring laughs. "Behind the velvet rope, as it were. It's a very specific kind of person who thinks my side of the desk is the VIP section."

"I'm a library superfan. I'm not sure you realize how much I needed this place when I was younger."

Mrs. Herring smiles. "I think I do. I always have a handful of patrons I look after, and you were one. Now, tell me what you've been up to. Start with college. Duke, was it?"

I tell her about majoring in finance, working in the Duke dining hall to help pay my incidentals even though my scholarship covered room and board. I'd even gotten a scholarship from the library, and it helped so much, but there were always expenses that fell outside of all the financial aid, and with a head for money, I knew it was best to keep my loans to an absolute minimum.

She wants to know all the details. Why did I choose finance? What kinds of jobs can you do with that? How did I end up at a hedge fund? What was the environment like?

I'm not used to people taking such a deep interest in the details, but it makes sense that a librarian wants to know everything. Mrs. Herring always seemed like one of those magical adults who knew everything about everything when I was a kid, and on the rare occasion she didn't know something, she took great pleasure in finding the answer. In fact, I think that's part of where my interest in trivia developed.

I answer all of her questions until she gets to the one I dislike discussing most.

"It sounds like you enjoyed Chicago," she says. "What made you decide to leave?"

The answer doesn't speak well of me. I make a face.

She laughs. "A man."

"How'd you know that?" I ask, startled by her guess.

"Dear, that's what that face always means. Every man in my life before my darling Cornell put that look on my face."

"Is it okay if we skip over that part?"

"Of course, dear. But I'd love to know why you came back to Harvest Hollow. I'm delighted you're here, but as I remember, you don't have much family here, do you?"

"An aunt and a few cousins," I say. "One of them works for me."

Neither of us mentions my dad. She'd dealt with him a couple of times when he'd come into the library looking for me, belligerent and loud.

"Then why Harvest Hollow?"

I consider my answer. "To give back to the community," I finally say. Sure, I meant to dish out to everyone who had forced me to take it, but Mrs. Herring has only ever been good to me, and she doesn't deserve my cynicism.

She looks at me for a long moment, as if she can hear the irony I kept out of the words, but she doesn't press me. Instead, she nods. "Excellent. I know where you can start. I want to offer a financial literacy class to our patrons one night a week, helping them figure out how to manage their spending and start building nest eggs and working toward their larger financial goals. Better housing or emergency car repair funds. That type of thing. You'd be perfect for the job. The unpaid, doing-it-out-of-the-goodness-of-your-heart job."

She's calling me on my claim. If this was the kind of giving back I'd meant, she's offering the perfect opportunity. I hedge, unable to give her an outright no. "Now isn't such a good time. Still trying to find my pace with the bar and all of that."

"I understand. Let's get through the fall tourist season, and when business goes back to normal, it'll feel so much less crazy than when you're dealing with the crowds. I'm sure teaching the class will fit neatly in your schedule. Let me check something." She types on her computer, and a minute later she says, "It looks like Mondays and Tuesdays are the slowest nights for most bars. We'll look at doing it on one of those nights."

I smile and shake my head. "You're not wrong. I'll check in with you after the apple season ends and see what makes sense." I won't make any promises, but if it were anyone besides Mrs. Herring, I would have already given a blunt no. We chat for a few more minutes, then I excuse myself to wander the stacks. A Katherine Center novel I've somehow missed catches my eye, so I check it out and say goodbye to Mrs. Herring.

As I step back into the gold autumn afternoon, I'm struck again by how less than an hour in the library has already recentered me. I can't believe I'd forgotten how this place and that woman had always been a good part of any day I stopped by.

Sure, some things didn't change and probably never would, like Sloane and her compulsive need to be a queen bee. But Lucas had changed for the better. And some things that hadn't changed . . .

I look over my shoulder at the library. Some things had been good all along.

"Whoa."

"Oof," I say, my breath leaving me as I walk into something solid. Solid and warm. Solid and warm and dressed in the familiar green of the Harvest Hollow sheriff's uniform.

Lucas's hands come up to steady me with a firm hold on my arms, and I step back, dabbing at his chest where I rammed a book into it like it's spilled cocoa instead.

"Sorry," I say. "I wasn't looking where I was going, obviously."

"I'm fine. You okay?" he asks.

His hands are still holding my upper arms, and we're barely a foot apart. I should step back more, but his hands are warm through the sleeves of my thin sweater in the creeping cool of late September, and for a moment, I can't bring myself to step away from the heat of his body.

It feels good, and I—

I step back immediately when I catch the drift of my thoughts toward how I want to stay right there, basking in his touch. Don't need any of that.

"I'm fine," I say. "Heading back to the Mockingbird."

"Sure. Hey, I'm glad I ran into you—"

"Technically, I ran into you."

He smiles. "Conceded. Anyway, I was going to see if you might be interested—"

I don't know what's going to come out of his mouth next, but I cut him off. I hold up my wrist with my watch. "Oh, Ry is texting. I need to go down and help out. Sorry again about the crash." I hurry down the sidewalk. His words might have been leading up to asking me out, and I need to outrace them. Because I need to say no. And I'm pretty sure I couldn't have.

Sheriff's bullet dodged.

Chapter Twenty-One

LUCAS

I watch Jolie walk away as fast as a woman can without it turning into a run.

She doesn't even have a smartwatch. It was just a regular watch with hands. No texts.

That settles the question of whether she's avoiding me. What I'm not sure about is why. I didn't date during the election two years ago, and then Brooklyn came along almost right after that, but I'm not a monk or even a hermit. I enjoy the company of women, and I think I read them pretty well. Even Jolie.

She gives major standoffish energy, but I'm not imagining the tension I sense between us—and I don't mean the angry kind that we had in high school. I feel a strong pull toward her. She's completely different from my usual type, which always ends up being women who were former cheerleaders and beauty queens, even when I don't know that going in.

Jolie is not that soft kind of pretty. She's . . . I don't know. She has the kind of face—or maybe it's the way she carries herself—that I'd expect to see in a museum oil portrait of important historical figures. Regal. Maybe that's the word. She's a specific kind of hot. Librarian hot. Teacher hot. Woman-in-authority hot.

The thing is, I've seen her crack a couple of times. And when she does, it animates everything about her. A warmth shines through, and it pulls me in.

Except she's pushing me away. That much is obvious. Could it be all our high school baggage? Is she still holding that against me? She's clearly got a chip on her shoulder over a lot of things, and from what I'm gathering in bits and pieces, she had way more going on outside of school than I would have imagined for the mousy book nerd forced into tutoring me. If I'd thought about her life outside of our time in the school library at all, it probably would have been to imagine her doing extra credit at home just for fun.

Law enforcement has taught me time and again that there is so much more going on behind closed doors than people would ever guess. It means that what Jolie has shared is likely the tip of the iceberg.

I'd like to learn more about her.

It's a good time, given that things are settling back down with Brooklyn. Every morning this week, I've still expected her to appear at the last possible minute at breakfast, her face a blank, her body hunched, the corners of her mouth turned down. She's been her usual self, but I sort of feel like I do when I pull over a vehicle for a traffic stop: they're routine—until they aren't. Until you get the wrong person at the wrong time, and they can suddenly become dangerous.

This is not so different from living with a tween.

I get no more time to stare after Jolie, mulling like a weirdo, because Becky pops out from the station. "Boss, Wayne Oakley is on the way over, and he's demanding to speak to you."

I nod and head in, settling in behind my desk and pulling up Harvest Hollow Happenings to see if there are any new updates that would tip me off as to why I'm about to get the dubious honor of his company.

The intercom beeps. "Mr. Oakley and his daughter are here to see you."

Sloane? I know her in passing, mostly, because she's often with her father at high-profile events. I don't know why she'd be here too. "Send them back."

I deliberately leave my office door shut, because Wayne Oakley is the kind of guy that needs strong signals and boundaries. Forcing him to knock and request entrance is one of them. I generally operate with an open-door policy for employees and citizens alike, but Wayne needs reminders.

The knock comes, and it even manages to sound irritated. I hide a smile and call, "Come on in."

The door opens to admit Wayne and Sloane, and I stand to shake their hands before waving them into the chairs on their side of my desk and taking my seat again. "How can I help you today?"

Wayne starts. "You have got to get the Doll Bandit. It's getting out of hand."

I raise an eyebrow. "I can understand the mayor's concern, but as far as I know, this hasn't affected any local businesses. They've all shown up at private residences. Why would the Chamber be worried about this?"

"Because one of them showed up on my porch this morning, and it is unacceptable," Sloane says.

Ah. Okay. I pull out my notepad to take down the pertinent information. "Let me call in Detective Slocum. She's lead on this, and we'll get the details."

"You don't need to investigate," she says. "I know who's doing this."

I lay my pen down and lean forward. "Tell me."

"Jolie McGraw."

The name falls between us and lies there like an undetonated bomb. I don't allow any change of expression. No one has better cop face than I do. "What leads you to believe that?"

"She's back in town."

"Sure. Bought Sullivan's. That's not exactly a smoking gun," I say.

"She's like one of those people who snaps and goes on a rampage," Sloane says.

"You need to put a stop to this, Lucas," Wayne says.

"That's Sheriff to you," I tell him, my voice calm and polite. He'll start calling me "boy" or "son" if I don't. "Can you elaborate on that, Sloane? I've spoken with her a few times since she opened the new place, and I don't get that impression." An axe to grind, yes. Never a "rampage" vibe.

"She hated me in high school. She was very resentful that my family had money, and she would do everything she could to undermine me. She disliked a lot of people, actually. I stopped by her bar the other night with some friends, and it was clear she still isn't over her high school insecurities. She was very rude to me. And then a creepy doll that looks like my daughter shows up on our porch?"

She leans forward, fixing me with a hard stare that I think is supposed to intimidate me. "It's no coincidence that those dolls started showing up right around the time Jolie McGraw came back to town."

I resist the urge to rub my suddenly throbbing temples. To be honest, I'd probably rather deal with the leader of the local biker gang than Sloane Oakley-Whatever any day of the week. She's got a major helping of her father's entitlement, and she's clearly ready to throw both their last name and his title around to make some noise.

"I understand why that would concern you, but correlation is not causation. I have one of my best investigators looking into this, and we'll figure out what's going on."

Wayne snorts. "Best? How good can she be if you still haven't cracked this? This isn't exactly a mastermind operation. We should have answers by now."

I stand and walk to my office door, an invitation to leave. "I hear you, Wayne. But if even the most dedicated Facebook detectives can't solve it with all their theories and gossip, maybe you can cut my deputy a bit of slack while she sorts through the possibilities. Thank you for stopping by. I'll keep you posted."

Spluttering follows as Wayne Oakley tries to wrap his head around being dismissed. I stand and say nothing for a few uncomfortable seconds until my visitors register that I mean it; I'm done. Then they leave, but of course, Wayne has to make it sound like it was his choice.

"I'll look forward to an update soon," he says as they walk out.

"You bet," I tell him, which means absolutely nothing. No one outside of this department will be briefed until we know what we're dealing with. I'm sympathetic to the parents who are worried about these dolls appearing, but technically, there has been no crime committed. We'll get to the bottom of it and figure out whether there's an imminent threat, but my gut says this is the community getting each other all worked up over something that has a benign explanation.

It happens all the time.

I don't even bother to watch them exit the building, closing my door almost as soon as they've cleared it. I plop down in my office chair with a grunt because whether I personally believe there's a crime afoot or not, Sloane Oakley-Whatever has handed me a viable motive. Not that I think for one second that Jolie has anything to do with this. But it will require an official follow-up, and I can't send a deputy to do that. It would be insulting. Which means I have to do it.

I've been trying to come up with a good reason to stop by and see her, but man.

This ain't it.

Chapter Twenty-Two

JOLIE

"Jo?" Ry pokes his head into my office. "I've got a bit of a situation here."

"What's up?"

"Tina's kid is sick, and she can't leave him with her sister because reasons. I didn't catch that part. But she can't make it in for her shift. I'm calling in one of the new hires, but he's not fully trained yet."

"I got it," I tell him. "I'll cover for Tina."

"Sorry about this, cuz," he says. "We'll get the staffing where we need it soon."

I shrug. "It's tough for everyone right now to stay fully staffed. Don't worry about it. I expected these kinds of things to happen with a new business. We'll figure it out over time." I stand and look down at my heels. These aren't going to work for a full shift, not even for me, and I'm used to being in heels. I'm just not used to serving drinks in them for six hours straight. "Let me do something about this shoe situation, and I'll be ready to help."

Twenty minutes later I'm back in a pair of black flats from a boutique down the street, and I jump in on Tina's prep work. By 4:00, we're half-full—mostly teachers from the nearest middle school—and I know that shortly after 5:00 we'll be hopping with businesspeople stopping by to unwind for a bit.

We end up busier within a half hour. Our new hire, Daniel, helps where he can, mostly assisting Ry at the bar, but Precious and I handle the tables. Sort of. I'm not brilliant at it, but I know our drink selection well enough to make it work, and I do plenty of small talking and schmoozing to make sure they're okay even if the service is slightly glitchy. I hope the tips are good enough to cover whatever Tina normally makes; I don't want her to come out short for the week because I'm not as good as she is, but I do my best.

By 5:00, I'm maxed. I can handle as many tables as I have but no more. I doubt I'll hit a groove, but I should at least be able to handle a normal night of business.

That's when Lucas walks in.

He's in uniform, and this time it's impossible not to notice how it fits over his shoulders. They are broad. And sexy. And there's no way that man is rocking that build without putting in gym time. Like five hundred pushups every night or something.

Not that I have time to pause and consider such idiotic things. I jerk back into motion as Ry nods at Lucas. Lucas wouldn't come in for a drink in his uniform, so he must be here for business, but after standing inside the door for a minute or two and surveying the bar, he takes a seat at an empty four-top near the front and removes his hat.

Unfortunately, he's in my zone, Precious being more capable of handling the busier back half of the tables.

As soon as I drop off the next round of drinks for a raucous table of English teachers (and why is it *always* the English teachers?), I stop at Lucas's table.

"Hey, Lucas. Can I get you something?"

"No. Just need to talk something over with you when you have a minute."

A patron at another table signals for me. "Sorry, hang on a second. Blue dolphin coming up. Thanks for your patience."

I swing by the bar and call, "Water for the sheriff!" to Daniel before I hurry over to the beckoning table and take their next round of orders. But in between every single move I make, I'm wondering why the heck he's here. No one would have called him because there's no trouble. I mean, besides being short-staffed. So what's he doing? Do I want to know? Maybe I don't want to know.

Once I put the new drinks in the order system, I pick up a glass of ice water for Lucas and deposit it in front of him. "Here you go. What's up?"

"Hey, Jolie. I was wondering—"

But now a different table is trying to get my attention, and Ry is too, and I have to cut him off again. "Sorry, Lucas. Hang on." I don't mind being saved from whatever this conversation is. I'm not even sure why I'm slightly anxious about it.

When I find a lull about five minutes later, I stop at his table again. "Sorry. You were saying?"

"I wanted to see if—"

The entrance opens and a passel of women in business suits come in. Maybe six of them? It's the banker crowd, and they're already in high spirits, their laughter drowning out whatever Lucas is trying to say.

Mary Louise meets my eyes, hers brimming with amusement, and nods to let the ladies know they've passed the commonsense age check, which is "You clearly look over twenty-one, so I won't card you." Mary Louise doesn't card unless someone looks young, but stopping everyone is silly if it's obvious they're the legal age to drink.

"I really am so sorry," I tell him again. "Tina's kid is sick, and I'm covering. Be right back." I head to the bar to pluck up drink menus for the new arrivals.

It doesn't get any better over the next twenty minutes, and Lucas seems to realize that there will be no time to chat. I'm hustling back and forth so hard that I don't even have time to glance his way for a good bit, and when I finally do, it's to see that he's left and two new people, a middle-aged couple, have taken his place.

"When did Lucas leave?" I ask Mary Louise, skimming past her on a bar run.

"About ten minutes ago."

On the way back with the couple's menus, I ask, "Did he say what he needed?"

She shakes her head. "I've got theories."

"Like?"

"He was acting odd. I think maybe he came by to ask you out."

I fight the impulse to race out of the door and chase after him.

This is the dumbest possible impulse. Why would I do that? It's not like I'd say yes. And maybe Mary Louise is wrong about what he wants. I start to ask her why she thinks this, but Ry needs me, and I'm nearly running for over two hours straight before the pace slows down enough that Precious can handle the tables on her own. By now, Daniel has started to get the hang of things, and he's on the floor working two of the smaller tables too.

I finally have a spare minute to check in with my head of security, who is imagining things. "Mary Louise, Lucas didn't tell you specifically why he was here?"

She shakes her head.

"Then why are you assuming he wanted to . . ." I can't finish the sentence because the weird swoop I get in my stomach from even considering it makes me feel like I'm back in high school. No. Worse. Middle school.

"He was nervous, kind of," she says. "Fidgeting. That's not like him."

"That's not evidence."

She gives me a faint smile. "Never took his eyes off you, either."

Warmth blooms in my cheeks, and I hope she doesn't notice. "That doesn't mean anything."

A faint shrug again. "Fine. My theory is wrong."

I glance toward the door, imagining walking out of it to look for Lucas. But that's stupid. He left two hours ago, for one.

And for two, if Mary Louise is right, and that's what he was here for, the last thing I need to do is follow up on that. Not when the idea makes me way more nervous than Shane Hardin reaching behind him ever did.

When it's slow enough for me to leave, I climb into my truck and drive the long way home. The way that won't take me by the sheriff's office or the turnoff to the Cole place.

I park in my garage and lock myself in the house.

Um, I mean, lock the door firmly behind me, then put myself to bed like a good girl who isn't pretending that she isn't wildly tempted to text the hot sheriff and see what he needs.

This much I do know: the last thing that man needs is *me*.

And vice freaking versa.

I hug my pillow. My muscles are screaming, I have blisters on both heels, and I smell like beer. Conclusion: waiting tables is skilled labor. In addition to the physical demands of being on your feet and constantly moving, it takes either a degree in clinical psychology or an innate talent with people to keep the good times rolling and the cash coming in.

I text Tina to see how her boy is doing, and when she tells me his fever is down, I give a sigh of relief. I just wanted to make sure he's okay, but knowing she can be back at work tomorrow is a bonus. Right now, I'm so wiped I'm sure that after a quick shower to knock the smell of fermented hops off me, I'm going to sleep the sleep of the righteous.

I do not.

I do not because one Lucas Cole keeps interrupting my efforts to fall asleep like my sleep is trying to run a stop sign on a country road at 2:00 in the morning.

Is Mary Louise right? Did he come in to ask me out?

I don't bother pretending that I wasn't highly aware of him the entire time he was in the bar. Even though I couldn't get to his table often, I could sense his restlessness. The fidgeting. He used to do that during tutoring, but as a full-grown man, the sheriff has a fascinating stillness about him. That coiled feeling of pent-up energy, the energy that revealed itself when he exploded into action to help Mary Louise subdue Shane. He doesn't fidget. He moves with intent. But not this afternoon. This afternoon he was twitchy.

Could it have been nerves? Lucas doesn't strike me as someone who is shy with women, but what do I know? I tried to pretend he didn't exist outside of tutoring, so I have no idea if he had a lot of girlfriends back then. He doesn't come across as a flirt, but I don't think I'm alone in my heightened awareness when we're near each other. I only have the evidence of a few small moments between us where nothing was said but the space was still full of words, in a way. Words in my head like *Close the distance* and *Don't close the distance* at the exact same time.

I replay every look, word, and movement from him this afternoon until late into the night.

I hate this. And I'm going to do something about it.

Chapter Twenty-Three

JOLIE

It took me so long to fall asleep that I wake up midmorning, disoriented by the intensity of the sunlight coming through the window. That's 10:30 AM sunshine, and I'm usually out in it, not waking up to it.

Mixed in with the sleepy confusion is an image of Lucas, watching me carefully, one side of his mouth hitched up in the tiniest smile. Have I even seen him smile that way before?

Yes. The night he pulled me over and I rattled off geometry theorems.

Was that when he started slipping past my guard?

Because that's the conclusion I've come to: Lucas Cole is one of the people I should be most on guard against, but I somehow keep forgetting to be. It's not okay. It needs to change. It *will* change. Which means having an awkward conversation.

I have been ruthless in suppressing exactly how awkward I feel in most of my life. College was a three-year exercise in blending in, avoiding notice so the awkward didn't show through. Would have been four years, but I finished early, of course.

I got several more years of practice at the hedge fund until I became such a world-class faker that I wasn't always sure if I'd become good enough to fool myself about my own awkwardness or if I'd finally become more comfortable in my own skin.

I am that. Comfortable in my own skin. But as I imagine the impending conversation with Lucas, it's obvious that still leaves room for awkwardness.

Has to be done, though. I can't have him popping up unexpectedly to put me on the spot about a date. Time to be proactive here and "nick this in the butt," as Precious has said twice now. Ry even corrected her, telling her it should be "nip this in the bud," but she'd fixed him with stern blue eyes and said, "I know how it goes. I say it how it *should* go." And that's been that.

I get up and get dressed, pulling on a pair of Vince Camuto pants. I own so many pairs of expensive black slacks. Why? No one needs this many suit pants, especially not someone who isn't working in an office anymore. But I'll be working with the new chef, Bonnie, today. She's coming in to make some different dishes for the staff to try, and I'm itching to get in the kitchen with her. I'm not a great cook, but I can wash vegetables and peel potatoes or whatever she needs. The inside of my brain itches, and the idea of being hands-on soothes it, a little. And black pants are going to be better for that.

But honestly? I eye the racks in my closet hung with jackets and slacks. This really is kind of a stupid number of suits. I think there's a Gap on the other side of town. Might be time to get to know it. I sort of went from thrifting straight to Bloomingdale's at my mentor's urging. I'd gravitated toward higher-end brands in the thrift shops, but I didn't know they were high-end until I was buying the same brands new off the rack in a department store that offered me complimentary seltzer water while I browsed. But I'd never had the GAP/Loft/Zara in-between stage. Maybe Tina could come advise me again . . .

I'm avoiding thoughts of Lucas and the conversation we need to have by doing a closet inventory. Another Young Jo move—avoiding friction.

But friction is how you stay sharp. So I choose a blouse I don't mind getting stains on, and I put it on, all while figuring out how I want to bring this up with Lucas. Then I catch my reflection and frown. Black pants and a gray shirt. How . . . drab? I pull off the shirt.

Maybe it's stupid to want to look cute in front of someone you're going to reject for a date, but whatever. I've got my pride. I choose a fitted ivory shirt that I would normally only wear under a buttoned blazer for the office. It looks good by itself.

It stays that way exactly as long as it takes me to step one foot in the garage and realize it's *chilly.* Then I duck back into the house and grab a sweater jacket, a long one in teal, and decide I like the pop of color anyway.

I have no more excuses to avoid the talk with Lucas. During the drive to the bar, I come up with a script that makes sense to me. Straightforward. To the point. Just dealing with things instead of pretending they'll go away if I ignore them.

Still, when I pull into my parking spot, my first impulse is to climb out of the truck and head straight to the library and disappear into the fiction shelves. Freaking Phillip flattened my real-world hopes for romance like roadkill, but a fictional escape into someone else's love story—one that I know will work out—*that* I can handle right now. It's *all* I can handle right now.

So, yeah. Time to talk to Lucas.

But I'll do it on the way to the library. Like when you get your lip waxed then the esthetician puts cooling gel on it. I will stop by the station—lip wax—and go from there to the library—cooling gel. And see if Mrs. Herring set the new Katherine Center release aside for me. That's like . . . that's like if the esthetician hands you a Candy Junction Choco-Mocha Bonbon on your way out.

Sure, you look like you're working for Franco's Birthday Clowns with your bright red mouth, but you're a clown with a *bonbon.*

I pull out my phone.

JOLIE: Need to run to the library. Can I chat with you for a minute while I'm down that way?

LUCAS: Sure. I have a meeting in thirty min, but I'm free before that. I'll tell Becky to send you back.

I don't love the idea of going into the station to talk to him. What will Becky think? Or his deputies? Also, maybe it's extra rude to reject someone in his own office? Seems like yes.

JOLIE: Want to consider it a mental health break and meet me on the sidewalk in a few minutes? Fresh air or whatever?

LUCAS: Sure

I hop down from the truck. It's stupid that it's lifted. I know that. I don't need a lifted truck. No one *needs* a lifted truck. That's sort of the point. But I bought it when I was mad at Phillip and the Freaking Horsleys. I don't know if my brain was anything more than white mist when I walked into the Chicago dealership, but if I had an internal monologue, it probably sounded like "You think I'm an unpedigreed redneck who will embarrass you at your country club? I'll show YOU redneck." And then I paid cash for the pickup every boy in my high school would have loved to have driven.

Do I regret it almost two months later when I have to climb in and out of it?

No. Not even a little. Maybe the Horsleys were right about me. Or maybe it's an awesome truck.

I cut to the sidewalk through the bar so I can leave my purse, then I'm heading down Maple toward my lip wax and bonbon.

Lucas comes down the station steps as I approach and waits for me, hands resting on his belt. What anti-feminist part of myself finds a man in uniform hot because suddenly he has *authority*? Lucas needs to come around wearing regular clothes sometimes so it's less distracting.

"Hey, Jo," he says.

Ry calls me Jo, so Tina and Precious call me Jo. I'm sure Daniel will be doing it before long, and no doubt Bonnie will pick it up over time too. I kind of love it. No one but Ry has called me that before, but he's so laidback with me that it's infecting everyone in a good way.

I don't like it when Lucas calls me Jo because I like it too much when Lucas calls me Jo.

Maybe I need to find a self-help book at the library for women whose brains stop working when a good-looking man in a uniform comes around. Just because he makes really good apologies and he's sweet with his niece and he's always trying to look out for me even when I don't need him to . . .

Wait, why am I here?

"You wanted to talk?" he asks.

Right. To tell him I'm not looking for any of those things in a man. Because I'm not looking for a man. So I'm not going on a date. Okay, okay, my speech is coming back to me.

I draw a deep breath, and his eyebrows fly up. "Sorry it was so busy when you came in yesterday," I say.

"No problem. It's not like I wanted—"

"You're a really nice guy, Lucas." I cut him off in the middle of his sentence, and he stops talking, his mouth slightly open for a second. Um, he really is so handsome in his uniform in a young Raylan Givens/*Justified* kind of way. Why am I hyperaware of this now, when I'm planning to push him permanently out of reach?

I have to do this before I forget to do this.

"Not words I ever thought I'd say to you at one point, but I guess we all grow up and change."

"Okay, thank you."

"But I can't go out with you."

His forehead furrows.

"I get why that's confusing, but it's not because of high school or anything. I just think it's a bad idea because of Brooklyn."

He looks even more confused. "Brooklyn?"

I nod. "I'd like to mentor her, if that's okay. Kind of like a Big Buddy thing but not official. If you think she'll go for it."

He gives his head a small shake like he's trying to clear it. "I hadn't thought about it, but probably?"

"Right, well." I slide my hands in my pockets and feel a small knot of thread in one. I roll it around in my fingers, relieved for somewhere to focus my nervous energy. "Glad you understand. Thanks for being cool about it. I'm going to go ahead to the library. So." We stand there looking at each other, the mother of all awkward pauses stretching between us, until I say, "Okay, bye."

"Jolie," Lucas says as I shift to step past him. "Did you just reject me for a date I didn't ask you on?"

I stop. "Yeah, Mary Louise told me that's why you stopped by yesterday. I figured it was better than letting you get it all out when I knew I would say no."

He scratches his chin, and it makes me want to know how soft his beard is for myself. I didn't think I was into beards, but I guess I hadn't seen the right guy in one. Not that he's the right guy for me. He's just the right guy to make a beard look good, that's all.

"Mary Louise said I stopped by to ask you out?"

I'd dreaded this whole conversation because I knew it would be awkward, but something in his tone tips me off that this is about to get much, much worse. "Yes?" I fight not to turn it into a question and lose.

"Why would she think that?"

Oh. No.

I definitely look like a clown now. The kind that trips over her own feet and falls flat on her face. I try to pull myself together, to channel the cool Jolie McGraw, top-performing portfolio manager at Blue Slate, telling our new guys they better straighten up and fly right if they want to stay in my division. "You didn't come in yesterday to ask me out?"

"I did not." Something like amusement lurks in his eyes. He's laughing at my expense, and I can't blame him.

"Ah. Well, then I guess we didn't need to have a chat after all." I pull my hands from my pockets and then in a move I can't stop—a move that feels like I'm watching it from out of body, a slow-motion scene in a disaster film so no one can miss a single excruciating detail—I hold out my hand for a shake.

A freaking handshake.

Lucas accepts it, his expression confused again.

I give him my best business grip. "Thanks again." *Whaaat?* "Bye."

"Jolie," he says, not letting my hand go, which results in me jerking to a halt because of my "getting the crud out of here" momentum. "I did come by to talk to you yesterday. I still need to."

I slide my hand from his and tuck my hair behind my ear, like that's somehow smooth. "Sure. About what?"

"We should talk about this in my office."

This has to be about Shane. Whatever this is, I'd prefer to hear it in the crisp air of late September and not inside his office. "It's fine," I say. "It might be nice to have some bad news to make me forget my total embarrassment." I expect him to smile.

He hesitates, no smile.

I give him a nod that is meant to say "Out with it," and it must say that, because out it comes.

"You've been named as the Doll Bandit."

I hear the words. I do not understand the words. I run them through my mind again. And then I turn on my heel, march up the stairs, and go looking for his office.

Chapter Twenty-Four

LUCAS

Not once has this woman done anything I've expected.

I follow Jolie up the stairs, nodding at Becky to buzz us through as we enter the lobby. "Through the door, hang a left, and go all the way down to the office that has my name on it."

Jolie doesn't acknowledge she's heard me, but she turns left and follows my directions, stopping at my office door. She stands to the side, waiting for me to open it and escort her in.

She heads straight to the chair in front of my desk and sinks down. "Who said what now?" She has the question out before I'm all the way seated.

"Someone came in here yesterday afternoon to report that one of the dolls was left for her daughter, and she thinks there's a correlation between your return to town and the dolls cropping up."

Her eyes narrow. "Who was it?"

I've been thinking about this since the Oakleys left. I spent some time checking both their social media and Jolie's. As best I can tell, Jolie only has Facebook, and her settings are too restricted to gather much. I'll need to compliment her on that. Sloane is on Facebook and Instagram, and she even stars in the TikToks of one of the elementary school PTAs. They're goofy, but she probably thinks they're cute. I couldn't find any trace of Jolie following any of those accounts.

I lean back in my chair. "What's your relationship with Sloane Oakley like?"

Her face darkens, her lips pressing together in a thin line before she answers. "We don't have one."

"But you recently had an interaction?"

She snorts. "Interaction. Yeah, we did."

"I've heard her version of it. What's yours?"

"Are you investigating me?" Her tone holds a trace of disbelief. "You don't believe her, do you?"

"This is why I came in yesterday, Jo. I do—"

"Don't you 'Jo' me, Lucas Cole. You do not get to investigate me for a bogus charge and still call me Jo."

I sigh. "Fine, Ms. McGraw." She frowns. "I went to the Mockingbird myself because I felt like it's the least I can do. I have a detective on this investigation, and technically, it should be her job. But I didn't feel right about sending her over without at least a heads-up, not after how you've helped me. So I came myself."

She studies me for a minute, gnawing the inside of her cheek, and I have a flashback to tutoring, watching her do the same thing. She did it when I was being especially moody, like I was the problem she was trying to solve instead of the problem sets in the math book.

"I appreciate that, but I didn't hear you say anywhere in there that you don't think it's me."

I don't, but she's part of an official investigation now, so I can't say that. "Ms. McGraw, this is standard operating procedure. I'm going to call in Detective Slocum right now to have her conduct this interview. We'll keep it official. That way, there won't be any question about whether we did our jobs correctly."

"This is an official interview now? Is that another word for interrogation? Do I need a lawyer for this?"

I shake my head. "You're not under arrest. We're trying to gather information. You can choose to have an attorney present."

Jolie gives me a long stare, and this time I sense contempt in it. I want to tell her I know it's not her. I don't blame her for feeling this way. That's exactly why I'm bringing in Slocum. She'll clear it up, Jolie can walk out without a new stress hanging over her, and then I can talk to her in my unofficial capacity as Lucas to find out why she rejected me for a date I didn't ask her on, and how I can change her answer when I ask her out for real.

"You can come back to my house, walk the whole thing right this second when I've had no warning, poke in every closet, open every drawer, and you're not going to find a doll anywhere," she says. "I didn't do it, so there is literally no way to charge me with anything. Bring her in."

I pick up my phone. "Slocum, Jolie McGraw is in my office to answer any questions you might have." I hang up and tell Jolie, "She'll be here in a minute."

Deputy Slocum knocks on my door in half that time, but those thirty seconds feel like forever while Jolie and I sit in silence, her stewing and refusing to meet my eyes.

"Sheriff," Slocum says when I call for her to enter.

I introduce her to Jolie. "She'll be glad to answer any questions you have." I haven't told Slocum about my friendship with Jolie because the moment it became relevant, it also became important that I not influence Slocum by making her think she needs to investigate Jolie differently based on our . . . acquaintance with each other.

"Thank you for coming in, Ms. McGraw," Slocum says. "I need to confer with the sheriff for a brief moment. Pardon me."

She hands me her cell phone, and I have to force myself to keep my expression blank as I realize what I'm looking at. It's a new post from first thing this morning in Happenings: "Sounds like the Doll Bandit is the owner of the new bar on Maple. These dolls started showing up when she got to town, and she's got bad blood with some of the moms of these girls."

I must not do a good enough job with my face because Jolie tenses. "What, Lucas?"

Slocum shifts at Jolie's use of my first name. She's one of my investigators because she's sharp, and that's not the kind of detail that will slip by her.

"Ms. McGraw, do you follow the Harvest Hollow Happenings Instagram, where they share town news—"

"Gossip, you mean?" She's already reaching into her pocket for her phone.

"That one," Slocum confirms.

"I do," Jolie says, tapping on her screen. She's quiet for a few seconds until she spots the post. She gives a small, irritated grunt. It's really cute. Not that I let that show in my face either. "Great. Looks like you aren't the only one Sloane ran her mouth off to."

"You know Sloane Oakley-Hunsaker?" Slocum asked.

"Well enough to kick her out of my bar the day before she decided to accuse me of being some doll weirdo."

Slocum and I exchange looks. That does cast Sloane's report in a different light.

Slocum pulls out her notebook and a pen. "Can I ask why you kicked her out?"

"Because she's awful?" Jolie's tone says she can't believe Slocum even has to ask this.

"Did she say or do anything in particular that night that led to your invitation to her to leave?"

I have to fight a smile at Slocum's phrasing. She's very good.

"Sloane Oakley is still mad I beat her for valedictorian. She worked hard enough to be the salutatorian, but I guess she thought she deserved the crown. In high school, she never missed a chance to harass me about something. My appearance. My address. She stopped in the other night with her coven and decided to relive those memories. I decided not to."

Her coven. She's killing me. Even Slocum's lips twitch.

"Where were you between midnight and 7 AM this morning?" Slocum asks.

"Home. I left the bar around 10:45 and didn't come back until this morning."

That's not great. Since she lives alone, she won't have anyone to corroborate her story.

"You can check the log on my security alarm," Jolie says. "I have to arm and disarm it when I come and go. It'll match up."

I want to cheer.

"That would do it." Slocum makes a note before tucking her notebook into her jacket. She hands Jolie a business card. "If you could notify your alarm company to email the log to me, it'll save us a lot of time on this end. Otherwise, I can make a formal request with a warrant if you prefer."

It's not a threat, and Jolie seems to sense that, nodding. "Thank you, detective. I'll have it sent over."

Slocum nods and leaves, pulling the door shut behind her.

That's when it feels safe to smile. "I knew you didn't do it, by the way."

This doesn't seem to thrill her. In fact, she looks even more frustrated than before. "Great. That's three of us plus anyone who actually knows me." She holds up her phone. "That only leaves everyone who sees this post suspecting me. What's that saying? That a lie can travel around the world in the time it takes the truth to put its shoes on?"

"You don't have anything to worry about."

"You don't get it." She stands and paces to the wall where a large map shows the different patrol districts. "It doesn't have to be true for it to cause me problems. I can't even go to the library now."

"The library?" I don't see the connection.

She turns to look at me, twin spots of color high in her cheeks. "I was on my way in to tell Mrs. Herring that I would be happy to volunteer. She wants me to teach an adult financial literacy class, and I don't really want to do that. It would have to be at night, and I'm usually going to be at the Mockingbird. But I could be free in the afternoons and be there for homework help when kids come in."

I didn't need any more proof, but those aren't the words of someone trying to terrorize small children in town. "That's a great idea, McGraw."

She shoots me a sharp look. "You can call me Jolie. And it *was* a good idea until this post showed up." She shakes her phone. "Who's going to want to send their kids for tutoring with someone who's been accused of a weird preoccupation with little girls and matching dolls?"

I grimace. "Yeah, okay."

"This sucks, Lucas." She jams her hand through her hair and turns back to the map. I think she doesn't want me to watch whatever she's feeling play out on her face. "I left Harvest Hollow because I felt like I didn't belong here. I was a loner kid, and I didn't fit anywhere or with anyone. I thought I'd go live a different life where I could find my place."

She slides her hand from her hair, and it's the first time I've seen it in anything but perfect condition, every strand in place. Now there are bumps and stray locks of hair, and I want to go over and smooth them. Anything to make her feel better right now, because under her anger, I hear the hurt. I wonder how many people in her life have known to listen for it?

Without turning around, she slips her hands into her pockets and continues. "I came back to Harvest Hollow because of a breakup, if you can believe that."

"What happened?"

She takes a long time to answer. "I built this whole life in Chicago where I thought I belonged." She flashes me a small but real smile and sits again. "The weirdest part was that even though Ry is the only person I've stayed in touch with here, all I wanted to do was come back to Harvest Hollow. I don't know why. But I couldn't let go of it. Every day, I'd show up to work and think about how much I didn't like it. I'd walk into my overpriced condo and think how it didn't look like me. After about a month, I felt like I was climbing the walls everywhere. The office. Home. I decided I was done."

"And you came here. Because this felt like home." I think she's going to argue, but she opens her mouth, says nothing, and snaps it shut. "Want to know how I know?"

She settles back in the chair. "Lay it on me."

"Because you didn't have to leave Chicago. You could have stayed. But we're mammals when we come right down to it, and when we need to burrow, we go home. Sounds like Harvest Hollow is in your DNA."

"Maybe my lizard brain," she grumbles.

"Can't argue with prehistoric programming."

"Can't I?"

I smile. "You're here, aren't you? Has it been that bad?"

She gives me a long look. "Today hasn't been great. How soon are you going to catch this bandit? Because I don't need this sticking to me."

"This case has gone to the top of my list."

"How is it that you're having to deal with two cases involving me in less than two months?"

"Just lucky, I guess." I grin, but she doesn't smile.

"I hate this, Lucas. Sloane pulled this because she wants to make sure I know I'm not welcome back. That I don't belong. The funny thing is, my overwhelming instinct right now is that I do." She leans forward, resting her hands on the edge of my desk. "I *do*. And I'm going to prove it."

"Jolie . . ." My tone is a warning.

"No, listen. I'm good at patterns. I can look at complex systems and see things other people don't. It's why I was good at my job before. Let me help your deputy. If you know I didn't do it, use me as a resource to help figure out who did."

"That's not a great idea." Honestly, I know how sharp she is. She'd be an asset—except for the optics of it. I wouldn't care if it was only going to cause me a headache, but it's going to cause her problems. Fanning the flames, basically.

As if reading my mind, she says, "I'll keep it quiet. Look at it in my office. Or better yet, my house. No one will see you coming or going and start stupid rumors. Or keep them going."

"They're all going to bounce back on you," I say. "Better not."

"Lucas, I know how this is going to sound, but I'm not sure you understand how good I am at this kind of thing. Seeing links, anticipating what comes next. I'm sure I can help. You know Sloane is only going to make this a bigger deal now that she gets to play victim. And that means her dad is going to be in here huffing and puffing regularly."

"He already is."

"Then it will be worse."

"It doesn't matter on my end, Jolie. We would have had to follow up that claim no matter who made it. Wayne Oakley doesn't tell me how to do my job, but I'll say this: him coming in here and throwing his weight around is why I decided to get involved directly. I don't take kindly to people making unsubstantiated claims against my friends."

"Friends?"

"If that's okay."

A long pause. "Yeah. That's okay." She scoots her chair closer so she can lean even farther across the desk. "Let me help." Like she senses that I'm about to shake my head, she adds, "I'm hoping it will make you forget that I barreled over here to . . . you know."

"Know what?" I ask in a far too innocent voice.

She sniffs. "I was laboring under a misapprehension. My apologies."

"Accepted."

"Let me make it right by helping you with this stupid doll thing that is trying to ruin my life."

"When you put it that way . . ."

"Yes!" She straightens and gives a quick clap of her hands.

It seriously might be the most adorable thing I've ever seen. This is such a bad idea. "All right, Jolie. I'll stop by your place in the next few days with the information."

She's out of her chair and heading for the door like she doesn't want to linger long enough for me to change my mind. "You can call me Jo. And you won't be sorry, Lucas."

Be sorry, future tense? She's right. Because I already am.

Chapter Twenty-Five

JOLIE

I feel better that Lucas is letting me help, but I still don't feel good. I want Sloane to keep my name out of her mouth, and I don't want anyone mentioning me in the same breath as this doll situation. It's going to be a problem, I know it.

I wasn't exaggerating when I told Lucas I couldn't volunteer until this is cleared up. Instead, I go back to the bar and meet Bonnie, who arrives right on time.

"So tell me about your menu," I say as we settle in at a table once Ry comes down.

"I'm thinking seasonal," she says. "We'll have some year-round items, but I want to make sure we're rotating specials often enough to keep people coming back. I have a good relationship with the growers around here, and I practically live at the farmer's market, so based on the growing season, here's what I'm looking at for fall."

She passes us each a menu, and while she'd shared some of her ideas in our interview, it's a whole new level of excitement to see it spelled out the way she plans to put it on the menu. "I'm going to spend today getting to know the kitchen and prepping. Family dinner tomorrow?"

I nod. Family dinner is actually the staff, who I'm paying to be here an hour earlier than a normal shift so they can try Bonnie's dishes and give their feedback.

"Great. Then I'm going to get in the kitchen and stake out my territory."

"Let me know when you get to prep," I tell her. "I'd like to help. I'm not a great cook, but I can help with the grunt work."

"You got it. I need all the help I can get. My first interviews aren't set up until Friday." She's planning to start dinner service in two weeks, eventually expanding to lunch by November. She'll be busy hiring, training, ordering, and prepping every day until then.

"Great," Ry says. "We'll do your final paperwork, I'll get you your keys, and the kitchen is yours."

Turns out, grunt work in the kitchen is the perfect thing for me today. There's something satisfying about rinsing dirt from fresh vegetables, cutting off inedible ends, peeling or grating as Bonnie needs. She's not much of a talker, and I like that. I'm not either. She answers questions I have, but otherwise we lapse into quiet other than the classic rock she's playing from a Bluetooth speaker she brought with her.

By the time Tina shows up for her shift, I'm almost relaxed. The cops—*Lucas*—believe I'm innocent, and I'll be able to put an end to Sloane's rumors once I can look at all their evidence and help them find whoever is doing this.

The relief lasts until about thirty minutes into Tina's shift. It's a Friday, and by now, we should have had the first trickle of customers coming in with a surge filling most of our tables by close to 6:00. But no one comes in.

An ugly hole opens inside my chest somewhere, and when another thirty minutes passes and brings us only half the customers we're used to, it grows bigger and bigger until it's a hungry void of dread that wants to snack on my internal organs, especially all the ones that help me breathe.

"I'll be in my office if you need me," I tell Ry.

He surveys the light crowd, a slight look of concern on his face. "Doubt we will. Weird night."

In my office, I check my phone to see if I'm right about the problem. I open Happenings to check the post from earlier, and it's as bad as I thought it would be. More people have piled on with comments from "How awful! I'm not giving her my business!" to

"I knew something was off about her when I went there with my wife. They water down their drinks too."

We do not.

Some people are pushing back, asking for evidence or saying they had a good experience at the bar. A handful of names I recognize say good things about me. But the negative comments outnumber them by two to one. The feeling in my chest is worse.

I remember this too well. When the buzzing in my head starts, I'm sure: I'm on the verge of a panic attack. It's been a long time since I had one. Years. But I had them way too often when I was a kid. It got like this when a situation felt bigger than anything I could do about it. Bringing home a request from school for money for a class party, knowing it could set off my dad. Getting a better grade on anything than Sloane did because it would mean skipping lunch so she couldn't be mean to me.

I won't let her do this again. I didn't have any tools to stand up to her then, but I do now. I take a deep breath then another and lean back in my chair.

I do one of the grounding exercises I learned when I googled these symptoms in college and discovered I was probably dealing with anxiety. *Name four things you can see.* "Dolly sayings calendar. A Book Smart magnet. My Cataloochee Coffee tumbler. My cell phone." *Name three things you can touch.* "My leather purse. The wooden desk. The plastic keyboard." *Name two things you can hear.* I close my eyes and listen. "The clink of glass. The music playing." *Name one thing you can smell.* I take another deep breath through my nose. "Orange oil for the wood."

I open my eyes and do box breathing. *Breathe in through the nose for four seconds, hold for four seconds, exhale through the mouth for four seconds.* I don't know if this is right, but it's the count that works for me, and after repeating the sequence a half-dozen times, the buzzing in my head is gone. I don't feel good, but I don't feel like I'm about to spin out either. And I don't have the overwhelming need to hide in my office anymore.

I go out to the floor to find Ry. "I think I can explain why we're probably seeing a drop in business tonight."

"It's homecoming for Harvest," he says.

For a moment, I perk up. That could definitely explain a slow night. But . . . that would only explain why Harvest High alumni aren't here.

We're behind the bar, and I hand Ry my phone. He takes it with a questioning look before he reads the post. His forehead wrinkles deeper with every comment. "Jolie, this is complete crap."

"I know. But it's Sloane's way of getting back at me for kicking her out the other night. One of these dolls was left at her house, and she and her dad went to Lucas and told him it was me because..."

"Because why? Did she confess to bullying you in high school so your 'revenge' makes sense?" The air quotes he puts around "revenge" are the most aggressive I've ever seen. I love him even more for it.

I shake my head. "Something about being jealous of her then and trying to get even? I don't know. But when Lucas questioned me—"

"When he did *what*?"

"He had to. I was mad about it too, but I get it."

"Jo, you know I'm the first to play peacemaker, but you are taking all of this way too calmly."

"You wouldn't think so if you'd seen me in my office fifteen minutes ago." When his face darkens even more, I rest a hand on his arm. "Lucas knows I didn't do it, and I've got logs from my alarm system to prove it."

"Then go on here and tell them you didn't do it." He thrusts the phone at me.

I slide it into my pocket. "They won't believe me."

"Then tell them the sheriff's department cleared you."

"They believe I'm guilty based on my move-in date and the word of a stranger," I say. "They're not going to believe I've been cleared."

"Then tell Lucas to make an official statement."

My eyebrows go up. That's a thought. "I'm not sure if he can do that in an open investigation. I don't know the rules."

"I'm sure he can if your name is being slandered. Or libeled. Or whatever posting those rumors is." He nods at my phone.

I find a small smile. "I'll ask him about that when he brings over the case file so I can help."

Ry's eyes widen. "Seriously?" He does a fist pump when I nod. "Yes. The doll creep is as good as caught. No one is better at puzzles than you."

"I hope so," I tell him. It's hard to know how good I'll be at this one because I don't know how many pieces I'll have to work with. "But to be honest, I think it's not going to be too helpful for me to be here tonight, so I'm going to take off. Don't want to put people off their beer."

He hauls me into his arms. Ry and his mom were the only people who showed me physical affection when I was a kid. I always felt awkward, but I still loved their spontaneous hugs.

"They're going to be so sorry they messed with you," he says into my hair. Then he lets me go and pushes me in the direction of my office. "Get out of here. Eat something bad for you and watch something that will rot your brain."

"Will do."

I almost stop at the burger joint a couple of blocks down, but halfway there, I turn and walk back to my truck. What if they believe the rumor too? I don't know who's on my side right now besides Lucas and my staff.

That's not nothing. I know that. But I still have that lonely feeling I remember too well of not knowing who's on my side and who's sucking up to Sloane. Wayne Oakley's position as Chamber president means he knows all the businesses around here, and who knows what he's been spreading around and to where.

I drive through a chain place and eat my uninspired value meal on the way home. I try watching a few different things on my laptop, but nothing holds my attention, so I give up and put in a meditation app to help me sleep.

The problem turns out not to have been homecoming. Business is terrible all weekend. So terrible that I'm glad when Lucas wakes me up an hour early on Monday morning by ringing my doorbell. When I see him in the app, standing on my porch in his uniform, holding up a bakery bag and smiling at my doorbell camera, I smile back even though he can't see me.

"Just woke up," I tell him through the intercom. "I'll meet you in my kitchen. Feel free to look for weird doll crap while you wait."

He shakes his head but walks in when I tell him the alarm system is disengaged.

I shuffle over to my closet, but there's nothing I want to wear. I have an urge to put on something cute. It's stupid. But I can still take pride in my appearance even if I'm not going to date Lucas. I want a soft sweater and a pair of jeans, but my one pair of jeans needs washing, and I don't own any casual sweaters. It's all suits and more suits and I'm sick of it. In fact, the longer I stand here staring, the more an idea takes shape in my head, and I yank all of the jackets off their bars and lay them on my bed.

"Jo? You good?" Lucas calls from the end of the hall, and I realize I've lost track of time.

"I'm good. Be there in a minute." I grab some joggers from my dresser and pull on a Duke sweatshirt. It's just Lucas; it shouldn't matter anyway.

I walk into the kitchen with an outstretched hand. "Coffee me."

Lucas does, and we sit in silence, each on a stool, drinking. It's an easy silence, and I appreciate that he remembers I need caffeine in my system before I'm fully sentient. Once it hits my bloodstream, I set the coffee down and look at the white pastry bag. There's also a file folder sitting near it.

I nod at the bag. "That has grease spots on it."

"Just makes you want it more, doesn't it?" he says.

"Yes. Please feed me."

He smiles over the rim of his coffee cup and pushes the bag toward me.

I open it to find an apple turnover. "Yesss."

"It's from Book Smart. The owner bakes them. Have you had a chance to try them yet?"

I shake my head. I've popped in to browse the books, but I haven't tried her café counter.

"You'll like it," he says.

A bite confirms his wisdom and judgment, which I tell him. "But don't let it go to your head," I add. "I'm just talking about pastries."

He chokes and spits a little bit of coffee, a few drops landing on me as he grabs for a paper napkin to wipe his mouth and the counter. "Sorry about that."

"What's wrong with you?"

"I heard something besides pastries at first."

I squinch my eyes at him, trying to figure that one out. Then it hits me. "Lucas! You thought I said 'pasties'?"

"Only for as long as it took me to choke on my coffee." He keeps his eyes on his cup, and I resist the urge to fold my arms over my chest.

We fall into an awkward silence.

"So I—"

"Did you—" we both say at the same time.

"Sorry, go ahead," he says.

"Did you bring the case stuff over?" I ask, nodding at the folder. "I'm awake enough to dig into it now."

"Yeah, that's it. Before we dive in, though, I need—"

"Is this where you tell me this is confidential and not to run my mouth about it?"

He nods.

"I got it. Lay it out for me?"

He walks around to stand across the island from me and pulls a paper from the folder, setting it down so it's facing me, upside down to him.

"This is a map of everywhere the dolls have been found so far. There have been eight."

Eight houses in one area have red circles drawn around them. "They're all in two neighborhoods."

He nods. "Makes sense that the Doll Creeper would know the kids in a single area by sight well enough to match them to dolls. This is where a lot of younger families live. In most cases, the girls receiving them are the oldest child or at least the oldest girl."

I study the houses and the street names. This area is about three miles north of downtown, where the city started spreading out with new housing tracts and shopping centers. I don't know it well. It wasn't half this big when I'd graduated.

"It's interesting to see Harvest Hollow on a map," I say. "It's grown a lot."

He nods. "Hinder can be irritating, but he's a good mayor. And I can't stand Oakley, but he has good business sense. He's talked a lot of developers into building here, and that brings in more business."

I nod, but I'm not about to join the Oakley fan club. "Tell me more about each of the girls."

"Youngest is seven, oldest is eleven. Each doll has the same hair color and eye color as the girl it's left for. Only half of them play with dolls, but not this particular kind."

"That's my next question. What do you know about the dolls?"

He unlocks his phone before he hands it over to me. "I've got pictures of each of them."

I'd seen three of them in that wretched comment thread last night, posted by the recipients—victims? "What's the crime, by the way?" I ask. "I didn't know leaving dolls was against the law."

He sighs. "That's what makes the whole thing a pain. Intent matters. If they're gifts, it's weird but sweet. If they're not, they could be considered harassment or even stalking. We need to find out who's doing this and clear that up so we can settle people down."

I look at the photos. "Fancy" is an understatement. Each doll has been shot from several angles. They have clothing from different eras, but it all looks well-made, no shiny polyester or anything. Real lace and velvet. A couple look like references to story characters, like one that might be from *Heidi*, but I only vaguely know the story.

"How big are these?" I ask as I scroll through more photos.

"About a foot tall."

"Have you done an image search on these?"

"Yes. They're all by the same maker. Cindy Dawton. The brand has been around since the late seventies. Collectible items. Did you see the red-haired one yet?" When I nod he says, "One like it sold on eBay last year for almost three hundred dollars."

I look at him, surprised out of words. I shouldn't be. Wealthy people pick up weird hobbies and interests. Maybe not weirder than poor people's hobbies. But definitely more expensive.

"I know," he says. "So now we have not just matchy dolls but expensive matchy dolls being left at girls" houses."

"Collectible," I murmur. "All left in the same area." I look at the map again. "Newer homes, younger families. Do you know anyone our age who collects dolls?"

He shakes his head. "No. I don't have sisters, and if Brooklyn was into them, she moved on before she came to me."

"How is she?" I ask, looking up to meet his eyes.

They soften with a smile. "Still seems happy. No trying to get out of school."

"Good. I mean it about being her unofficial Big Buddy. I can do it however it makes you comfortable."

"It's a great idea," he says. "What do you think is the best way to approach it? You'd know better than I would."

"Honesty," I answer immediately. "I'll share enough about my background for her to understand why I'd want to do it and explain the idea of mentoring. I'll ask if she wants to be my protégé."

He laughs. "She likes big words. I have a feeling she'll sign right up to be mentored."

"I hope so. I noticed when I was at Book Smart the other day that they're having an author come for a signing. Sasha Liu? She writes this great fantasy series I think Brooklyn would like."

"Don't know who that is, but I'm sure Brooklyn would love that. I'll ask her and let you know."

"Could I do it? Ask her, I mean? I want her to know the invitation is sincere, not something her uncle set up."

"Oh, sure." He gives me a long look. "You really do care about her."

I shrug. "Can't help it. I *was* her."

"Should I bring her by the Mockingbird after school, or . . ."

"Maybe I should stop by your place. Make it feel more personal. Neighborly."

"That would work. I'm home by 6:00 most days."

"Cool. But could, you, uh, not . . ." I shift, not sure how to phrase what I'm going to say next. Maybe it's strange. Or rude?

"Not what?"

"Your uniform." I nod at him. "Could you not wear it?"

He looks down at it. "I usually don't at home, but why? Is something wrong with it?"

I shake my head. "It's more like . . . I don't know. You're very official. And I don't want her to feel like I'm there for anything official? It's the neighborly thing again."

"So something more casual. Approachable." His eyes glint. "Maybe even inviting. Like, say, pasties?"

"Lucas!"

He gives me an innocent look. "Not pasties? Maybe sweats then?"

Why is the image of him in joggers so sexy? Why, brain? Whyyyyy? "Pasties are not inviting. Pasties would make me run away."

He gives me a serious nod. "Got it. I don't know why you keep bringing them up."

"Lucas!"

"I'm trying to talk business here. Speaking of which . . ."

I watched girls in high school hit boys who teased them. I never got it until now. My palms itch to give his forearm a smack and also maybe to feel the muscles in it . . .

Oh, my gosh. *Pull it together, girl.* "Right. Business. Clearing my name of being the Doll Bandit." I look back at the map and run the doll pictures through my mind. "At this stage, do you call this evidence or clues?"

He looks startled. "We don't use the word clues, but I guess that's what it is. When we're sure something is connected to an investigation, we call it evidence."

"Do you have any conclusions based on these clues?" I ask.

He watches me with a small smile. "Do you?"

I nod.

"Lay it out for me."

"I don't know who it is, but I have some guesses about where to start looking."

He gestures for me to continue.

"Let me do a couple of quick searches first?"

"Sure."

I search a few social media groups, look at Craigslist and the classifieds page for the local paper. Lucas keeps himself busy on his phone, so I don't feel rushed. After about ten minutes, I say, "Okay, I've got a place to start."

I point on the map at a senior living community. "This is new, right? I don't remember it." It's near the newer tract homes.

He nods. "Yeah. We need more of them. Boomers are aging and all that."

"There's a woman named Judy who has responded to a couple of posts made by other people who were offering up collectible dolls for sale or giveaway. I looked up her address and she lives in that community. Don't know if it's her leaving them, but she might know other collectors or have an idea of how to track some down."

He looks at the screenshots I've traced and back to the map. "Still a genius, huh?"

"Yep."

He looks up and meets my eyes, smiling. I smile back. And somehow the moment stretches into something longer, and the texture of it changes. He leans over and rests his forearms on the counter, his eyes not leaving mine.

"Jo," he says. It's soft, and something about it makes my stomach flip. "You're amazing."

"I'm not," I say. "I pay attention, that's all."

"But to everything. It's impressive as heck. To the details here. To Brooklyn. To your staff and what they need beyond their jobs."

My eyebrows fly up.

His smile gets wider. "I pay attention too. Especially when it comes to you, lately."

Oh, that is a big, giant swoopy flip inside my stomach, and there is no mistaking why. "Lucas . . ."

"Wait." He straightens. "Whatever you're going to say, can you wait about twenty minutes to say it?"

"I guess?" I say, because I'm not actually sure what was about to come out of my mouth.

"Twenty minutes," he says.

I nod and he scoops up everything that goes in the file and leaves.

Which means I have twenty minutes to brush my teeth and figure out the most diplomatic way to say that despite whatever these little moments are, Lucas and I are *not* happening.

Chapter Twenty-Six

LUCAS

Jolie only lives five minutes from me, so I run into my house, change my clothes, and drive back in my own car—a Ford Ranger I bought when I won the election. When I knock on Jolie's door seventeen minutes later, I'm in my most broken-in jeans, a blue plaid shirt, and my good boots, my truck in her driveway, my service vehicle back in mine.

She opens the door and looks like she can't decide if she's confused or amused.

I hold out my arms to my sides, presenting myself for inspection. "I'm here as a civilian, not the sheriff."

She steps back. "Okay, civilian. Come on in."

I follow her inside and she stops to turn and face me.

"Wait, do civilians still come to the kitchen, or do we need to sit in my living room?" She gestures to her sofa set. "I got those two weeks ago, and I think I've only sat on them once."

"Living room," I say. "I'll give you an unbiased opinion on your sofa comfort." This makes her blush, and I grin. I hadn't meant anything by it, but if she's blushing, it's because she imagined a very interesting way to test the sofas. Good. We're on a shared wavelength, because business-type meetings over her kitchen counter are not on my mind.

I'm here to ask her out. Despite her preemptive date rejection the other night, the mood and tone of this morning feel different.

More relaxed. Even flirtatious. For the first time since she's been back, Jolie seems *open*.

She chooses an armchair and waves me to the couch. "Are you going to explain why you changed clothes?"

"Yes, ma'am," I say to tease her. It works. She smiles. "I'm glad you're home again in Harvest Hollow, Jolie McGraw. I wasn't too bright in high school, but I'm smart enough to see it now: you're a cool person, and I wondered if you might like to grab lunch sometime and talk about things besides our jobs."

The tops of her cheekbones are light pink, and I can't tell if it's still the last blush or a new one. She bites her lip and gives me the same look she used to get when she was solving a particularly tough equation.

"I'm talking about a date, Jo, if that clears it up for you at all."

She nods but doesn't smile. "We talk about Brooklyn."

"We do." Is this a precursor to telling me she doesn't want to date a dad? Because that's what I am. My brother isn't getting out of prison until Brooklyn is done with college, and that's only with good behavior, which isn't his strong suit.

"So no."

I blink. I hadn't expected her to say no, and I rethink those couple of minutes in her kitchen and the other times I've sensed a connection. "No to a date?"

"Right. No to a date." She gives a single, quick nod, like she's punctuating her answer.

"Have I misread the situation? I haven't been on a date since I got Brooklyn, so maybe I'm way out of practice, but I thought..." I trail off as she shakes her head.

"You haven't misread things. I'm sure any woman would tell me I'm crazy for saying no right now, but it does come down to Brooklyn. If you and I don't work out—and my track record says we won't—I can't be for her what she needs."

I sit back and study her. "That's a lot to pick through. I'm trying to figure out where to start. How about with your 'track record.' What does that mean?"

"It means I ended up back in Harvest Hollow because the one serious relationship I've ever had fell apart when I had no clue there were problems. And suddenly, I realized I didn't have what it took to be in that relationship. Or my job. Or even Chicago."

Whew, that's a lot. "I have so many questions. But I guess the main one is clarifying: if you weren't getting over your breakup, you're saying you would still say no because of Brooklyn?" When she confirms it, I think about this for a second. "Explain to me why it would be an issue for you to mentor her if you and I go out on a terrible date?"

She's biting her lip again, worrying at it like it's going to reveal the answer. Got it: this is the thing she does when she's having a hard time spitting out what she thinks she needs to say.

"It's okay, Jo. Lay it on me. I can take it."

She sighs. "Do you think it would be one date? Just one? If it was, that wouldn't be a big deal, I agree. We'd be like 'oh, well,' and I'd be fine coming by for Brooklyn whenever. But what if it goes well? What if it's not one date? What if it's one, then five, then a relationship? And when that doesn't work out, it gets super awkward for everyone, especially Brooklyn. She's the last person who needs to come up short in any me-and-you scenario."

I love that she's so focused on doing right by Brooklyn, but I'm also torn between laughing at how far into the future she's thinking or asking the half-dozen more questions her concerns have raised in my mind. I do the only thing that makes sense, and I stand and cross to where she's sitting to get down on one knee in front of her. She looks surprised at first, and when I reach out and take both her hands in mine, she looks downright nervous.

"Jolie McGraw. You are absolutely right. I should be taking this all way more seriously."

She tugs her hands. "Lucas—"

"Wait." I keep a light grip on them and continue. "Jolie." I look as deep into her eyes as she'll let me, hers blinking rapidly as she fights the urge to look away. "I'm not proposing marriage, Jo," I say in my most earnest voice. "I was thinking more like a burger."

She freezes, her eyes locked on mine. Then she busts out laughing, pulls her hand away, and shoves me hard enough to topple me sideways. I grin at her from the floor.

"Thanks for clearing that up," she says as I pick myself up and go back to the sofa. "But I'm not a casual dater. And that means I have to think through all the consequences."

"What if I'm a casual dater?"

She gives me a funny look. "Are you?"

I think about this. "No? I haven't had a lot of relationships because I can tell by a third date or so if we're going to work out, and if the woman isn't looking for something convenient and casual, I make it clear that I don't have more to offer."

Now she's looking at me like I'm a bug or something. "So if she says she wants something long-term, you say 'See you, bye'? That's not awesome."

"I say that if I know we're not a good long-term fit. I've had long-term relationships where it wasn't true love or anything, but we both knew that. I haven't been in love before. I've been in like. I've been in comfort. I figure it'll help me recognize love when I see it, and when I do, I'll be all in. But like I said, I haven't dated since I got custody of Brooklyn." I sit back and give her a long look. "You're sure a date is off the table for the two of us?"

She hesitates, her eyes traveling over my face—and, I'm conceited enough to notice, my pecs—and I get the sense she's weighing the pros and cons. "I'm sure."

"No problem." I slap my thighs in that "conversation over" way that old men have and stand. "In that case, could you excuse me again for about three more minutes?"

She stands too. "Uh, sure. You need the bathroom or something?"

"Nope. Be back in a couple." I walk out to my truck and put on my Appies hat. Then I climb the three steps to her porch and knock again.

She yanks the door open like she was waiting for me. "What are you—"

"Hey, friend." I give her a big, friendly smile.

"Hey," she answers, still obviously confused.

"I put on my friendship hat." I point to it. "I thought I better make it literal so you could tell the difference between Date Lucas and Friend Lucas."

"You're ridiculous," she says.

I shrug. "I don't want to talk you into a date. So now I'm here as your friend."

She leans against the doorframe, and a twitch at the corner of her mouth gives away her amusement. "This isn't a trick to get in the friend zone where you're going to bide your time until I change my mind, is it?"

"No, ma'am. Sheriff-friend's honor."

She steps back again and lets me in.

I walk past her but stop and turn after a couple of steps. "Where do friends hang out? Kitchen or living room?"

"How about the kitchen while I scramble some eggs?"

I beeline for the kitchen. "Don't have to offer me food twice," I call over my shoulder.

She closes the door, and by the time she reaches me, I'm already on a stool, chin propped on my hand, waiting.

"Did I mention you're ridiculous?"

"I'm not," I inform her. "I'm just sitting here, waiting for a breakfast I was offered. Sounds like common sense to me."

She shakes her head but goes to her fridge and pulls out a carton of eggs, setting them on the counter before she starts digging through drawers.

"So as a friend, and a guy who likes to solve mysteries, tell me how this last relationship of yours went so wrong that you're terrified of lunch with a good-looking man?"

She shoots me a quelling look. I lift my eyebrows and wait.

She gets a fork and a bowl and cracks an egg on the rim. "Phillip Freaking Horsley."

"That guy is a tool. Tell me more." I get an almost-snicker from her.

"He was a stock trader at the hedge fund that recruited me out of college. We started working together more when I became a portfolio manager. And then we started dating."

"I mean, that's juicy stuff, Jo."

She rolls her eyes. "It wasn't dramatic. We started doing late dinners at the office, then he asked me to be his plus-one at a wedding for one of his college buddies, and then we were dating."

"So y'all kind of fell into it. Romantic," I say.

"Lucas . . ."

"He didn't even do a costume change. That's all I'm saying." This time I do get a laugh, one that's more like a breath through the nose, but still, it's a laugh. "Don't stop now. It's getting good. You have very predictable work dinners and civilized wedding dates, and this goes on for how long?"

She shakes her head, a half smile on her face as she whisks the eggs. "Two years."

"That's a long time, but I guess that makes sense when you're with someone out of habit."

"It wasn't habit." She whisks faster. "I liked him."

"*Liked* him? Liked him enough to up and leave an entire city when it didn't work out?"

"I loved him." There's a furious *clink clink clink* of the fork against the glass of the bowl. "Probably?"

"Now we're getting somewhere. If you were with him for two years, you definitely loved him. But something happened."

She slams the fork down, and a bit of egg yolk spatters on the counter. She doesn't notice, crouching instead to dig through what sounds like a drawer of medieval armor before the clanging stops and she stands with a skillet in her hands. She sets it on the stove and starts the burner.

"Roger Galbraith Horsley happened."

"His . . . dog?"

This time, she smiles. "His father. His father, the state senator, whose father was once the mayor of the fine city of Chicago. His father and mother, who live in Glencoe, the most exclusive suburb of Chicago, in a house worth more than ten of mine, with a pristine view of Lake Michigan."

I glance around the kitchen. "This was not a cheap house."

"No, it was not." Her tone is almost grim, not proud like I might have expected. But then again, I'm still trying to figure out what to expect from this fascinating zigzagger. "Anyway, when you have that kind of political pedigree and that zip code and that job title, you don't want your only son getting too serious about a girl from nowhere without people of her own."

"You've got people. I've been to your bar. I've seen it." It's easy to tell that Ry or Mary Louise would take a bullet for her, mainly because I saw them both try.

"I have no distinguished ancestors. Certainly not from a respectable Midwestern family that built their wealth during the Industrial Revolution. Anyway, one night Phillip tells me he wants to come over and talk to me. He has flowers delivered, and I get nervous. I think he's going to propose. I stress over what to wear. How to do my hair. I think, 'This is a moment for the wedding slide show, better look good.' Then Phillip comes over to my place, which was half the size of this house but cost way more. And do you think he proposed?"

"I think he did not. Also, I'm sorry I was a massive jerk with my fake-out proposal earlier. You were so worried about a date, and I was trying to make you laugh by taking things to a ridiculous extreme." Could I have done anything more thoughtless?

She waves off my apology. "It was almost funny."

"Thanks?"

"At least it didn't send me into a doom spiral."

"Fine. I'll take it. So Phillip comes over and does not propose."

"He does not. But he comes to tell me that he was going to. According to Phillip, he went to request his grandmother's ring for the proposal, but instead, he got a lecture. His dad feels I'm not an asset to his son's ambitions."

"Please tell me that when Phillip Freaking Horsley said this, you flipped over a table, told him to kiss your assets, and kicked him out."

She smiles. "I did kick him out."

"Yes!" I do a fist pump. "And then you realized you were better off without him, and you wouldn't waste an ounce of emotion on him or on regretting your choices."

She drops a pat of butter into the skillet where it makes a satisfying sizzle. She keeps an eye on it, but I suspect she's not seeing it as much as she's watching a replay of events in her mind. "Yes, no, and no."

"Meaning?"

She tips the pan this way and that to spread the butter. "Meaning I definitely realized I was better off without him. But I also realized that I'd somehow built my life around him to the point that when we broke up, I didn't know what to do with myself. I couldn't think of anyone I could call to hang out with. No one from the office. And all my other 'friends,' I knew through Phillip."

She gives the pan a hard shake, and I feel bad for it.

"I felt like I was waking up from a spell." She picks up the bowl and brings it to the stove. "He'd done this magic trick of being from a stable family. A respected one, even. They had money and connections, the same house his whole life, a vacation home. A Christmas card list."

The spatula scrapes softly across the pan as she moves the eggs around, and I decide now is not the time to tell her that she shouldn't be using a metal spatula on a nonstick pan.

"We broke up, and then, I don't know." She shakes her head. "I realized I wanted the stability and the Christmas card family more than I wanted Phillip. I realized I hated my job and didn't like the people I worked with that much. Too single-minded. I realized I didn't like my too-modern condo. And worst of all, I didn't like myself."

"Jolie." I know my voice sounds strained, but I can't help it. "I don't like hearing you say that. Permission to approach and hug?"

"Stand down, Sheriff. I don't need a hug."

But *I* need to hug her. Still, I say only, "Understood. Continue. Does Phillip come slinking back, realizing he's made the biggest mistake of his life?"

"I wish. But it's worse."

I wince.

"Yeah. That about sums up what happens next, which is that after I've stewed about it for a couple of days, I gather the few things of his he's left at my place, like a beanie that always looked stupid on him and a Nintendo Switch. Do you know how pathetic that is? How did I not see that in two years, he was subtly signaling how little he wanted our lives to overlap?"

The pan gets another angry shake.

"I text Phillip to come get his stuff. Phillip does not come over. Phillip's mother comes over."

"You're kidding."

She glances over her shoulder at me. "No. She thought maybe I was trying to win Phillip back, so she wanted to be clear about a few things. She said I lacked breeding, and I wasn't fit for their lifestyle. She said I had showed too much of my origins, from my accent to my table manners, and that while I had done an admirable job of trying to refine myself, in times of duress, like wedding planning and political campaigns, people's roots show true, and that wasn't the kind of liability Phillip needed."

"I—what—she—ungh." I'm too stunned by Phillip Freaking Horsley's mother's nerve to form a sentence. I try again. "This woman had the gall to come over and say all that to you?"

Jolie pulls out some plates, but she has to check a couple cabinets to find them, like she uses them so little that she doesn't remember where she keeps them.

"Different words, but it's what she meant." Jolie slides eggs onto each plate. "I'll hand it to her, it was the nicest way I've ever been called a hillbilly."

She sets a plate of eggs with a fork down in front of me, then takes a stool across from me and pokes at her own eggs. "Maybe I should have been the kind of person who rose above it. Given her Phillip's pathetic box, showed her the door, and then gone back to work and kicked butt to prove none of it bothered me. But I couldn't. I was furious, but at the same time, part of me felt like she'd told the truth about the parts of my life I'd tried to leave behind."

I scoop up a bite of scrambled eggs and chew. They're fine. The kitchen clearly isn't where Jolie is going to find her mojo. "So coming back here was . . . what? Confirming what she thought about you?"

"Yep. I knew I didn't want to stay in Chicago, but I didn't have anywhere else to go. When I left for college, I was so happy to be leaving but also nervous because I'd never been more than a hundred miles from Harvest Hollow. Ry told me not to worry, that if I hated Durham and college, Harvest Hollow could always be my fall back plan."

She eats a couple bites of her eggs, but I stay quiet, sensing she isn't finished talking. "Never thought I'd need it, honestly. But when Priscilla Horsley pressed on all my bruises, I figured I'd show them how country I could be. So I handed in my notice, bought the place I hated most in this town, hired movers, and bought every country boy's dream truck and drove it h . . . ere."

I wonder if she'd been about to say "home." "Has it been all bad? Coming back and living down to her judgments of you?" I hate that she thinks of being in Harvest Hollow that way, but I'm trying to be a friend, and I push my sense of offense aside.

"All? No." She sighs. "Surprisingly."

"But some?"

She nods. "Enough."

This frustrates me, but I think about Wayne Oakley marching in with Sloane to accuse Jolie of some nonsense simply because they've had beef since high school. "I'd like to argue with you, but I can't, having just spent an hour with you trying to clear your name of bogus charges."

"The lack of deep-dish pizza is also a negative. And I got used to good shopping." She smiles to show me she's choosing things that don't matter in an effort to downplay the hard parts of coming back. But it's the kind of smile that squeezes my heart because she's forcing it.

"I can think of one fully excellent, purely good thing you get here and not there," I tell her.

She pauses with her fork halfway to her mouth. "If you say it's you, I'm going to flick my last forkful of eggs at you."

"Good thing I'm going to say Brooklyn."

She smiles and takes her bite. "Fair."

"So let's figure out how to keep that purely good thing going, and then we'll figure out the rest of it."

"All right, Lucas Cole. Using Brooklyn is a cheat code, but it's going to work every time."

"Good," I tell her. "But I'm not using Brooklyn. I'm using you."

She gives me a sharp look.

"Look, if a gorgeous woman with a smarter brain than anyone I know wants to spend time with my kid, I'm sorry, but I'm not going to say no."

She drops her fork to her plate with a loud clatter and jumps up from her stool. "That's it, Lucas Cole. Come over here and get that hug right now."

Jolie *offering* a hug? Yeah. Don't have to tell me twice.

We both round the island and meet at one end, and she steps into my arms, sliding hers around my waist. Her chin doesn't quite reach my shoulder, so she rests her head against my chest while she squeezes.

I wrap my arms around her shoulders and hold her there, a soft laugh rumbling out of me. "All I have to do for hugs is call you gorgeous and smart?"

"No. I'm hugging you for working so hard to take care of Brooklyn."

Well, dang. That almost makes my eyes water. I tighten the hug, wishing I knew the words to tell this prickly armful of woman how special she is in a way that she'll believe me. She hugs me back harder too, and I decide that this is the definition of a perfect morning. Even with the crime stuff.

But it can't last, because all too soon, more-than-friendly feelings build in my chest, and the pure femininity of this contrary woman has my attention.

I clear my throat. "Jo?"

"Hmm?" It's a quiet, lazy sound, the response of a woman who is content in my arms.

"The last thing I want to do is let you go and walk out the door, but I need to if we're going to stay just friends."

A beat passes before she stirs. Then she slowly straightens and steps away from me with a resigned "Right. Yeah."

I reach out and graze my fingertip along the faint dusting of freckles on one of her cheekbones. I haven't been close enough to see them before, they're so light. "Sorry about that, but I really do hear you when you say you only have friendship to offer. Me being honest is how we stay on that footing."

"I get it. And I appreciate it."

I swear it almost sounds like a question at the end, like she's not so sure she does, and I allow myself a smile, the kind that'll keep her guessing. Keeping Jolie McGraw on her toes is about to become my new favorite pastime.

"I'll let Brooklyn know you're coming by. And if I catch us a doll-leaving degenerate in the meantime, I'll be in touch. See you, Jo."

I walk out of the kitchen, and I feel her eyes on my back all the way to the door. Matter of fact, I'd bet it was my back *end*, because I knew exactly what I was doing when I picked these jeans.

I drive home to change back into my uniform, whistling the whole way. It may be that when I catch this Doll Bandit, I'll shake their hand instead of cuffing them, because they have inadvertently done me the favor of keeping Jo firmly in my sights.

She ends up being literally in my sights that afternoon. I'm walking across Maple for a coffee break when I spot her truck parked in front of the consignment shop.

Jolie walks out of the store, opens her passenger door, and pulls out a heaping armload of what looks like suits. Grays, navy, black.

I could stop in to say hey and see what she's doing. But no, she probably needs some space after our conversation this morning. I continue to the café, and when her truck is still outside after I get my order, I duck into the general store and invent an errand for myself, killing about ten minutes while I look for stuff I can use at my office. I leave with a bag of WD-40 for my squeaky desk drawer and a package of the pens I'd noticed on Jolie's desk.

I don't know why I'm buying her pens.

That's a lie. I'm buying her pens so I can go to the bar and give them to her the next time I need an excuse to see her. I'm trying to stay in the friend zone. I am. But friends buy pens for each other, right?

Her truck is gone, and I stop into the consignment shop. This is nosy and inappropriate, but knowing that can't override my need to understand more pieces of Jolie. Besides, I've given myself a good excuse.

Inside, the clerk behind the counter is switching out the hangers in a big pile of suiting to the hangers the store uses. She looks up when the bell over the door announces me.

"Hi, Officer. Can I help you?" she asks.

"I'm Sheriff Cole," I tell her. "You have a minute?"

She stops what she's doing and looks nervous. "Sure. Is there a problem?"

"Nothing like that," I say. "Just wondered if y'all ever sell dolls here. The fancy kind?" A glance around the store shows that it's mostly clothing, but there do seem to be a few home goods on shelves along the wall.

Her eyes widen. "Oh, is this about the creepy Doll Bandit? I've been following that on Instagram."

I suppress a grimace. Freaking Happenings, man. "I can't comment on an ongoing investigation."

"Right, right, of course." She's nodding her head and looking thrilled to be in a conversation with law enforcement where the phrase "ongoing investigation" has been used. "We don't get dolls in here. We mostly handle clothing."

She indicates the pile in front of her, and I take the opening. "Big pile. That's all from one person?"

"Yes. Nicest lady, too. We have a program called Women to Work that helps women re-entering the workforce put together a few professional outfits for free. This stuff is all designer, if you can believe that, and she's not even putting it on consignment." She picks up the jacket at the top of the pile and holds it against herself. "This is Theory," she says. "It's a five-hundred-dollar jacket, and she's giving it away."

Just more proof that Jolie is amazing, even if she's buying five-hundred-dollar jackets for some reason. Must be the kind of thing that matters in Chicago. And that must be exactly why she's shedding them. It's all part of burrowing into Harvest Hollow, and this makes me stupid happy.

"I'll let you get back to work," I tell the woman. "Thank you for your time."

"Sure, Sheriff. If I find any clues, I'll let you know."

I hide a cringe. She means well. "I appreciate that, ma'am, but don't worry. My deputies will have this sorted soon."

I walk back to the station and settle into my desk chair, but a hunch has me checking Happenings before I can tackle any real work.

Sure enough, there's a post two minutes old. "The sheriff is asking around town about who sells porcelain dolls. Hope he's also asking if the Mockingbird owner has bought any of them."

I groan. I just indirectly fed the HHH fire. I consider myself to be a smart guy, but I swear, something about Jolie regularly makes me lose my common sense.

Chapter Twenty-Seven

JOLIE

I examine my reflection, not sure how I feel.

I'm about to head to the bar dressed in jeans and an olive green sweater Tina made me buy yesterday. She was delighted to come shopping after I donated almost all my old clothes the day before and spent three hours bossing me in and out of dressing rooms.

The sweater is long sleeved and fitted but not tight. The thing is, it has a cutout in the chest area, an oval shape where it looks like I'm wearing a long-sleeved crop top over a matching shell, kind of? The cutout is only about five inches wide and doesn't even show a hint of cleavage, but it still feels sort of scandalous?

Man, I've been in suits for too long.

I add some brown leather booties with a stacked heel, and suddenly I feel like exactly the customer Tequila Mockingbird is supposed to cater to: a trendy young professional out for a fun evening.

Not that I expect work to be fun. Last night's numbers were dismal. I built lulls into my first-year operating costs, knowing it would take time to get a new place off the ground and develop a clientele of regulars. But that assumes steady growth. We're going the other direction this week.

That's okay if it's only a week. But I still remember a popular sandwich shop going out of business when I was in high school—Hogg Jay's—because someone spread a rumor that they found a fingertip in their chicken salad. Never mind that all the store workers had all their fingertips; the rumor was enough, everyone claiming to have "seen a picture" of it, but no one ever being able to produce that photo.

Interestingly, three members of the baseball team had been kicked out the day before the rumor started due to rowdiness, but the fingertip story was too good to pass up sharing, so *that* was the story that made the rounds, and Hogg Jay's disappeared.

"It was just one bad week, right?" I say to Ry when he pops by my office.

"I put Precious on call instead of scheduling her tonight because there weren't enough tips for Tina and Daniel to split last night and buy even a gallon of gas."

I wince but shake my head and fix a smile on my face anyway. "One bad week," I repeat.

"One bad week." He gives me a tired smile.

"Ry? Jolie?" It's Sophie, hollering from the front entrance.

We walk out as she's on her way to the office.

"Don't you believe them," Sophie says, shaking her phone.

Ry and I trade confused looks. "Believe what?" he asks.

Her eyes shift between us before she slumps a tiny bit. "You didn't see yet?"

I doubt I want to know, but I ask. "See what?"

She hands me her phone, the Trip Planner app open. It's the most popular app for tourists or anyone wanting to check out a local business online. A one-star review dated today catches my eye first since it's the top review. "Pretentious wannabe bar with second-rate décor. Perfect if you want to overpay for watered-down drinks," I read aloud. I suck my teeth. "Tell us how you really feel, reviewer 'Captain HH.'"

Ry has his phone out now. "Only go here if you want to hang out with a criminal creeper. Just watch the owner. You'll see." He rubs his forehead as he reads.

"You ignore those, y'all," Sophie says, her expression fierce. "There's plenty of good ones here too."

"Like this one?" I ask. "'Quit hating on a really cool new local spot just because you can't get over high school, you has-been downhillers.' That's from a Sophie D." I turn to Ry with a pretend puzzled look. "You know anyone who could be Sophie D?"

Sophie folds her arms across her chest. "I'm not wrong. And it's not only me saying nice things."

I skim a few more. She's right. There are people defending the Mockingbird, but it's half and half, and a handful of five stars won't help when there are just as many one stars.

"I appreciate you trying," I tell Sophie.

"Oh, I'm not going to try. We're going to shut her up. She gave our store two stars last year and said we're 'unskilled jewelers who lack an eye for quality,' but that's because my dad graded the diamond in her wedding ring and told her it was a cubic zirconia. Which it *was*," she says with so much satisfaction that Ry laughs, and I have to smile. "I emailed her and let her know she could take the review down or we'd post an owner response to her review explaining she was mad because her husband lied to her about the ring he bought her."

"Dang, girl," Ry says. "Remind me never to cross you."

"I've survived two toddlers," she says. "You think I'm scared of her?"

"I assume the 'her' is Sloane?" When Sophie nods, I say, "We don't know that this was her for sure."

"Don't we, though?" she asks.

I sigh. Of course it was. She doesn't forgive or forget, which sounds a lot like a person I see in the mirror every morning. I'm thinking it's not such a good look.

"It'll be fine," I say. "This is a speed bump. The sheriff's office is closing in on a suspect, and since it's not me, when they catch the person, all this can stop."

"The sheriff's office meaning your very special friend, the extremely fine Lucas Cole?" Sophie asks.

"I mean the sheriff's office. Period."

Ry smiles. "Then why are you blushing?"

"Quiet," I grumble. "I'm not."

"Well, I want to launch trivia night," Sophie says. "I've been stockpiling my questions, and I want to start getting the word out *now*. We should ramp up, not down."

I don't think this is a good idea. My gut instinct combined with experience growing up in Harvest Hollow says it won't work. But I haven't had a lot of people sling a bat over their shoulder and fall into step beside me like Sophie is clearly determined to do. And I'm not going to say no.

"Sounds good," I say. "Let's do it. Let me know what you need."

"I need you to check with Bonnie and see if she's good with cooking for it. It'll be sooner than she planned."

"I'll talk to her," I say. "What else?"

"I'll let you know. I'm going to start pulling this together." She pauses at the exit to thrust her fist in the air and yell, "Goonies never say die!"

Ry responds with his upraised fist, and I finally laugh. "Get out of here, crazy."

She leaves with a grin.

Despite Sophie's bravado, it's an even slower Wednesday than usual.

I try to be positive about Thursday, but after anemic afternoon sales, Ry tells me to go home. "I know you have a scary-good poker face. Go find it, then come back with it tomorrow. Let's not do any real worrying until we see how the weekend goes."

"You're right." I rub at the space between my eyebrows where my "worry brackets" show up. "I need to think good thoughts. If you can hold it down here, I'll be back tomorrow."

He shoos me with a cheerful "Get out of here."

It's dinner time, the normal lull for us, one that we're hoping to bolster when dinner service starts, but things feel less certain than they did last week. I text Lucas to see if it's okay for me to stop by and visit Brooklyn because I don't want to interrupt their supper. He tells me to come on over.

Am I hoping he'll remember he has an update on the case to give me that has slipped his mind until now? Maybe. I really need this to be fixed.

I pull into his driveway—his grandfather's driveway?—the Cole driveway and park. Today I'm in a pintuck-ruffle short-sleeved blouse in a soft peach color with jeans and my booties. Did I pick it because it makes me feel extra feminine and I sort of thought I might see Lucas today?

It's a nice shirt. That's all. Really.

But I pull on my long cardigan and tie it around the waist to remind myself that I'm not trying to look pretty for Lucas. There. Now I'm dressed comfortably for my *friend*.

Lucas opens the door before I can even knock. "Hey," he says, smiling at me and holding out his other arm for a *friendly* hug.

Does it feel way warmer than a Ry hug? Does it feel way shorter than I want it to?

I choose not to entertain these questions.

"Come on in and let me take your sweater," he says. "You've met Pops."

"Hey, Mr. John," I say, but I'm wondering what Lucas thinks of my top.

"Hey, honey." He's pushing up from his recliner in front of the local evening news. "Let me get you some tea."

"Oh, no thank you. Truly, I'm fine. You stay comfortable. Is Brooklyn here?"

"Hey."

I turn to see her standing at the opening to a hallway. "Hey, Brooklyn. I was wondering if we could talk for a few minutes, about good things, I hope."

She shoots a look at her uncle, who nods. He wears a small smile but says nothing.

"Uncle Lucas says we can have some ice cream if you want to come in the kitchen?"

"Ice cream is only my favorite," I say.

"Mine too," she says, still shy but looking less nervous. "Um, you can follow me?"

Lucas sits on the sofa to make it clear he's giving us space, and I follow Brooklyn to the kitchen.

"We only have chocolate chip ice cream," she says. "It's my favorite. Is that okay?"

I sigh and shrug. "It's only my second favorite, but I guess I'll live. Why don't you tell me where the bowls are?"

She smiles and points, then asks for my first favorite flavor while she rummages through the freezer.

"Butter pecan because I was apparently born with the tastes of an eighty-year-old woman," I tell her as I scan the cabinets. I spot the bowls I want and pull them down, grinning, then dig through the silverware drawer.

Brooklyn turns around with the carton of ice cream the same time I turn around with two large salad bowls and two serving spoons instead of cereal spoons.

"These look like the right size," I say.

That wins a big grin and a happy nod as we settle in at the table.

"Why don't you scoop?" I say, and she digs in, piling about half the carton in my bowl. I smile as I watch her, asking questions to relax the atmosphere even further. "Did you get a chance to read *Keeper of the Lost Cities* yet?"

Her face lights up. "Oh, my gosh. I just finished the second book. It's soooo good," she says in that particular squeal only girls her age can do. I love it, and I listen to her chatter about the characters and plot points as she dishes the other half of the entire carton into her bowl.

I nod in approval when she's finished serving. "This is how it should be done."

"Oh, wait, one more thing!" She goes to the pantry and comes back with a bottle I haven't seen in forever.

"Magic Shell," I say with delight. "I haven't had that in years."

"It's *so* good, Miss Jolie," she says.

"You can just call me Jolie. So how's life?"

She shellacs our ice cream with the topper as we fall into an easy conversation about school. It doesn't sound like she hates it, so that's a win.

When she winds down, I set my spoon in my bowl. I'm only halfway through my ice cream, and I'm going to need a rest to finish it, which I have every intention of doing. "Did your uncle tell you why I wanted to come over tonight?"

"Kind of. I don't know if I totally get it," she admits.

"I know we've only talked a couple of times, but I feel like we have a lot in common. We laugh at the same jokes, for example."

"And like the same books," she adds.

"Totally. We have something else in common too. I grew up with no mom, only my dad."

Her eyes widen. "I kind of forget that grownups used to be kids."

"I get it. Lucas has told me a little about your dad. And how he thinks it might be rough being the only girl in your house sometimes."

"Yeah. I mean, Uncle Lucas always says I can tell him anything, but . . ." She trails off and casts her eyes in the direction of the living room. "But, like, I don't really want to talk to him about some stuff. I told him I need deodorant the other day, and he cleared his throat, like, five times and said okay, but he looked kind of funny. Kind of embarrassed?"

"Tuff Lady Fresh," I tell her. "Stupid name, best deodorant. I buy a five-pack. I'll give you one so you can see what you think. But you know how I figured that out?"

She shakes her head no.

"My dad was an alcoholic. If he'd ever been sober enough to think about what I needed, I still don't think stuff like deodorant would cross his mind. But every now and then, my aunt would have me come stay the night, and one morning she said, 'Jolie, you stink. Take this deodorant, and if you run out, just tell me.' But I never would. I'd just buy it whenever I had enough extra at the grocery store."

Her eyes grow round. "My dad has drug problems. And anger problems? And I think stealing problems."

"This is kind of what I mean about having things in common. I could have used a female mentor, an adult in my life who could understand what I was going through and the kinds of questions I might have or things that I might need. My aunt did her best, but she worked a lot, and I slipped off her radar more often than not."

"Uncle Lucas keeps me on his radar pretty good. And Pops."

I nod. "Good men. But I hope you'll still consider being my protégé."

"Protégé." She repeats the word. "Uncle Lucas used that word too, but I couldn't figure out how to spell it to look up what it means."

I point to my chest. "Mentor." I point to her. "Mentee." Her expression clears. "But the proper word is protégé. So that's what I'm here to ask you. Would you be my protégé? We'd mostly hang out and talk about books or do nerdy things, but you'd be able to ask me questions about anything, any time. Like deodorant. Or bras. Or boys, although I still don't really understand them. Or prom dresses. Whatever you want. What do you think?"

"Do you like K-pop?" she asks, her expression serious.

"Don't know much about it, but I'm happy to learn."

"Okay. I'd like to be your Mentos."

"Mentee, you mean?"

"Yeah, but Mentos is funnier." She grins, and like the brief glimpse I caught on our shopping trip, I see the full Brooklyn coming through.

"You're right, Mentos. Want to hang out Saturday morning before I go to work? I'm thinking get some more ice cream and maybe hit the bookstore for a book signing with Sasha Liu."

Her eyes grow huge. "No way."

"Oh, very much yes way."

I get another squeal and it makes me laugh. "So I'll see you Saturday morning."

"Yes. For sure."

"Great. Let's finish our ice cream, and I'll explain the plan to your uncle."

Brooklyn tucks into the rest of her dessert, peppering in information about her K-pop that she feels it's important for me to know. When we return to the living room ten minutes later, she tells Lucas, "We're going to be Mentos."

She grins up at me, and I smile at him. "She said yes," I explain. "Could you bring her over Saturday morning? We're going to hang out."

"Sure," he says. "Happy to."

"Thanks. Anyway, I better go." I need to trade the warm glow of this Brooklyn situation and Lucas's smile for an evening of trying to fight off the impending failure of the Mockingbird, which is sort of the key element of my now-shaky fall back plan. I don't want to think so negatively, but the part of me that learned life on hard mode knows it's the only way to keep things stable.

"I'll walk you out," Lucas says, shoving up from the sofa while Brooklyn settles in to watch the *Wheel* with her great-grandfather.

When we reach my truck, he hauls me into a hug. He doesn't ask, but I don't need him to, which surprises me.

"Thanks for all of this," he murmurs, his breath stirring strands of my hair.

"No problem." I hug him back and listen to the steady thump of his heart.

"It's a big deal to everyone in our house," he says. "And I'm sorry I don't have anything specific to tell you about the doll situation yet. Slocum has narrowed it down to two suspects. She's interviewing one tomorrow, and the other is out of town for a few more days, according to a neighbor."

I lean back. "Do you know when that one left?"

"Saturday." His eyes are glinting in the light of a bright half-moon.

"And when was the last time someone reported getting a doll?" I ask.

"The day before that."

I let out a pent-up breath, realizing he's probably found his culprit, and relax against his chest. "I'm so ready for this to be over."

He hugs me tighter. "I know."

We stand there quietly for several moments before I hear the steady beats of his heart increasing. He lets me go.

"Better get in your truck, friend," he says.

"I wore a cute shirt," I blurt.

"You, uh . . . yes? You did. I noticed."

I climb into the truck, shut the door, and lower the window, which means I'm looking down at him. "I don't know why I wore a cute shirt to come talk to a ten-year-old."

Lucas rests his hand on the truck door, a slow smile spreading over his face. "I don't know, Jo. Sounds like you got yourself another mystery."

"It wasn't for you." I'm going to speak it into truth for myself.

"'Course not," he says. "Sleep well. I'll have answers for you soon."

I pull away with a bunch more questions and make the short drive to my house.

No, only one question.

What is wrong with me?

I left Chicago because my perfectly planned life fell apart. I came back to Harvest Hollow to get it all back under control again. And it was. Until the first time I saw grown-up Lucas Cole.

And it spun out even more with the appearance of Sloane Oakley-Hunsaker.

I don't want this. I want things to be sane. Ordered. Structured. Predictable.

And profitable, if my plan is going to work. Somewhere along the way, the plan went from "show the freaking Horsleys how Appalachian I am while rubbing my success in the face of my hometown haters" to "make a life here."

I fall asleep thinking about that, and I drive to the Mockingbird the next day with a heavy heart, hoping Lucas clears my name soon but not sure even that will be enough.

THE FALL BACK PLAN

A chalkboard sign on the sidewalk in front of the bar startles me as I'm turning in to park, and I get out of the truck to walk back around and read it instead of entering through the back.

"Friday Drink Special: Drink with an outlaw! Bourbon Bandits and Dolly Derbies, half price!"

I walk in through the front. Ry is behind the bar with a highball glass and a bottle of Weldon Select, a North Carolina bourbon.

"Bourbon Bandits?" I say.

He smiles. "Leaning into it. People who don't know about this mess will be interested in the name, and I figure the ones who do know will realize no one who is guilty would pull a stunt like this. Bourbon, bitters, amaro, and an orange twist. I'm practicing now."

I watch as he makes the cocktail. "Best part of your job?"

"Taste testing? Obviously."

"And what's the Dolly Derby?"

"Gin, peach bitters, and mint."

I watch as he takes a sip of his Bandit and makes a satisfied face. "You sure about this?"

"Did it make you laugh when you saw the sign?"

"Yes."

"There's your answer. Embrace the notoriety, cousin. And check this out." He texts me something, and I open my phone to find a flyer done like an Old West "wanted" poster.

I read it aloud. "Since we're trying and convicting people in the court of public opinion in Harvest Hollow like the old days, may as well come drink with the town's most notorious outlaw."

"I'm posting that in all my social media groups," he says. "Everyone on staff is going to send it to their friends, and we'll see."

I put my phone away, shaking my head. "I hope you're right about this, cousin." But inside, I have warm fuzzies, a thing happening more often lately, because I'm beginning to realize Ry and Mrs. Herring aren't my only people.

As it turns out, Ry is right about leaning into the whole situation. I hang around the whole night, even after Ry reveals the final part of his plan when the first customers come in: he has me carry a ragged baby doll around the whole evening for a photo op, and the more people who snap and post the picture, the more business we get. It's still about twenty percent less in sales than our last good Friday, but we're close to full at a few points in the night.

When I finally head home after midnight, I fall into bed exhausted but looking forward to the next day for the first time all week. Ry really might have turned things around. Once Lucas confirms the true Doll Bandit, everything will be okay.

Am I also looking forward to seeing Lucas in the morning when he brings Brooklyn by?

"That has nothing to do with it," I inform my empty bedroom.

But even I don't believe me.

Chapter Twenty-Eight

LUCAS

Brooklyn and I walk up to Jolie's door at 10:00 Saturday morning. She opens it with a smile.

There is no point at which this woman hasn't looked beautiful, but this morning she looks especially good in jeans and a plaid jacket with tan suede boots that go all the way to her knees.

She's covered from neck to ankle, so why does she look so sexy?

"What's that?" Jolie asks.

I blink, confused until I remember I'm holding a picnic basket. "Oh, public relations? You mentioned getting ice cream, but I wondered what you would think about me crashing the first part of your hangout. What if we did a picnic on the library lawn? I thought if I hang out with you so publicly, it might make a few people question whether the sheriff and his child would really fraternize with a criminal."

"That's so thoughtful," Jolie says. "I could use all the help I can get. Brooklyn, is that okay with you?"

"Fine with me, Miss Jo. I think it'll be fun."

Jolie's face softens a bit when Brooklyn uses her nickname, and I'm thankful again to this woman for seeing a need and filling it.

"Let's do it," Jolie says. "You want to ride with me, Brooklyn?"

"Yes!"

"I'll follow y'all over and go to my office when we're done. Brooklyn doesn't have any other commitments today, so take as much time as you want."

We head out and I park behind the station and walk over to meet them on the library lawn, where Brooklyn is smoothing out the blanket we brought.

"What's in here?" Jolie asks as she opens the basket.

"Pops packed," I confess. "We'll see."

We pull out a ham sandwich lunch with plastic baggies of plain chips and more with sliced carrots. He's even put a whole bottle of ranch dressing inside. Dessert is a Little Debbie oatmeal creme pie for everyone.

"Not so fancy," I say, by way of apology. "But I promise, he uses the good bread and ham."

"Are you kidding?" Jolie asks as she unwraps a sandwich. "This is perfect." After a bite she adds, "Good bread and good ham."

"Why are we doing all this?" Brooklyn says. "Because we're trying to prove what?"

We spend the next several minutes taking turns explaining the doll situation to Brooklyn, who looks increasingly baffled.

"Why would anyone care if you gave their kid a doll? A girl in my class got one, and she likes hers."

"People get odd about strangers giving their kids gifts," I tell her. "And there's nothing wrong with being alert. The problem here is certain folks going around accusing Jolie of doing it without any proof and implying she's up to something . . ." I'm trying to find a word, but Brooklyn supplies it.

"Nefarious?"

I grin. "Yes, nefarious, vocab genius. How do you know all these words?"

She shrugs. "Reading. Speaking of that, I know we're going to the bookstore, but can we go to the library too? I want to see what's on the new release shelf."

"Works for me," Jolie says, but her enthusiasm feels forced.

I gather up the trash and put it into the Walmart plastic bag Pops also provided. "Brooklyn, can you go throw this away?"

She jumps up to do it, and when she's out of earshot, I turn to Jolie. "You don't have to take her to the library."

She shakes her head. "No, it's fine. Remember I told you Mrs. Herring wants me to volunteer there? I've been avoiding her since I became public enemy number one."

"I know Roberta Herring. She isn't going to believe the rumors."

"Probably not," Jolie says. "But she'll recognize that it's no bueno having me around kids right now."

"Jo." I want to take her hands in mine and squeeze them, reassure her that she's going to be okay. But I'm rationing how often I'll let myself touch her because I'm trying to respect her boundaries.

Instead, I shift so I'm sitting beside her, and that means we're now both facing toward the busy general store and the weekend foot traffic mountain towns get when the temperatures cool. "I know it seems like everyone in the world is on Sloane's side, but I promise you, this town is way bigger than her. There are way more people who haven't even heard about this situation than who have. It'll make you feel better if you can remember that."

She nods and climbs to her feet as Brooklyn comes back. "Ready for the library?"

"Ready," Brooklyn says.

"Can I tag along for this part too if I swear to leave you alone for the rest?" I ask as I fold the blanket.

Brooklyn rolls her eyes but says, "Okay, Uncle Lucas. But you don't have to protect me so much. Miss Jo is safe."

"I know," I tell her. "This just sounds way more fun than the paperwork waiting for me."

"Let's go then."

We walk into the library a minute later, and Roberta Herring greets us with a smile. Brooklyn peels off to the circulation room after a quick wave to the librarian.

"Hello there, friends," Mrs. Herring says. "I'd say I'm surprised to see you all together, but Brooklyn has been telling me all about your book recommendations to her, Jolie."

"Guilty," Jolie says, and I think she almost winces. Not a great choice of words, considering everything.

"I'm glad you're here," Mrs. Herring continues. "Jolie, I expected to see you before now. Have you considered my proposal?"

"I have," Jolie says. She hesitates, then sighs. "I was going to tell you that I'd like to volunteer, but not to teach financial literacy classes. I think I could be more helpful doing some afterschool tutoring."

"Wonderful," Mrs. Herring says. "When can you start?"

There's another almost wince. "There's kind of a situation right now, Mrs. Herring. I don't think this is a good time."

"What kind of situation?" the librarian asks.

Jolie closes her eyes and breathes out through her nose for a few counts. Then she opens them and says, "It's honestly so stupid, but I've been accused of leaving dolls at some people's houses to harass them, I guess? Right now, it's about like inviting the boogeyman to come tutor."

"That *is* ridiculous," Mrs. Herring says. "Whoever is suggesting that has a good enough imagination to be making up stories I could shelve here. And it changes nothing for me. When would you like to start volunteering?"

"Are you sure?" Jolie asks. She sounds so uncertain but hopeful, and it breaks my heart a little. It also makes me want to write Sloane Oakley-Hunsaker at least a dozen citations for being a public nuisance.

"Am I sure that someone who had the Dewey decimal system memorized by sixth grade would be a good tutor for some of the kids who hang around here after school?" Mrs. Herring's eyes twinkle. "Quite sure, Jolie. So, next week?"

"That would work," Jolie says. "Thank you."

Mrs. Herring shakes her head. "You don't need to thank me for doing me a favor. Goodness, girl. I'm planning to bring you a pie on your first day."

Jolie looks so pleased by this that I immediately resolve to learn how to make pie. I want her to look as happy to see me as she does about getting that pie.

"You have a deal," she tells Mrs. Herring.

We excuse ourselves to trail after Brooklyn, but when it becomes clear that she and Jolie speak a book language I have no way of understanding, I let them know I'm going to head over to my office.

They barely lift their eyes from the map inside of some fantasy book to tell me goodbye.

I walk out smiling, but it fades as I cross the street to the station.

It's time to get down to business, which means putting Jolie and her insanely kissable-looking lips out of mind.

Ha.

Or at least trying to.

Chapter Twenty-Nine

JOLIE

When Sophie said she was going to "run with trivia night," I don't think I'd understood exactly how excited she was about it. She must have spent her entire Sunday working on this, because when I drive into town on Monday, at least half the store windows are displaying a bright blue flyer advertising Thursday Trivia.

I park and walk down Maple, looking at the posters, crossing over to get some Cataloochee coffee at the café so I can stroll up the other way and enjoy the view. Each bright spot of blue releases a tiny, happy flutter in my chest.

Once I have my coffee, I walk back up Maple, again spotting trivia posters in nearly every other window. I nip into the bookstore to see if they have any new events scheduled to take Brooklyn to. As I pass the old men and a young woman who always hang out there, one of them calls, "Hey, there, gal."

I check over my shoulder, but he clucks and says, "Yes, I mean you. Come on over here for a minute if you don't mind a few old men."

I walk closer. "Can I help you with something?"

"Maybe," he says. "I'm Henry and these are my friends, Floyd, Jean, and Hazel. You're the gal that owns the new place? The bird bar?"

"The Mockingbird, yes. That's me." Am I about to be interrogated about the dolls? My stomach tightens, and I brace myself.

"Is there an age limit on that trivia night?" he asks.

Oh. "You have to be twenty-one."

"That's a minimum. I'm asking if three old coots and Hazel can be a team."

Oh! I smile. "Technically, yes, but I'll need to check with my quizmaster. Y'all might have an unfair advantage due to your having lived through most of history."

One of his buddies hoots, and Henry grins at me. "Too bad. We'll be there Thursday. We're going to win and treat ourselves to brunch at the fancy hotel where Don Douglas had his birthday."

"Fifty-seven," one of them snorts. Floyd, I think? "That's not even a real birthday. Seventy-five. That's a real birthday."

"Hear, hear," another of them says. He has a faint French accent. Must be Jean. "Old enough to have made lots of friends with a fair amount of them still alive to come by for the party."

"I'd love to see you win," I tell them. "Your odds are pretty good since I'm not sure we'll have many other teams."

One of them gets a cranky look on his face. "The Lady Librarians will be there, and they're talking a big enough game that I'm looking forward to hushing them like they always do us in the library."

Oh, Mrs. Herring. Having my back again.

"The showdown of the decade," I say. "If you're there on Thursday, you each get an applejack on me."

They give me their solemn vows that nothing will keep them away now, and I head to the Mockingbird. When I walk in, the next surprise awaits me: every table has a small bright blue placard with the trivia night info and a QR code for people to scan and sign up.

I hand Ry his coffee. "You and Sophie have been busy. I saw the signs all over Maple."

"That's mostly Sophie. We've already had so many signups thanks to Lucas, and we haven't been open for regular business since we posted them."

"Lucas? What does he have to do with this?"

He taps his cell phone and hands it to me. "That's the app Sophie is using. Look at the teams so far. Lucas saw a sign and called the bar this morning," he explains as I read through the list. "Said he was signing up and challenging the firefighters. Said he was going to recruit other teams too."

The Tin Stars, Captain: Lucas. Hot Shots, Captain: Jace. The Lady Librarians, Captain: Roberta. The Hazy Codgers, Captain: Henry. There are at least five more team names on the list. Sophie is requiring teams of four, and that's almost forty people plus their friends coming in to drink and eat and spend money in the bar.

"This is awesome," I say.

"Yeah, and Sophie might even be able to get some of the Appies players to compete. I guess the team owner is one of their customers."

"Does Bonnie know?" She'd said she'd be happy to treat it as a soft launch for the happy hour menu, but I'm suddenly realizing we may have far more business than I bargained for.

"I'll tell her when she gets in today. I bet she'll be excited."

I pull out a table and sit. It's an inelegant thump. "I can't believe all these signups."

Ry smirks. "I can. That dude has the hots for you."

That makes me blush, but it's not like it's news. Lucas told me himself. And he knows the attraction isn't one-sided, even if I said I didn't want to act on it.

The man has shown up for me again and again in a way that no one but Ry ever has. And Mrs. Herring. And Sophie. And Tina. And . . .

What if I'm wrong? In every possible way, Lucas is different from Phillip. He makes my pulse hammer harder than Phillip ever did, and I haven't even kissed the man. Thought about it constantly, yes. But we haven't shared anything more than a hug.

What if I took a risk on him? Lucas shows up for everyone in his life, over and over again. The town. His Pops. Brooklyn.

Me.

He knows everything about me, and instead of judging it, he understands because of his own messed up family. But he's let it make him strong and good, not brittle. I've become brittle, afraid to bend in case I break.

But what am I protecting myself from? People who have no reason to have to care about me but do anyway? Sure, Sloane with her daddy issues tried to make me feel like a loser again, but so many other people have shown me that I belong.

I, Jolie McGraw, belong in Harvest Hollow.

I look around the bar at what we're building. At what I'm now sure we'll be able to continue building.

I, Jolie McGraw, *choose* Harvest Hollow. This place isn't my fall back plan; it's my endgame.

"I'm an idiot," I say.

Ry looks up. "You are many things, but that isn't one of them."

"About Lucas. I've been an idiot."

Ry studies me. "An idiot like you realize you should one hundred percent take him up on all that sweet, sweet love he's trying to throw your way?"

I look at him uncertainly. "I think . . . yes?"

He grabs a bar towel and whips it over his head like a propeller. "Hallelujah! Definitely yes. Heck yes to all the yeses. You need to go and get your man, cuz!"

A grin is spreading over my face. "What do I do? Just drop in at the station and be like 'Let's date'?"

"Sure. Or grab him and lay a big, juicy smooch on him. That's my vote. But yes. Go!"

I'm laughing now, and I jump to my feet. "Okay, okay, I'm going. I'll be back." I text Lucas as I head toward the exit.

JOLIE: I'm coming to see you. Right now. It's good. I think.

LUCAS: You have my attention.

I'm still grinning as I push open the rear exit door, still grinning as I read his response, still grinning as I reach for my truck door, still grinning as I notice a cream-colored envelope tucked into the window.

I pluck it out and open it, and then I freeze as the words sink in.

To the owner of the Mockingbird,

Meet me at Green Oaks cemetery by the weeping mother statue tonight at 8:00. It's time to end the doll terror.

It's handwritten in fine cursive and unsigned, and it wipes my smile right out.

Chapter Thirty

JOLIE

"This is the good thing you wanted to see me about?" Lucas says, accepting the note I hand to him.

"Not exactly. Found it on my truck when I walked out of the bar. Read it."

He scans and his eyes shoot to mine. "No way. You're not going to meet an anonymous stranger in a cemetery after dark."

His objection isn't a surprise, but it bugs me anyway. "At the risk of sounding fifteen again, you are not the boss of me."

He waves his hand around his office. "I'm the boss of this investigation. And possibly your common sense. Show me a single word in there that suggests to you it would be a good idea to do what the note says. At best, this is a joke and some dumb teenagers are going to jump out from behind tombstones and scare you. It's not a coincidence that today is the first day of October. We'll have a spike in nuisance complaints like we do every year."

I try to hold on to my patience. I know this whole doll situation has been an irritant to him too, but it hasn't upended his life the way it has mine for the last ten days. "You sound very condescending right now."

He sighs. "I'm not trying to. But do you understand from my perspective why this sounds like a bad idea?"

I lean forward in my chair across the desk from him. "I do. I know I don't have any proof, but my gut tells me this isn't a joke. Maybe it's the handwriting. It's old school. Proper. Trained.

It reminds me of Mrs. Herring's. If it was kids, would they even handwrite it? On nice stationery? And how could they fake that older-style cursive?"

He keeps his eyes on mine for a few seconds before he looks down and picks up the note in front of him, rubbing the paper between his fingers. Two deep grooves, a mirror of my worry brackets, appear between his eyebrows.

"I need to be done with this. I don't need your permission, but I was hoping for your support." For the three months after Phillip dumped me and I started putting together my Chicago exit plan, coming back to Harvest Hollow had felt like the next and final step. I'd move here, run a bar, and live down to the McGraw reputation. I didn't see much beyond that, and my whole life, I'd always been thinking about what came next. About when my real life would start once I left this town.

Coming back? That had been the whole plan. I was too worn out inside to think of what anything past opening the bar would look like. No thoughts of expansion, weaving into the town fabric. Nothing like volunteering at the library or making new friends in town. Harvest Hollow was somewhere familiar, even if unloved. By me, at least.

Now, barely a month into all this, I see glimpses of what comes next. There's always Ry, Mary Louise, Tina, and Precious. There's Bonnie and the new staff coming on. There's laughing with Sophie, talking with Mrs. Herring, hot cups of Cataloochee coffee. And always Lucas and Brooklyn.

What isn't in this peek at the near future is the little black rain cloud of Sloane Oakley-Hunsaker dampening all the good vibes.

"I'm taking any chance to be done with this, Lucas. Please be on my side." It's so hard to say those words, and I try not to show it.

"I am. One hundred percent." He pushes the note back across the desk toward me. "I'm going with you. I'll stay out of sight, but I'll be watching. You'll keep your cell phone with you and leave it on an open call so I can hear what's happening. Can you agree to that?"

"Yes." I smile and it wobbles, and the end of my nose is stinging. Am I going to cry? Why would I cry? This makes no sense. I didn't cry when Lucas told me about the accusations in the first place. Why now?

I get up from the chair, heading for the door as fast as possible. If I'm going to cry, I'm doing it where no one can see me, since I wouldn't be able to explain my tears to anyone. "I'll meet you back here at 7:30?"

He's getting up to walk around his desk, and I grab the handle before he can get to me. "Okay, thanks, bye." I dart out and close it behind me. I stand there for a couple of seconds, drawing a steadying breath as I survey the open office space and the different employees working at desks, some in uniform, some not.

Why would I run away from Lucas?

I turn and open the door again, pushing it as Lucas pulls, and I nearly fall into him. He steps back and steadies me as I lose my balance.

"Whoa, you okay?"

I nod and close the door behind me, leaning against it. Lucas is close enough for me to graze my finger over the star on his chest, and I want to. Badly. He's studying me with a look of concern, like he's trying to read my face and figure out what to do next.

He's right that I've lost my common sense. It's the only thing that explains what happens next, as I reach out and hook my fingers beneath the hems on each of his short sleeves to pull him toward me. His eyes widen right as I close mine, and I press my lips to his.

It's a soft touch. I am not a kiss-first woman, or I never have been until Lucas Cole. But I'm a kiss-first woman now, and after a split second of stillness from him—barely the time it takes to catch a breath—the sheriff of Harvest Hollow makes very sure I don't regret it.

His hands come up to cradle my head as he kisses me back, his fingers sure and warm as he slides them behind my neck, his thumbs feathering against my jaw. He brushes his lips against mine, once, twice, until I make a soft, impatient sound, and feel his mouth curve into a smile.

Then he's kissing me, really kissing me, like he's thought for days—weeks—about how he wants to do this, his lips warm and insistent. My hands drift from his ridiculous biceps to his chest, and though his shirts are never tight, they're so well fitted that I can't even grab a fistful, but only slide my fingers between the second and third button to pull him closer.

It tips him off-balance and one of his hands flies up to brace against the door beside my head, and oh my stars, *why* does that make me want to kiss him even more? But it does, and I do.

Quiet weaves around us, a cottony, pillowy silence where I'm wrapped up in the warmth of Lucas, everything else falling away except the sound of my own heartbeat pulsing in my ears, the feel of his drumming against the backs of my fingers as I hold him there.

A shrill desk phone right outside his office pierces the quiet, and the spell breaks.

I let go of his shirt and push lightly. His head comes up to meet my eyes, his glinting with something I can't name. Surprise? Confusion? He blinks, like he's emerging from a daydream.

"Sorry." His voice is gruff but quiet.

"You didn't do anything." When his eyes flash, I correct myself. "You did good, I mean. That was . . . uh, good. You're very . . ." I am babbling. I do *not* babble.

"Good?" he finishes.

"Very good. If we're being specific."

He's taken a step back, but he's still close enough to almost feel his body heat. "I appreciate your evaluation. Want to tell me what that was?"

"No." I wince when his eyebrows go up. "I don't know. If I did, I'd tell you."

He gives me a long look followed by a short nod. "Fair enough."

He shifts again to make room for me to leave.

I turn and put my hand on the doorknob when he stops me with a question.

"Do you regret it?"

I rest my head against the door, squeezing my eyes shut. Do I? Not at the moment. But will I, when it sinks in what I—we—just did? "I don't know."

He doesn't answer, and I slip out of the door without looking back.

I meet Lucas at 7:30 at the station like we agreed. He texted me to meet him near the Elm Street exit, which is where department employees park, and when I drive up, he's waiting beside the electronic gate to buzz me in.

As it closes behind me, I roll down my truck window and look down at him. He looks all business, a lawman who was definitely not making out with his old high school tutor in his office that afternoon. His face is serious, his jaw tight.

"How are we doing this?" I ask.

"I ran home and got my truck," he says. "I'll park on Odell and stay by the Oakley family vault."

Green Oaks is a modest cemetery. It holds maybe only two or three other statues besides the weeping mother one the note's author specified, all smaller. The Oakley vault is the only grand thing in it, and these days, Oakleys are cremated and interred in the columbarium that was added to the side of the vault when Wayne Oakley's grandfather passed a while back. It's for only their family remains; a larger columbarium for everyone else was built a while ago to accommodate the rise in cremations versus burials.

I know, because the director told me all about it when I called to make arrangements for my father's body.

"I can see straight to the weeping mother from beside the vault," Lucas continues. "It's only thirty yards, and I can run it fast if I need to. When you park at the cemetery, call me as soon as you get out of the truck and keep your phone somewhere I can easily hear you."

I pick up the coat next to me and hold it up. "Deep front pocket. I'll put my phone in there."

"Ready?" he asks.

"For this to be over? Past ready."

His eyes soften. "I hope this actually does get you answers and it's not a hoax."

I can't accept any other outcome. I want to step into all the ideas and plans that Ry and Sophie are percolating without any reservations. "I'll see you over there."

He presses the button to open the gate and watches as I back out then straighten the truck and wave before heading down Elm and northwest toward Green Oaks.

Ten minutes later, I pull into the cemetery parking lot and wait until my dashboard clock says 7:55. Then I cut the engine and call Lucas.

"I'm here," he says. "I'm by the vault. Go ahead and put your phone in your pocket. Tell me why you're here."

I put on my coat, a well-lined wool topcoat that had worked well with my suits in the frigid Chicago winters. I slide the phone into the pocket. "Hey, it's me. I'm here to solve the dumbest crime spree to ever hit Harvest Hollow." I pull the phone back out. "Did that work?"

"Heard you loud and clear. Head for the statue whenever you're ready."

I put the phone back and climb down from the truck, deciding not to lock it in case I need to jump in it fast. I try not to dwell on why I would need to do that. The night air is chilly, and I slip my hands into my side pockets. I follow the paved road that divides the cemetery into the older and newer graves until I reach a point where I can cross the grass and walk straight to the statue.

Whoever I'm meeting, they will most likely be coming from one of two directions, and since I didn't hear anyone behind me, I turn toward the east gate, the one that opens from the sidewalk on Dunn for pedestrians. That's the older part of the cemetery, and it has mature trees shading the sidewalk path that leads toward me. It's nearly impossible to make out anything in the dark.

I huddle and wait, trying not to flinch at the rustle of every tree branch or soft owl call. "I'm glad you're here," I say quietly, hoping Lucas will hear me. "I still would have done this by myself, but I feel better knowing you're out there spying on me like a weirdo." A few seconds later, my phone vibrates with a text, no doubt Lucas responding. I'll check it later. I don't want to take my eyes off the east path.

After about two more minutes, I hear the scrape of soft footsteps from that direction. I can't tell much from the sound. "I hear someone coming," I say very quietly. "I don't think they're very heavy. That's all I can tell."

A few seconds later, the lamps lighting the cemetery road illuminate a small figure emerging from the darkness. Technically, these grounds are closed after dark, so it's hard to see the graves once you leave the road. But these lamps are intended for safe road navigation, and it's enough for me to see that this small figure is female.

She draws closer, slowly, like she doesn't want to be walking this way at all. I straighten and step farther from the statue so she can see me.

"Jolie McGraw?" she calls.

"Yes. Who are you?"

She takes a few more steps into the west side of the road and stops about ten feet away. "Hello, dear."

And the lamp reveals a face I've known and resented for years. It's Janice Sullivan.

Chapter Thirty-One

JOLIE

I give a soft gasp. "Janice?"

"Hello, dear. I'm afraid I've caused you quite a bit of trouble."

She looks as if she's aged twenty years since I last saw her, not ten. Her hair is more salt than pepper now, and her wrinkles are even deeper. But the stubborn angle of her chin is the same, and her eyes have the same observant watchfulness I remember from the many times I came to fetch my dad from her barstool.

I have no idea what to say, so I say nothing.

She sighs. "I suppose you're wondering why we're here."

"You wrote the note on my truck?"

"I did."

This doesn't make any sense. "Why all the spooky atmosphere? And the mystery?"

She looks startled. "What do you mean?"

"Why did you drag me out to a cemetery after closing to meet you at the creepiest statue to 'put an end to the doll terror'? I'm freaked out. Should I be freaked out?" My voice is getting fast and high as the adrenaline I've been running on for the last twenty minutes begins to subside.

"I . . ." She looks around the cemetery. "Oh, no. Oh, this isn't at all how I meant for this to go. I only picked this statue because Tom is buried right there, and I come to visit every week." She points to our left, and the angle of her arm makes it seem as if his grave is fairly close, but it's outside the pool of the lamplight, and I can't see exactly where she means.

I look at her again. "Why at night?"

She lifts and drops her shoulders. "I'm embarrassed. I didn't want anyone to see me."

"Is that why you didn't sign the note?" I ask.

She shakes her head. "I didn't sign it because I didn't think you'd come if you knew it was from me."

I understand all the words she's saying, but somehow, none of this is making any sense yet. "And putting the end to the 'doll terror'?"

Her mouth forms a wordless O, opening and closing, fish-like a few times, until she says, "It sounds very, very bad when you put it all together that way."

"I didn't put it together that way, Janice. You did." My words are curt as the reality of standing in front of this woman settles in. She was one of my dad's biggest enablers.

"You're right." A long sigh. "You're right. I'm so sorry, Jolie. I believe I have some things to explain to you. There's a bench over there. A little dark but more comfortable than standing here. Would that be all right?"

I hesitate. I'm not inclined to do anything helpful for Janice Sullivan, but neither am I a monster. "Sure," I say. "My phone has a flashlight." I pull it from my pocket and see that the call with Lucas is still open. I send a quick text.

JOLIE: No danger
LUCAS: Keep the line open

I do, turning on the phone's flashlight and following Janice's directions to the cement bench I wouldn't have found in the dark.

She sits, but I don't. She pats the spot next to her. "Would you like to get comfortable?"

Like we're about to have freaking tea. "I'll stand."

She nods and gives another soft sigh. "I've been leaving the dolls. I never dreamed anyone would see something scary about it. And of course, in the worst of all possible scenarios, the suspicion fell on you. It's the last thing I would have ever wanted."

Her tone is sincere, but I don't really care. I'm not here to make her feel better, so I say nothing.

"Tom died two years ago," she says. "I tried to keep the bar open, but it was far too much work without him. And I didn't want to do it anyway. It was always his baby more than mine. And now, it's yours." She turns her head up to me. "Why did you buy it?"

I answer with my own question. "Would you have sold it to me if you knew it was me?"

She hesitates, like she's thinking hard about this. "No. Pardon me for saying so, but it doesn't seem like a healthy thing for you to do."

"So you would have said no to protect me?" I can't believe she's saying this with a straight face.

"Yes." It's simple. And it makes me believe her, but it also makes me angrier.

"Why start now?" I snap. "That would have been helpful when I was seven. Or twelve. Or seventeen."

"I know it doesn't seem like it, Jolie, but I tried then too."

I can only give her an incredulous laugh. "Fetching my dad home from your bar was always the worst part of my day."

"I know it. And believe it or not, I did what I could. Your dad was—"

"He was a drunk."

"Yes." She acknowledges. "One of the worst cases I've seen."

"But you kept serving him."

She sighs. "Maybe you haven't owned your place long enough to understand this, but there are some cases where all you can do is keep a person where you can keep an eye on them."

"So you're the patron saint of alcoholics now?"

"It wouldn't have mattered if I banned your father, Jolie. He would have found somewhere else to drink. Somewhere farther from your place, where he could get into more trouble trying to get home. Somewhere no one was keeping an eye on him, just taking his money until he was too drunk to pay and then they'd pitch him outside. I hoped keeping him at the bar until he was drunk enough not to resist would keep him out of trouble. Tom took him home any chance he could, but sometimes it was too busy, and then we'd call you."

She looks down at her hands. "I'm ashamed of that. In my mind, I was doing something good. I told myself it was more than anyone else would have done for him. But I should have cut him off. Or done more for you."

Unbelievable. "I have no absolution for you."

She nods. "I understand. I want you to know I'm sorry all the same. I cared about both of you. I'd have gone to his funeral if I'd known about it. I visit him sometimes." She glances toward the columbarium. It gives off a muted glow from the landscape lights trained on it. "I've told him I'm sorry many times. I'm glad I get to say it to you now."

My flashlight catches the glint of tears in her eyes as she turns back toward me, and I'm shocked at the sight of them. I think she's trying to hide them from me, and that more than anything convinces me that she means it.

"What do you want from me?" I sound tired to my own ears. "Forgiveness?"

She shakes her head and stays silent for a long time, staring into the dark in the direction of Tom's grave. "You know the Harvest Hollow Library Distinguished Scholarship award you won?"

"The scholar . . . yes?" It closed the gap on a few things my university-sponsored financial aid package didn't cover. Books every semester, because the total always exceeded the stipend the school gave me. A warm jacket when mine tore my sophomore year. A new pair of rain boots. A new pair of glasses when my prescription changed. The kinds of things that I would have had to do without if I didn't have that award renew every year.

"That was your dad."

"What do you mean? My dad never had an extra dollar he didn't drink away."

"You're right," she said. "But from the time he complained about you one night when you were a junior and you'd asked to go look at a few colleges in driving distance, I started setting aside every cent he spent on drinking. Tom and I figured that money should have been going to you, so we made sure it did. We kept it after you graduated until he passed. I have a couple thousand more to give you when you want it."

I can't process what she's saying. "That scholarship was from the library."

She sighs. "I knew you wouldn't take it if you knew where it was coming from. Roberta Herring worked with us to set that up. You were its one and only winner."

I remember Mrs. Herring urging me to apply for it, telling me that no one deserved it more.

"So I never earned that?"

She makes a sharp, impatient sound. "Of course you did. You'd have won it if it had been a real one too. It was money your dad should have been putting toward your education the whole time. You did the work. You made the grades. You got yourself into college. We just made sure he did his part."

I sit beside her on the bench, stunned into silence. "Mrs. Herring never breathed a word about it."

"Of course not. She knew you would have turned it down if you knew. And we never told your father what we were up to. He would have gone down to Durham and insisted you owed it to him."

She's right. I'd had to lie about how much I earned at my part-time jobs, giving him enough to appease him so he'd go spend it in a bar while I squirreled the rest of it away. I knew what he would do with the money, and I still gave it to him because it was the only way to make sure I kept some too, or he would have taken it all.

Maybe I can see the path Janice Sullivan's illogic took when she kept serving him to keep an eye on him.

I don't know what to do with all of this info, but I know it's a bigger thing than I can hold, so I grab for something I can. "The dolls."

She gives a pained laugh. "I have never been more embarrassed, and you're the last person I ever thought would have ended up in the bull's-eye of this mess."

"I'd definitely like to know how they led us to a cemetery after dark."

"I collect them," she says. "I never liked to tell anyone because it sounded strange for a woman with no children. I couldn't pretend they were anyone else's, so I just kept my habit quiet. Tom thought it was pure foolishness even though he never said a word about it. But he was too practical to understand why I bought an expensive, elaborate doll every year, then kept them all in a locked room I never let anyone else enter."

She shudders. "Good heavens, I sound like an insane person. It's unintentional. I only kept them hidden because I never wanted to explain to anyone who visited why I had a room full of dolls. I'm not totally sure myself. What you must have thought when you got that unsigned note about doll terror on your truck." She gives a choked, disbelieving laugh. "You probably thought you were coming to meet a psychopath."

I turn my phone so she can see the screen. "I do have Lucas Cole on the other end of this call. He's over by the Oakley vault."

We both turn and squint in that direction, but even knowing he's there, I can't see him. We turn back around.

"Can't blame you. It's good thinking." She leans toward the phone. "Hello, Lucas."

"Hey, Miss Janice." It's not on speaker, but we can hear him clearly enough.

"I'm going to keep him on the line," I tell her. "These dolls have been a headache for him too."

"I had no idea what an uproar they were causing until I got back to town yesterday," she says. "I went to church and heard people buzzing about it in the sanctuary after services. I don't use social media much, but I asked enough questions to figure out where these ideas were coming from, then checked that gossip Instagram myself. I about died when I realized what had blown up in my absence. I mean it almost literally." She pats my thigh. "I'm old, Jolie."

"So . . . why?" It's the most obvious question. "Why were you leaving dolls anonymously?"

She heaves her deepest sigh of all here. "I don't like attention. Never have. I only told you about the scholarship so you'd know that at least we found an indirect way to make your dad pay. Those dolls, they're collectibles. A lot of dolls people buy and try to sell aren't, but these are the real deal. Maybe I bought one for each version of the daughters I might have had. I don't know. But I bought the high-end ones. It's my only vice."

"So you didn't want people to know it was you giving them expensive dolls. Why give them at all? Why not sell them?"

She shrugs. "I didn't need the money. I'm not wealthy, but I moved into the senior living center after you bought the bar. I sold the house, and between the two, I have more than enough to cover what few years I have left. But when the movers boxed up the dolls and hauled them to my new place, I had to admit my foolishness in having collected them. And if I knew that was foolish, then I decided it would be better to give them to people who might enjoy them. I worked in my church's children's ministry until Tom died, and I lost the joy. But I've had a lot of little girls come through there over the years."

I'm beginning to understand. "Which church do you go to?"

"Church of the Master."

It's been around forever, but it's on the unofficial boundary where the new developments begin. "So most of the congregants who worship there are from the newer subdivisions."

She nods. "I decided to give them away, matching each doll with a girl who shared the same coloring. I thought it would be sweet." She finishes with a choked laugh, like she can't believe her own naivete.

"Then with no note explaining who they were from, and you dropping them off before dawn—"

"I sleep less than I used to as I get older," she says. "Or at least I do at night. Can't deny I also take more naps than I used to."

"So someone gets panicked—"

"Which is more contagious than flu," Lucas adds from my phone, making me and Janice both jump.

We smile at each other, and mine is sincere. Not how I thought seeing Janice Sullivan face-to-face would ever go. "Someone gets panicked and suddenly we've got a shady stalker on the loose."

Janice drops her face in her hands. "This is mortifying. Please don't think less of me if I admit that I feel terrible about scaring folks, but not bad enough that I want to admit to being the one behind it." She straightens and lowers her hands. "Still, I'm not letting you take the blame. I wanted to let you know that I have once again been adjacent to events ruining your life, but at least this one I can fix. I'll turn myself in officially tomorrow," she says into my phone.

"No need." Lucas's voice comes from behind us, and we turn to see him walking toward us. "You didn't commit a crime."

"But we need to clear Jolie," Janice protests.

He draws close enough to speak without raising his voice, and I end the call and tuck my phone away.

"Don't worry about it," he says. "I know how to clear her name and keep yours out of it at the same time. You've both worried about this enough. Consider it handled."

Janice and I exchange looks, and I suspect we have the same question. We look at him and ask, "How?"

"Just trust me."

Another pause, then both of us say, "No."

Lucas laughs, and even I have to smile. "If you need the gory details, I'm going to shoot my public information officer an email in a few minutes and ask her to fancy my words up so they make an official-sounding statement which she will put out as a press release. It'll explain the investigation has been concluded and that the dolls were left with the best intentions. She'll write it up without identifying anyone by name and make sure Harvest Hollow Happenings gets it too. I promise because it happens every time within minutes of release. Just like that, it'll be over."

I sit there, absorbing that. I can't believe it. By dinner tomorrow, this will all be settled.

"Miss Janice, did you drive here?" Lucas asks.

"I did."

"Can I take you home? I'll have an officer bring your vehicle to you in the morning."

"No need," she says. "My eyes are still sharp. Just passed a license test in June. But you can walk me to my car."

"My pleasure." Lucas holds out a hand to help her up, which she accepts.

She turns to meet my eyes again. "I'm sorry for everything, Jolie. Every bit of it. And maybe this will make you mad, but I promise I'm trying to help." She pulls a business card from her pocket and hands it to me. "You're doing right by the new place, Jolie McGraw. And more importantly, you're going to do good." Then with a nod, she takes Lucas's arm and heads back down the east path with him.

When he returns a few minutes later, he sits beside me. "How are you?"

I consider the question. "I'm all right. Maybe even good?"

He nods. "Can I ask what she gave you?"

I slide my hand in my pocket and touch the card's pointed corner. It has the information for two local Al-Anon meetings for supporting family members of alcoholics. I handed Shane Hardin that pamphlet with the same hope and doubt that I saw on Janice's face when she handed me the card.

Looking at Lucas, his face barely discernible in the dark, I give him a true answer. "She gave me a step in the right direction."

He accepts that without comment, and we fall into silence. My thoughts wander to the columbarium, and I shift to look at it. "That's where I had them put my dad's ashes. I haven't been in there."

"Do you want to go?"

I stare at it for a few more moments. "No."

He only nods, and I wonder if he thinks I'm heartless. Or broken. I know I'm not heartless. I'm not so sure about broken.

"I'll go eventually," I tell him.

"It's none of my business."

He's right, and it bothers me. I want it to be his business, and I can't lie to myself about what that means in the bigger picture.

"Coming back here hasn't gone at all like I thought it would. Ry is exactly the same. Sloane is exactly the same. But everyone else..."

"Everyone else is different?"

"Yeah."

"Even the sainted Mrs. Herring?"

I smile. "Caught on that I'm a bit obsessed with her, huh?"

"Do you think she'd adopt me?" he asks. "Because I get it."

"She's even more saintly than I thought," I say. "She was looking out for me in more ways than I ever knew." I look out in the darkness, but my mind is elsewhere, traveling down Maple Street and the near-constant stream of surprises it's given me. "So many people have had my back here. People I barely knew when I was growing up. People who I'm barely meeting. And they've all been..." I wave my hand, not sure how to describe it. "I don't get it. Why?"

Lucas leans over to give my shoulder a soft bump with his. "Why not? Harvest Hollow is about like most places, I imagine. Five percent of the folks here are Sloanes. It's inevitable. But eighty percent are like Roberta Herring."

"What about the other fifteen percent?"

There's a smile in his answer. "Those are your odd ducks like Janice Sullivan."

"Where do you think you fall, Lucas?" I know the answer. I wonder how he sees himself.

"I'd like to think I'm the eighty percent."

I shake my head. "No." I say it softly.

"No?"

"No, Lucas Cole. You are one of a kind."

"Shoot, Jolie." He fidgets a bit, like he's scraping his nail against his uniform jacket. "Confession: I'm having those more-than-friendly feelings again."

I turn my face toward his. We're almost close enough for me to feel his breath, which I know from experience now will smell faintly of cinnamon. "Confession: that's all right by me."

Lucas goes still, and I wait in those few full, delicious seconds for him to lean in, but when he moves, it's to stand. "Jo, you've had an intense night. The kind that would leave anyone feeling vulnerable. No one could blame you if your thoughts are too much of a mess to make clear choices right now. I won't take advantage of that. When you've got some clarity, I'll be waiting. These more-than-friends feelings . . ." He makes a sound somewhere between a laugh and a sigh. "They aren't going anywhere."

Lucas, the good sheriff. The good friend. The good man. I wouldn't expect anything less. But . . .

"Small problem," I say. "I'm always a mess lately. How will you know when it's okay?"

This time, there's definitely a chuckle. "Don't worry, Jolie Mc-Graw. I'm sure there'll be a sign I can't miss."

Chapter Thirty-Two

JOLIE

Lucas is right about one thing: there is a lot going on in my head. After he walked me to my car, I stayed up late into the night, thinking about all the revelations from Janice Sullivan.

On Tuesday morning around 10:00, a text from Ry wakes me up. It's just five exclamation points with a picture attached. I expand it and find the press release from the sheriff's department explaining that the mystery of the porch dolls has been solved: They were intended as a gift by a senior citizen who thought the recipients might enjoy having dolls that looked like them, and she's sincerely sorry to have caused so much trouble.

His public information officer has done an excellent job of keeping the giver's details vague enough that it could be just about any woman of retirement age in Harvest Hollow.

Ry follows this up with a picture of the sidewalk chalkboard which now reads "She didn't do it. Sorry we lied. Pink-Faced Liar cocktails half off tonight."

I send back a laughing face and text informing him I'll be in later. I have some business to attend to first.

An hour later, I walk into the library. When Mrs. Herring smiles and greets me, I raise an eyebrow and say, "The Harvest Hollow Library Distinguished Scholarship?"

She looks guilty for a second, then pulls her shoulders back and sniffs. "You deserved it. I'm not sorry."

"Good, because I'm here to say thank you."

We visit for an hour, working on my volunteer schedule in between helping the occasional patron, and when my stomach rumbles to inform me it has demands, I stroll out at noon and pause to study the sheriff's station.

I definitely woke with a clearer mind, but I'm not ready to talk to Lucas yet. I know what I want: him. I haven't figured out what "sign" to give him except marching in to make out with him again. I sense he's waiting for something more than that.

I walk up Maple instead, dipping into the café for a turkey sandwich and continuing on, window-shopping and enjoying all the warm fall décor appearing in store windows and doors in preparation for the big Harvest Festival this weekend. It's a family event, not really the crowd for drinks we sell, but I make a mental note to have Ry work up some apple-themed mocktails that everyone can enjoy next year.

This year, we'll count on tourists finding us in the evenings this weekend. If Sloane's reviews are still up when I check this afternoon, I'll be tracking her down and having a conversation with her about removing them. It will not be a request.

As I near the Mockingbird, Sophie steps from the jewelry store and calls a hello.

"Hey," I say. "Ready for Thursday?"

"Can't wait," she says. "We've had six more teams sign up, and news of your innocence has hit Harvest Hollow Happenings, so maybe we'll get even more. It's going to be a packed house."

"You're awesome," I tell her.

"And Thursday, everyone will find out exactly how awesome." She disappears into the store with a sassy grin.

I'm almost to the bar when her words sink in. *Thursday . . . everyone.*

Packed house. Teams. The Tin Stars.

I have a plan.

When Mr. John gets home with Brooklyn after school, I'm waiting on their front steps.

"Hey, Miss Jo," she says, hopping from his car and running toward me. "What are you doing here?"

"I came to see if you might help me with a project," I tell her.

"Sure."

I smile. "You don't even know what it is yet."

She shrugs. "Everything you do is fun."

I have to clear a knot in my throat. Imagine anyone—especially a kid—thinking I'm "fun." But she's waiting for me to reveal my plan with bright eyes and all the trust that it'll be something cool.

I hope it is.

"I kind of have a thing for your uncle."

"What thing? A present?"

"No, I mean I like him. *Like* him." I wish I knew what the slang is now for this. Maybe ten-year-olds didn't even think about that kind of stuff.

But Brooklyn's expression clears. "Oh, like a boyfriend? That's how you like him?"

It barely scratches the surface of the big feelings simmering beneath the surface, but it'll do. "Yeah. Like a boyfriend. Is that okay?"

She shrugs. "Sure. If you get married, can I be a flower girl?"

I laugh, both at the big jump to marriage, and with relief that she's fine with us dating. "He and I probably need to have a first date before we think about that."

"Okay. Go on a date."

I laugh again. She makes it sound so easy. And maybe when it comes right down to it, it is. "Speaking of that, I wondered if you could help me with some trivia about your Uncle Lucas."

She wrinkles her nose. "I guess? Not sure how much I know."

"Do you know his favorite TV show? Food? Sport?"

"Yes."

I grin at her. "Then between you and your Pops, this will work just fine."

For the next hour, I alternate between getting all kinds of info about Lucas and hearing about Brooklyn's week so far at school. Before I leave we make plans to go to the festival on Saturday morning and agree that we'll let Lucas come with us if we're feeling generous.

I head back to the Mockingbird and arrive around the same time our first group of teachers does for happy hour, and Ry smiles when I come in.

"Looking like we'll have a solid night," he says.

Bonnie is thrilled because she gets to serve previews of her dishes, and several tables demand she come out so they can pay their compliments.

No one outright apologizes to me because it would mean admitting they believed the story in the first place, but I don't need them to. They show they're sorry by being extra friendly and tipping generously. Ry had called in Daniel at 6:00 to help with the crowd, and the laughter and conversation go strong until around 9:00. Not at all bad for a Tuesday. When I check the sales numbers around 10:00, it shows it's our best Tuesday since we opened.

It's okay. Everything is going to be okay.

No. Better than that. Everything is good.

And if I can pull off my plan for Thursday night, then maybe, for the first time for me in Harvest Hollow, everything will be perfect.

Chapter Thirty-Three

LUCAS

Pops starts trying to shove me out of the door almost as soon as I walk through it after work on Thursday.

"Don't you have that trivia night at 7:00? You better get on it."

"I barely got home."

"Well, yeah. But you have to change and, you know, fix stuff."

"Fix what?" I have no idea what he's talking about. I can fix things, but he likes to. I don't even know what's broken.

"Your hair. You got hat hair."

I stare at him, totally confused.

"You need to brush your hair and get ready for trivia night."

"It's true," Brooklyn says. "You need to fix your hair."

"I'm feeling picked on," I say.

"You've heard worse from the rougher elements of Harvest Hollow. Go brush your hair."

Maybe in spite of their urging rather than because of it, I make it to the Mockingbird fifteen minutes before trivia starts. It's the first time I've been here in my civilian clothes, and it feels good to come as a private citizen, no problems to solve.

None except Jolie.

I'm not worried, exactly. Janice Sullivan laid a lot on her, and while I think most of it will help Jolie in some healing, she hasn't come to talk to me about it. I wish she would. I wish she could know how ready I am to listen to anything she wants to tell me. I wish I could tell her that my more-than-friends feelings started the second she pinned me with a glance that first night and kicked me out of her bar.

I knew then. She'd captured my attention in a way no woman ever has. I was telling her the truth when I said I'd never been in love but I'd know when I was, and that I would be all in. The moment I'd been sure was when she said she couldn't date me because she needed to be there for Brooklyn.

I know she's going to take more time to get there. She guards her heart more fiercely than anyone I've ever known, and there may even be a chance that she'll never open it to me at all. But I don't think so. My instincts tell me that there's more than just a mutual attraction at play here. I think she'd fall for me if she let herself.

Will she? I hope so. *When* will she?

I sigh as I step into the bar. There is absolutely no telling with Jolie McGraw. I'd thought we'd have texted or chatted by now, but I've heard nothing from her since I walked her to her truck Monday night. Maybe I should have brought her those pens? I know I need to let her set the pace on this, but I admit I'm glad I have a reason to be on her turf tonight to get a read on her, see what kind of energy she's giving off.

Mary Louise nods when I come in. "Sheriff."

"I'm just Lucas tonight."

"If you say so, Sheriff. I believe some of your teammates have already arrived."

The tables have been reconfigured to face the stage. I don't think they've started booking live acts yet, so this must be the first time putting it to use.

Sophie is standing on it talking to her husband, Joe. Every table is set for four with a sheet of paper and a pencil.

I recruited Slocum and Becky to my team, and they wave me over to their table. Jace Janssen, a firefighter, gives me a chin jerk and a smirk as I pass. I look at the placard with his team name.

"Hot Shots, Janssen? That's not even original."

He smirks. "Get your licks in now, Sheriff, because we're going to wipe the floor with you."

I grin at the trash-talking. There's already a good energy running through the Mockingbird, and the door has opened twice behind me to admit more laughing, chattering people.

All the tables have at least some of their members, and some—like Roberta Herring's—have them all. Of course, the librarians would be here and ready early.

Ry is at the bar, and Tina and a couple of other servers are circulating, taking food and drink orders. I sit with my teammates and watch it all, the whole time keeping an eye out for Jolie.

"Looking for someone?" Becky asks. She asks it in her very smart-aleck way that says she knows exactly who I'm looking for.

"Mind your business," I tell her.

Slocum snorts. "When has she ever?"

Becky only grins. "Jolie is in her office. I'm sure she'll be out soon."

By 7:00, the Mockingbird is packed with players and spectators in the booths, and Sophie takes the stage.

"Welcome to our first-ever Trivia Night at the Tequila Mockingbird!" she calls into the mic, and everyone cheers.

"Tonight is general trivia, and to thank you for coming out, we're offering some very generous prizes. Would my lovely assistant please tell the people about them?"

That's when I spot Jolie heading for the stage. She's in jeans but also black heels that are high and sexy enough to make my mouth go dry. She's wearing a black Tequila Mockingbird T-shirt with the bar's name in glittery gold letters, and her hair is down and loose. Still more polished than any other woman in the bar, but with a softness I've only seen in her when she's with Brooklyn.

"Welcome," she says. "We will not be giving out any dolls tonight, so sorry if you came for that." This elicits cheers and catcalls, and she smiles as she waits for them to subside. "What we do have are cash prizes and free beer for the winners!"

More cheers.

"A hundred dollars and a drink on us for first. Forty dollars and a drink on us for second. And third place gets a drink on us. We've got a full kitchen tonight, so let our service staff know if you get hungry, and we'll get you the best pub food in the city. Without further ado, let's play!"

She hands off the mic to Sophie and steps down from the stage to applause. As Sophie explains the rules of the night, Jolie heads toward Ry, her eyes stopping at my table and resting on me. She gives me a smile. An uncomplicated, happy smile. No, that's not exactly right. There's something about it, maybe a tinge of . . . something. A secret?

All I know for sure is that relief warms my chest as I confirm Jolie isn't upset with me. That's good. I can work with that.

There are twenty teams total playing, and the four lowest-scoring teams will be eliminated after each round. That means the final round will be a four-way face-off.

Sophie is funny but sharp, and twice when players challenge her answers, she gives them the source and shuts them down. There's a lot of laughter and more good-natured smack talk, and the atmosphere gets looser by the question.

It's been a long time since I had this much fun, and the only thing that would make it better would be having Jolie with me, sharing the jokes. But she keeps circulating among the teams, checking in with the kitchen, and generally playing a good host.

The Hot Shots go out in the second round, and I send over a round of beers with orders to Precious to tell them the sheriff sends his condolences. Jace shakes his head but toasts me, and then repays the favor when the Tin Stars go out in the next round.

I doubt anyone is surprised when the Lady Librarians and the Hazy Codgers are in the finals, along with a team of middle school teachers. The only surprise is that the fourth team is . . . the hockey players? But Alec, the Appies team captain, knows a metric ton of trivial things.

The final round plays out with the rest of us shouting our encouragement and shushing anyone we think is guessing the answers too loudly. As the time on the final question runs out, I look around for Jolie, hoping she's enjoying every part of tonight. Trivia night at the Mockingbird is going to be legendary, and I allow myself a small smile of satisfaction as I look at the teams I personally recruited.

As Sophie orders the teams to trade papers and begins revealing the answers, I still haven't spotted Jolie. She must be in the kitchen. Or maybe her office?

Five minutes later, still no Jolie, and Sophie is calling for the team captains to write the final score on the papers and return them to the teams they belong to.

"Captains, hands up if your team got at least fifteen." Four captains' hands go up. "Sixteen?" Still four. "Seventeen?" The teacher captain drops his hand. "Eighteen?" Now the hockey players are out with some grumbling.

It turns out that the Lady Librarians and the Hazy Codgers have tied with a perfect score in the final round.

"Well, well, well," says Sophie. "Time for a tiebreaker. Send up your captains to get your answer sheets." Mrs. Herring and Henry go up to get their papers. When they sit down, all the heads at each table lean in to study it as Sophie continues with her instructions. "I've prepared a special set of five Harvest Hollow–themed questions for this scenario, and spelling counts. Is everyone ready?" Seven silver-haired heads plus the young woman with the Codgers all nod. "Here we go. Who is the youngest person ever to be elected sheriff of Harvest Hollow?"

The teams whisper and their pencils scratch. Becky nudges me, and I'm glad the lighting isn't strong enough for anyone to notice that my neck is looking overwarm.

"Number two: what is his favorite TV show?"

Oh, ha ha. They're going to have some fun with me, I guess. Pops must have given Sophie the answers. I cross my arms and shake my head, waiting to see what comes next.

"Number three: what cartoon character is on the sheriff's sleep shirt?"

That elicits a wave of laughter, and Jace smirks at me again. It's possible Becky and Slocum wouldn't need to look hard now to see my face is getting warm.

"Number four: what song does the sheriff sing in the shower every morning?"

I narrow my eyes at Sophie. I know Miley Cyrus got all serious with her career, but "Party in the USA" is still a banger, and there's no way Pops would ever sell me out on that. This has Brooklyn written all over it.

Sophie doesn't glance in my direction once. "Last question: which high school nemesis of the sheriff went by the name Gappy and never got to play spin the bottle or seven minutes in heaven or any other dumb teenage party game when she was a kid?"

What in the world . . . ? Is the answer . . . no. Right? But who else would it be?

The teams whisper. No pencils scratch.

"Time's up," Sophie says. "Trade papers and we'll find out who won. Who is the youngest elected sheriff in Harvest Hollow history?"

"Lucas Cole," Mrs. Herring says.

"Correct. And what is his favorite TV show?"

"*Little House on the Prairie*," Henry says, and the bar cracks up.

Brooklyn for sure. I'm going to have to explain why that's *inside*-the-house information. Not that I can put the genie back in the bottle on this one. I will no doubt be finding thirst trap photos of Melissa Gilbert and Michael Landon all over the station now.

"Correct," Sophie says, and the laughs get louder. "What cartoon is on the sheriff's sleep shirt?"

"Scooby Doo," Mrs. Herring says.

"No shame in my game," I call. "The dog solves crimes!"

Becky looks like she can't breathe, she's laughing so hard.

"Number four," Sophie continues when the laughter dies down. "What is the sheriff's favorite song to sing in the shower?"

I slouch, but there's no avoiding this.

"Party in the USA," Mrs. Herring says.

"Correct," Sophie says.

Jace is on his feet. "Yeah-ah-yeah-ah-yeaaaaaaah," he sings, and half the bar finishes with "It's a party in the USA!"

"I'm a patriot," I call, and that gets laughs and whistles.

"Last question," Sophie says, and now I'm curious. "Who is his high school nemesis who everyone called Gappy and who never got to play any party kissing games?"

Neither captain raises their hand.

"Lady Librarians?" Sophie asks. They shake their heads. "Hazy Codgers?" Another no.

"I know the answer," another voice calls. We all turn to look at Jolie, who is leaning against the wall in the hallway leading to her office. "Before I got this dental implant, I was Gappy."

"Are you telling me you've never played spin the bottle?" Sophie asks with extremely fake surprise.

"I have not," Jolie calls back.

"Or seven minutes in heaven?"

"That either," Jolie says.

"Well, we better fix that," Sophie announces. "Anyone in here willing to volunteer for spin the bottle?"

I'm on my feet, but so is Jace. Why is he even up here? He's dating someone. I look out at the audience and spot his girlfriend grinning at her man.

Two of the codgers get up, and so do two of the hockey players. I glare at all of them.

"Just so happens I have a bottle here," Sophie says. More cheers. "Gentlemen, if you could form a circle up here on the stage, I'll spin this bottle and we'll see where that gets us."

I shoot a look at Jolie, who is watching me with a smile. If she thinks I'm letting anyone else get the kiss, she has sorely misread me.

I scowl at the rest of the men in the circle, but Sophie has already slipped between two of them and crouched to set the bottle down. Then she gives it a hard spin and steps out of the circle again.

"Okay, y'all, not my best work. One, two, three times around and it's slowing . . . slowing . . . slowing . . ."

I haven't been watching the bottle because I've been too busy shooting death looks at my competition, but I look down now.

The bottle stops, pointing in the direction of one of the hockey players. He nudges it with his toe, and it spins to Floyd, who nudges it and points it at the other hockey player. He nudges it to point to Henry, who points it Jace's way. Slow as molasses, Jace crouches and turns the bottle so it points straight at me.

"Looks like we have a winner," he says. And when all the other men grin, I realize I have been played. Using my Scooby powers of reasoning, I figure out what Jolie was up to when she was flitting around among the tables all night.

I push my way through the circle to the sound of the crowd cheering, and it only gets louder as I hop off the stage and stride across the bar to Jolie. When I reach her, I swoop her up and throw her over my shoulder and keep going down the hall.

"Lucas!" Jolie calls. "Put me down."

I answer with a smack on her very pert behind, and then the crowd loses it. Sophie can't even get them settled down because she's laughing too hard.

Jolie's office door is open and I walk right in, not letting her down until I slam the door shut and deposit her on her feet, backed up against it.

"Jolie McGraw," I say, ducking so our eyes are even. "Did you see that bottle land on me?"

Her mouth twitches. "Yes."

"You know what we call that?"

"A sign?"

"A sign." Then I capture her lips in a kiss that I feel to the soles of my feet, every one of my nerve endings lighting up as the sweetness that is Jolie floods through me.

She leans into the kiss, her hands fisting in the dark blue button-down shirt I wore because Brooklyn said it would make my eyes look nice, and I wanted Jolie to think I had nice eyes.

I don't know how long that kiss goes, but it changes tone and intensity before either of us comes up for air.

"Jo," I say, resting my forehead against hers.

"Talk later," she murmurs, pressing kisses along my jawline.

I oblige, going back in for another kiss that once again erases all sense of time—

Until there's a sharp rapping on the door that startles Jolie into a squeak as she springs away from the sudden noise.

"It's been seven minutes in heaven," Mrs. Herring calls, "which means time is up and we want an update."

I growl and yank the door open. Mrs. Herring stands there looking not even remotely intimidated. "An update? Are you kidding?"

"I am not."

"Here's your update," I call loud enough for the rest of the bar to hear. It helps that they've all fallen silent. "Harvest Hollow Sheriff Falls for Doll Bandit." Then I close the door in Mrs. Herring's smiling face.

I draw Jolie against me again, and she rests her hands on my chest and smiles up at me. "You're falling for me, Lucas?"

"Already fallen for you," I correct her. "Which leads me to a question. Jolie McGraw, can I be your fall forward plan?"

She peers up at me through her dark lashes. "Why, Lucas Cole, I thought you'd never ask. If I say yes, can I have another seven minutes in heaven?"

"You can have as many as you want forever, Jo. All of mine are yours. But Brooklyn is still going to get it when I get home."

And I steal her laugh with another kiss.

Epilogue

JOLIE

One Year Later. . .

The fall garlands are all up on Maple again. Without question, this is my favorite time of year in Harvest Hollow. It's dusk as I step out of the bookstore, the Hazy Codgers behind me, Henry nagging at me to get a move on so we don't miss trivia night.

"Gal, step it up. The Lady Librarians are going to get the good table."

"Settle down, Henry," Hazel says, her voice full of patient amusement. "We're still early."

I slide the brand-new copy of *The Lion of Lark-Hayes Manor* into my tote bag for Brooklyn. A middle grade fantasy about a sixth grader who loves fantasy books? Check. I need to make sure we're still set for our girl day on Saturday too. We're getting blowouts and pedicures, and I only feel a little bit bad for Lucas for introducing Brooklyn to these expensive luxuries. He'll do anything to spoil her, and I'm just helping him by giving him another way to do it.

I lead my quarreling band of trivia fiends to the Mockingbird and step into the warmth of the bar and the Billy Strings song playing over the PA. I stop inside the door, surprised by the crowd.

"Everything good?" I ask Mary Louise.

She nods. "Always is."

This is true. We've got a rotating staff of twelve servers now to handle our very full lunch crowd—thanks to our delicious menu—and our evening patrons. And Bonnie is about to level up again by adding weekend brunch starting in October, and she'll no doubt make the Blue Ridge Mountain Best List again. People can't get enough of her food that manages to be local, simple, and still inventive. We have plenty of business and a happy wait staff.

The team tables are almost all full, all the regulars in their spots. The Lady Librarians and Hazy Codgers always battle over the same table, which is ridiculous, because no matter which group gets it, the other team ends up seated right next to them. The view is exactly the same. They just like arguing. The Lady Librarians get the table tonight, but they'll all bicker again next week.

"Get outta here, boss," Mary Louise says. "We're set."

I'm usually "home" by dinner these days, home being Lucas's place so we can all eat together. Mr. John is a better cook than any of us, so I have no complaints. No, that's an understatement: it's become my favorite part of the day.

"All right, see you tomorrow." I leave through the back exit, pleased with the warmth and chatter I'm leaving behind. I don't know what I thought the Mockingbird would become when I decided to open it. It had been a whim born from anger.

I don't think I realized how much of my life I'd spent being angry until it became safe to say how very, very mad I was.

It's one of the things I've learned from Lucas over the last year. That I don't have to be afraid of my feelings, good or bad. The bad ones can't swallow me whole, and it's fine to let the good ones consume me. There's not a limit on how many times I can be happy.

In truth, contentment is my baseline now, and I never knew it wasn't before. I'd confused security and stability for happiness, but they are very different things. Security is a place to start, but it's not happiness itself, just the foundation to build on.

I climb into my truck and get on the road toward home. I need a quick shower before I go over to Lucas's place.

That makes me happy. My impractical truck, my home with a linen closet full of fluffy towels, and dresser drawers full of the sweaters I just rotated in for the cooling weather.

It's the simple things. It's the best things.

As I drive down the stretch of road just past the four-way stop that Lucas pulled me over for missing last year, I see flashing lights in my rearview mirror and groan.

I'm pretty sure I didn't miss a sign and that I wasn't speeding, but if I was, there's no way I'm using my "status" as the sheriff's girlfriend to get out of a ticket. If it's a patrol officer who recognizes me, it might happen anyway, but when I check my side mirror, I don't know the deputy approaching.

I roll down my window and place my hands on the steering wheel.

"Evening, ma'am," he says when he reaches me and shines his light inside.

"Good evening, deputy. Is there a problem?"

"Unfortunately, there is, ma'am. Your vehicle matches the description of a truck recently reported as the getaway vehicle in a robbery."

I stare at him, then blink. It's so obviously not me that I'm not even worried about it. Just confused.

"License and registration, ma'am?"

I sigh but reach for my glove compartment and hand over the registration plus my license. I'll have to tell Lucas about this, but I'll leave out the deputy's name. I just need to make sure they have my license plate number in the system as *not* the culprit so I don't get pulled over again for no reason.

"Thank you, ma'am. I'll run these and be back shortly."

I sigh and settle in to wait. This shouldn't make me too late for dinner if we can resolve it in the next few minutes, but honestly, it's kind of ridiculous that this deputy wouldn't take one look at me and realize I'm not a thief. He's on the younger side, so it's probably a question of experience.

A minute or so later, I hear the crunch of his shoes on the shoulder gravel, and I'm glad that this is taking even less time than I expected. I start to extend my hand through the window to take back my documentation, but the deputy says, "Whoa, ma'am. Easy there."

I pull my hand back and lean slightly out of the window. "I'm sorry?"

"Ma'am, I'm going to need you to step out of your vehicle." He moves back to give me plenty of room to climb down.

I don't. I stay where I am. It's full dark, and I have no desire to be on the road shoulder. "Why?"

"You've been implicated as the primary robbery suspect."

"What?" I know I sound incredulous, but why wouldn't I? Robbery? I cannot believe I'm even going to have to do this, but I take a breath to settle my rising irritation and say, "Can we call Sheriff Cole, please? He'll vouch for me."

"I'm going to ask you again politely, ma'am. Please step out of the vehicle."

"This has to be a mistake. I'm—"

"Ma'am. Please." This deputy might be new to the job, but he has cop face down pat.

That's it. I'm definitely telling Lucas about this.

I open the door and get down. "Who reported me?" I ask as my ankle boots meet the dirt.

"I did," says a deep voice that is *not* the deputy's. Lucas walks out of the dark, not in uniform. He's wearing my favorite flannel, and he gives his deputy a serious nod. "I'll take it from here, deputy. Thank you."

"Yes, sir," the deputy says, walking back to his car.

"Don't make this difficult, Jolie."

"Lucas . . ." I'm not worried, but I'm more confused than ever.

"One year ago, in this very spot, you stole my heart," he says, and I start to get it. He reaches out to take my hands. "It took me a few weeks to realize it, but I was a goner. Robbery, Jolie. Do you deny it?"

A huge smile has hijacked my face. I shake my head. "I don't deny it, Lucas. And what's more, I'm not sorry."

"Shameless," he says with mock gravity.

"Guilty and I don't care."

"I do," he says. "More than I ever thought I could. Jo, this has been the happiest year of my life, and I'm hoping you feel the same. *You* are my heart, Jolie, and I'm wondering if you might consider being with me always."

The end of my nose is stinging. "Yes, Lucas. Right after I kill you for that trick you just pulled on me."

He pulls me close and rests his head on mine. We stand like this often because I love listening to the beat of his heart. "I love you, Jolie McGraw."

"I love you too, Lucas Cole." We've said it countless times over the last year, and I never get tired of it.

He pulls back a little. "To be clear, I'm asking you to marry me."

I smile up at him, his face visible in the headlights of the deputy's cruiser. "To be clear, I'm saying yes."

"Whoohoo!" That's Brooklyn's voice, and I look up to catch her and Pops coming at us from the other side of the cop car, where apparently they'd been waiting in the backseat. Brooklyn flings her arms around us. "We're a family!"

And as Lucas gathers us both close while Pops grins, I let the tears fall, because there is no possible way to keep in this much happiness.

More Lucas and Jolie?

For a sneak peek into Lucas and Jolie's future—and a most inter-esting turn of events for Sloane Oakley-Hunsaker, sign up for my newsletter at www.melaniejacobson.net!

Acknowledgments

Thank you to Courtney Walsh and especially Emma St. Clair for inviting me to part of this series, and for all their hard work in coordinating it. Thank you to my fellow series authors for making it so fun to collaborate on the ins-and-outs of Harvest Hollow: Julie Christianson, Carina Taylor, Savannah Scott, and Jenny Proctor. Thank you to the several law enforcement friends who helped answer lots of little questions, but most especially to Captain Alan Corn of the Henderson County Sherrif's Office in North Carolina. Thank you to Hector at Mulleady's in Mission Viejo, CA for patiently answering a teetotaler's questions about drinks and pub logistics. Thank you to my wingman and best friend, Kenny Jacobson, for coming along to trivia nights at breweries and sports bars for research and fun. Thank you to Jeanna Stay for her sharp-eyed proofread, Kaylee Baldwin for her complete beta read despite her own projects, and my subject area experts Melody Williams, Meredith Logan, Samantha Martin, and Sabrina Mock-Rossi for helping me to get the little things right. Thank you to my ARC readers for their typo catches and for helping me to get the word out about my books. Thank you to my assistants, Cathy Jeppsen, Stacia Jacobson, and all of my kids for helping me keep the business side of writing going. Lastly, thank you to Scooter for his constant interruptions so I remember to get up from my desk now and then.